I0574467

THE FALL OF THE House of Otter

HOUSE OF OTTER

THE FALL OF THE
House
of Otter

LEO SPARX

4 Horsemen
Publications, Inc.

4 Horsemen
Publications, Inc.

Published By: 4 Horsemen Publications, Inc.

4 Horsemen Publications, Inc.
PO Box 417
Sylva, NC 28779
4horsemenpublications.com
info@4horsemenpublications.com

Cover & Typesetting by Valerie Willis
Edited by Tilde M. Cooke

Library of Congress Control Number: 2023930649

Paperback ISBN-13: 978-1-64450-817-6
Audiobook ISBN-13: 978-1-64450-819-0
Ebook ISBN-13: 978-1-64450-818-3

QUEER ZOOLOGY

Otter (n): a man who is leaner than a cub or bear
but still covered in fur

Contents

LEO SPARX

Before ALEXANDER

The fall of the *House of Otter*

Dedication

To the writer's groups,
otterwise none of this would be possible.

BEFORE...

I was naked in a hotel room, somewhere in France, where everything sparkled. The drapes on either side of the long windows were illuminated by the afternoon sun in a city I still hadn't seen, but there was still no sign of the man who had brought me there. On my lap, a shining silver tray sat balanced between my bare legs. In contrast to the dark hair of my thighs, orange slices were stacked on a platter, vibrant as the last sunset I could remember. The one in a little beach town where people called the closest body of water an ocean, but never the sea.

It was brave to have white sheets, I thought, while my lips curved around the flesh of the juicy fruit. Small droplets from my bite landed on the pristine linens, and I rubbed the nearly translucent liquid into the flawless fibers. I didn't know when the man would return, but I didn't want him to determine me ungrateful for everything he'd offered since our trip began.

There were still defined burn lines on my waist and mid-thigh from waking up shirtless only the morning before. In a different place, I'd spent a starlit night pressed to a flat lounge chair squished into the sand. When the man hung over me in a business suit, silhouetted by the newly risen sun and cloudless teal sky, my body was not yet ready to face the day. In the brief hours before the tourists would arrive to knock down the remnants of forgotten sandcastles, I was half-asleep with my stomach against the stretchy plastic when I pretended not to hear him approaching. From the corner of my eye, the man's charcoal shadow in the warming tan grains said, "Turn over, boy."

Complying to the demands of mysterious men wasn't entirely new to me, but I still hesitated before scooping my sunglasses from the shady area under my chair and slipping them across my eyes. With the saturation of the rays toned down behind the lenses of borrowed glasses, I turned on my side, expecting to see a ranger hat or some indication of law enforcement staring back. But in the sudden clarity, it was easier to decipher the shadow's appearance. His skin and maintained scruff, the tie with the perfect knot near his Adam's apple, and his polished shoes hovering on the sand— this man wasn't a cop; he wasn't even working-class. He was *money*.

Speaking didn't seem necessary before I blinked a few times and continued adjusting to the reality I had awoken in. I completed the rotation to my back to let my chest welcome the sky. Sweat pooled in my chest hair, and I still smelled like warm coconut from the suntan lotion I'd been using in place of soap. It had been the closest thing I'd managed to find since bumming around the beach in this new town, using only what I scavenged from bags the visitors left behind.

The man appeared pleased the instant I moved my body, and I laid with my hands behind my head to let him take in the full view. A fraying white drawstring hung in the pubic hair peeking from the top of my swim trunks, and I could feel him concentrating on the area. Aside from the seagulls calling to dawn and a pelican scoping breakfast from an unusually low tide, no one else heard him ask me to pull down my bathing suit.

Looking past the tops of my feet, beyond the end of the lounge chair, rainbow abalone reflected iridescent as the waves rippled in and out. I still had my hands behind my head while small multi-colored coquinas surfaced with the salty flow before burrowing back into the wet sand and bubbling from their hiding spots. It was how I often felt when a man dug me out of my own safety. When his presence felt like forceful hands trying to remove me from the ground and open my shell. Like I couldn't be beautiful without being bothered.

"Let me see your cock, boy," he repeated. Maybe he hadn't realized that behind my tinted barrier, I hadn't been looking at him. But now, I moved my gaze from the surf back to his jawline.

I pulled my sunglasses down just enough for him to see my eyes. "I'm feeling generous. Are you?" I asked, smirking at his Windsor knot and shiny loafers.

He laughed, unexpectedly bending in his linen dress pants until his knees rested in the sand near my lounge chair. The ocean air made the sweat on my body feel like sea salt ice cream, and when he brought his mouth close to my waistband, I hoped I tasted just as sweet.

"Very generous," he said, using his fingers to toy with the rogue drawstring in the dark forest connected by a single line to my stomach hair. Tracing the pattern north, his hand followed the path up my abdomen until the thick follicles expanded again on my chest. My nipples were starting to get hard, fighting their way through lush curls. Noticing the towers, he brought his index finger and thumb together, circling the perimeter with a light touch before pinching them between his prints.

When my mouth opened to let a quiet moan escape, the stranger seized the opportunity to move his fingers to my tongue. He slid them in and out of my mouth until they were coated with my own slippery spit while he used his other hand to remove my glasses and toss them back into the sand. With his eyes looking into mine, he moved the moisture back to my erect nipples. Immediately, my cock awoke, swelling until it filled the space in my thin trunks.

They were short at the bottom, several inches above my knee and settling at my upper thigh. The man could have easily slid his hand through one of the legs to grip me, but he didn't. Even after moving his attention from my chest and back to the bulge still growing beneath the only fabric on my body, he didn't touch it. Instead, he brought his tongue down to the top of the waistband and tasted the sweat just below my navel. The warmth of his salvia against the chilled breeze made me thicker, but he still avoided the pulsing, now just centimeters from his mouth.

Bracing myself for him to pull me out and devour my length, I was surprised when the warmth of his tongue went missing. He used the metal piping of my chair to push himself up and back in his position above me. Starting at where his fancy shoes found their soles back in the sediment, I watched his shadow again grow tall. The dark image brought his own hand to his lips and sucked my sweat from each of his fingers.

After a final suckling sound, his eyes were on the ocean, not me, when he said, "I believe I instructed you to take out your cock, boy." This was the third time he'd asked. With no further hesitation, I let my thumbs untie the twisted white knot keeping the short trunks around my waist. Whether he paid or not, I wanted to cum, and I wanted him to watch.

Whomever had been the original owner of the bathing suit I'd been wearing, the person who'd selected the fluorescent colors and obtuse triangles from a rack amongst more muted colors and designs, had notable taste. I had noticed, since pulling them from the shade below the boardwalk and bathrooms, that the strange print looked great against my skin.

Perhaps my own sense of fashion had the tendency to sway somewhere toward unique, but it had been quite a while since I'd had the opportunity to choose from anything that hadn't already been left behind or forgotten. Everything I wore these days was retro out of necessity, and I hoped as the man smirked at the sight of my flesh poking through the elastic band, he'd determined my appearance as an appreciation for vintage style instead of an indicator of involuntary poverty.

Out of habit, I flicked at my exposed head before pulling the elastic band farther down my shaft. I could feel his eyes on me still, following the fraying white string until it landed just below my balls and tickled at them. As I grabbed a fist full of my hardness, the man's gaze shifted from my body to something behind me. I craved nothing less than his full admiration and released my cock to turn in the direction he was looking. A blue heron stretched its long beak and legs near a cabana but didn't seem interested in us.

"Haven't seen a heron before?" I asked the man, turning back toward him. His attention returned to me before he spoke. It wasn't the first time I'd seen a tourist impressed by a scavenger.

"We have sea birds in France, just none so..." His words trailed off for a moment while he fixated back on my firm cock dripping with precum in the open air, "large and..." Pressing his lips together and running his tongue across the bottom to moisten them, he finished his thought, "beautiful."

I hadn't noticed his accent before, and I didn't try to stop myself from smirking when I asked plainly, "Why would you vacation here if you live in France?"

The man smiled and broke his gaze with my cock before he walked closer to where I lay on the lounger. He was in my reach again as he bent just far enough down to grab one of the hands I had resting in my pubic hair.

Reaching toward his chest, I was determined to do something sexy; to pull his smooth looking tie until his lips were closer to my body. I didn't get anywhere near my goal before he palmed my other hand and brought them both together so he could hold them both at the wrists.

His grip was firm as he edged his way onto the chair next to me and used a single strong hand to pin my hands above me. With his other, he took hold of my cock and just before pumping at it hard and fast, whispered, "This isn't a vacation, boy."

I wasn't sure if I wanted to ask what he meant, but it didn't matter once he was stroking me from base to tip with my own precum and the briny mist as lubricant. His expert rhythm made the combination of liquids more than enough, and as he pressed my wrists firmly into the plastic ribbons of the lounge chair, all I could see was the intensity in his dark eyes.

The morning dew lingering in the sand filled my senses until I started holding my breath. My head pounded in time with the pulsing of my cock, already prepared to shoot, as my vision and taste disappeared. Everything was replaced with the sound of my own heartbeat and the crashing waves in time with each other, until the man's voice said, "Cum, boy. Give it to me." At his words, for a moment, the world instantly went quiet and dark.

When I opened my eyes again, I saw him staring down and followed his eyeline to the droplets being absorbed into the sediment. I'd always been able to get some distance when I came hard, and it seemed there had been enough power to propel every drip to the sand near my chair. The man appeared both impressed and disappointed.

"I would have liked to have tasted you," he said, releasing my hands and cock to pull a cloth handkerchief from his breast pocket. "Next time, I suppose, boy."

All I wanted to do in that moment was tuck my soft dick into my shorts and fall back to sleep. Maybe find a cabana I could sneak into before the beach rangers began patrolling the area between the surf and shops. The man had drained me so quickly I felt exhausted. He stood back in his original position, and the sun seemed brighter somehow, outlining his frame in a halo of morning light.

Tired and empty as I was, I still expected him to unzip and position his cock for me to exchange the favor. My body fought to stay relaxed, but I prepared myself mentally to get on my knees and suck the stranger to the hilt. Instead, the shadow adjusted his fitted slacks and asked, "Have you been to France, boy?"

My head turned to one side nearly on its own, and I peeked one eye open at him. A smile cracked across my face while I shook my head in response and simply said, "Nope."

He smiled back and laughed a bit, shifting his weight to his heels. "Gather your shirt and shoes, boy," he said. It wasn't a question.

Grabbing my sunglasses from the sand and pushing them flush with my face, I turned back toward the sea. "Don't have any."

The tide was higher now, and on any other day, I'd be running down to let the ocean cleanse me before the beach filled with umbrellas, blankets, and french-cut bikinis. It seemed the man had other ideas for my future.

An orange sun ray glistened from a gold ring while he laughed again, scratching his temple with a single finger. I could still see his shadow in the sand, but I didn't want him to know I was paying that much attention. "Well, we've got some shopping to do then," he said, turning his shoes in the grains. He began walking toward the boardwalk and away from me. "Come along, boy."

The tide in front of me continued to wax and wane over the colored shells. Small rainbow clams bubbled for breath from where they had buried themselves. I admired their sense of freedom in a place where most creatures would be drowned or smothered.

Taking a long inhale of salt and young coconut, I turned my head to see the man was halfway through the cattails and up the wooden steps to the boardwalk. He stopped in place and watched me watch him with the wind blowing at his suit jacket.

Even in the building humidity, I was frozen for a moment, taking in his full frame for the first time. Like my delay in recognizing his French accent, I somehow hadn't noticed before he was incredibly handsome. With my calmed cock tucked into my shorts, I hung my legs over the chair and let my bare feet touch the crushed shell. Standing between two horizons, I knew adventure had led me to this town, and now, it was leading me somewhere else.

My expectation was that a man like this one would be staying somewhere with an ocean view. A room with coral-colored carpet, turquoise painted walls, and a mirror that made the sitting area look even bigger than it was. Perhaps there would be a kitchenette and a balcony so high nothing could get in aside from the sea breeze. But the trajectory of my fantasy changed as I followed him past the resort buildings to the road where a long black town car waited beyond the small shops lining the boardwalk.

One of the back doors was open, held by a young man wearing white gloves and a chauffeur's hat. He reminded me of a Tom of Finland drawing but less broad in the chest. The moving sketch didn't speak as I tiptoed across the heated pavement, but he did extend his white-gloved hand toward the interior. I looked back at my host, who straightened his tie as he nodded to the driver. He slid through the door and across the dark leather inside, leaving room for me while I stood paralyzed with gravel between my toes.

"Get in, boy," he said, leaning over to give me a slight smile. Before I could question the possible cons of jumping into a car with a rich stranger, my naked back was sticking to the smooth seat, and the car was rolling over the rocky fragments of the road with light popping sounds.

The windows were so tinted I could hardly see out. There was no way to view our direction through the windshield since it was closed off by a partition between us and the driver. Glass bottles with etched geometric designs glimmered from the sunlight of dawn turned officially to morning, but it was still too early for the stores to be open anywhere in town.

What I wanted was a shopping spree montage in the bustling daybreak of Beachside. Store-branded bags with braided handles and garments folded by soft hands. I wanted the man to look at my endless reflection in the parallel mirrors of a well-lit boutique and dress me in an ascot or a bowtie like I'd seen in movies, then buy everything I draped over the checkout counter with a satin-finished credit card.

Unintentionally, I was creating a fantasy of him parading me around to his wealthy friends and showing them the scuffed penny he'd found on the beach then buffed to perfection. Even if it was only for a night. Even if that was all he wanted from me.

The duration of our time together was already abnormal compared to the usual quick bangs in semi-private locations. Still, he seemed determined to keep me to himself, or at least away from the people in town seeing us together.

I hadn't been in the beach community long enough to know it well, I just knew the tourists were drawn directly to the ocean upon their arrival. Not only were they forgetful enough from the frozen drinks to leave their belongings behind, but the pressure of having a story to bring back from their vacation to a place where it snowed often meant they were willing to spend ridiculous amounts of money to assure a good time. It was a rare night when I didn't come across a man who had strayed from his family or friends, far enough down the moonlit shore, with a few bucks to spare for a blowjob under the boardwalk.

Even if everything I'd learned about my most recent home had been from the underside of beach showers and public restrooms, I knew enough to sense we were heading west in the town car and had gotten pretty far away from town. When the seagulls stopped cawing and the open sky was replaced with towering greenery, the car stopped in front of a gate covered so entirely with twisted ivy the only legible word was "Otter."

I'd heard the word before, used by men to describe me and men who looked like me. It was the body hair on my compact frame that seemed to hold their fascination. That I didn't feel the need or desire to be smooth but wasn't large enough to be considered a bear, or whatever other queer zoology term the community had decided on to differentiate between our body types or fur. Words like that were the language we used to sort each other out but also to make sure everyone was included. Each animal or category was a term of endearment and for some—perhaps like my host—even a fetish, something you could request by name like a cocktail or ripe fruit.

I probably should have been more concerned when the driver forced the gate open and drove through the long stretch to a horse-shoe driveway before coming to another full stop in the pebbles. The overgrown vines extended well beyond the first entryway and climbed every inch of the exterior brick. There seemed to be a large wooden door framed by an archway, but it wasn't until the driver opened my door that I was able to get a closer look at the expansive structure.

Something breathed colder on this new side of town where, instead of surf, there were dense trees on either side. The small rocks under my feet almost felt chilled while I craned my neck to take in each story of the house piled on top of the other. It seemed endlessly tall, and by the time I reached the top to visually swallow a single window in a tower, the man spoke, breaking me from drinking the building in.

"Over here, boy." He was holding a long black key and picking the broken plants away as he pushed open the entrance and beck-oned me to pass the threshold. I must have hesitated at the blackness which seemed to be lurking on the other side because he checked his expensive watch and tapped at its face with a sigh.

I hadn't realized we were in a hurry, but the bottoms of my feet moved forward on their own at the thought of disappointing him. It was a new feeling for me, caring what a man wanted more than my own comfort. Even a man as rich as he seemed to be had never been enough of a reason for me to respond to commands, but here I was, crossing over the boundary and into the dark house without further question.

With my exposed chest near him, the man slipped by me to press his hand to a wall and flip a switch. Nothing happened.

"Hmm," he said and flicked the switch a few more times. Nothing. "Well, no matter. Up the stairs, boy."

From the light of a morning sun peeking through the door, I could see the general shape of a giant staircase and slowly walked toward it. With my hand stroking the smooth wooden banister, the man followed close behind through lush carpet and art I couldn't make out through the dimness. It seemed strange to me as we climbed higher that despite the opulence of the interior, no one had remembered to pay the electric bill.

"To your right, boy," the man said and pointed toward a hallway lined with closed wooden doors. On either side of the corridor, the furniture lining the walls was covered by off-white sheets. I supposed it was to keep the pieces from getting dusty, but it certainly didn't help with the eerie vibe of the large, and seemingly empty, house.

In this wing with the doors shut and windows covered in the same sheets, the natural light had completely disappeared, but the man continued following close behind. Aside from his occasional directions, the only sound came from boards creaking beneath my steps in time with his rhythmic breath.

When I turned around to look at the man, I heard a sliding sound followed by a thump coming from the end of the hallway. I jumped and stopped where I stood, giving the sound my attention instead of the man. It was difficult to focus my vision on something so far away, but I could make out what seemed to be a sheet on the ground below a painting still hanging on the wall.

Thinking the cover must have slid off the piece of art, I was drawn in that moment directly to the panting. As if it were calling to me. Beckoning me to acknowledge its beauty. I had to know what or who was in the deep-colored portrait. All I could make out aside from the colors was the shape of a figure, next to another that may have been shorter. Maybe an older man in a suit with a younger man sitting next to him—naked.

My feet moved down the hallway without my permission. Toward the two painted men. As I got closer, it was certain, one was seated and the other was kneeling. All I wanted to do was take them in, but in my trance, I felt a furry hand on my bare shoulder. "Back here, boy."

Spinning me back to face a door, he turned the knob and opened it to a massive room. The man had stopped me halfway down the hall, more importantly, halfway from the painting. I could still hear the artful figures calling—something wanted me to reach them—but the man shuffled me over the threshold, clearing his throat and blocking the male voices invading my mind. He closed the door behind us.

Inside, most of the area was filled with a massive bed framed with four posts. This was an orgy bed. A gangbang ring. A circle-jerk pillow fight battleground. But the mattress, like almost everything I'd seen in the house so far, was covered with the same sheeting as though it had been decades since it had been used.

Light from a single window illuminated a giant wardrobe on the opposite wall, and the man, completely ignoring the perfect setting for group sex only a few feet away, opened the hinged doors to reveal hanging clothes. Below were drawers that he pulled open one at a time to rummage through garments. I couldn't see them from where I stood, but he turned with an armful of options. "Take off your clothes, boy."

I assumed he was referring to the bathing suit. We both knew I wasn't wearing anything else unless the sunglasses I'd pushed up to rest in my shaggy hair counted as more than an accessory.

There wasn't much hesitation on my end to pull the elastic band down. It wasn't just because he had already seen the goods. Truth was, if I could be naked all the time, I would be. Given the universal okay to just be dick-out with as little on as possible, I'd go for it. Already I had gone at least a year without even a pair of designated flip-flops. What I'd learned in that time was: people put way too much thought into what they wear in hopes people will ask them to remove it.

So here I was, ratty drawstring around my ankles, my hairy ass not far from a king-sized bed already covered and protected from potential bodily fluids. If he wanted to, he could have bent me over right there. I could have put my back flat on the sheet and put my legs in the air.

No money had been exchanged, but the feeling was the same as any other time I'd been purchased. Or more so my time and my body. But unlike other men, instead of taking advantage of his new action figure's moving parts, he seemed more interested in dressing me. He handed me a jockstrap with a colorful band, then another, and another. He asked me to try on each and spin around until he found the color he liked best on my skin.

"That's the one, boy," he finally said, smirking each time he got a view of my furry ass. I could see he was hard under his slacks before he threw a pair of jeans, t-shirt, and set of boots on the bed near me. They all bounced against the mattress, and I thought about what it would be like to be under him in the spot the clothes landed when he said, "These look like they were made for you."

He seemed pleased enough, but while he was closing the wardrobe drawers, I heard whispers coming through the door. I couldn't be sure if it was the older or younger man in the picture, but one of them told me I wasn't trying hard enough. They spoke in strange words I couldn't understand as more than a feeling, but the sensation of their expectations running through me brought me to my knees in front of the door.

When the man turned around, I ran a hand through my hair to remove the glasses from where they sat perched in my beachy hair then threw them to the side. I spread my legs on the carpet to make sure he could get a full view of my package resting in the new underwear and opened my mouth, wide and inviting. Looking into his eyes as he stepped closer, I swirled my tongue toward the zipper of his pants. His hand was on my shoulder again, and for a moment, I thought I had him.

With a smile, he looked down at me and stroked my tongue with two fingers. I closed my lips around them and sucked as he thrust them deeper inside. He smirked, then sighed, catching a glimpse of his watch not far from my mouth. "We do not have the time, boy," he said, dragging his salty fingertips across my bottom lips as they exited the wet hole. Grabbing the door knob behind me, he motioned to the clothes still sitting on the bed, instructing me nonverbally to get dressed. He made his way to the hallway, leaving me on my knees, hard and waiting.

A sense of disappointment lingered as I waited for my firmness to subside before attempting to close the fly of the tight jeans. It felt strange, as if the house were communicating with me. As if I had a connection with it somehow. But for the moment, it was quiet. Possibly angry. The real life man was getting what he wanted, but the ones in the portrait seemed to want more than I was able to deliver. Maybe I just needed to eat something.

Convincing myself a real breakfast would clear my head, I finished dressing and carried the boots into the hall. I wished I could have explored the room more; there seemed to be an expansive bathroom with just the corner of a purple bathtub peeking through. A shower, bath, even just a quick splash of water would have been nice. But instead of letting me use the amenities of the massive house, the man tapped at his watch just outside the door. "Hurry up, boy."

Back in the hallway, cobwebs I hadn't noticed before were gathered in nearly every corner and around devices that looked like old speakers all wired together. The man was already down the stairs ahead of me, but when he reached the final landing, he stared up, waiting.

When my foot hit the first step, I couldn't help but swing my head back toward the portrait at the end of the hallway. The men in the painting didn't move or speak, but something told me it wouldn't be the last time I'd see them.

The man stopped in the doorway between the interior and front stoop where the car waited to take us away to wherever we were going. When I stood across from him on the threshold, he smiled and brushed a piece of hair from my cheek. Passion rose hot and electric within me. I wanted to kiss him. He leaned in close for a moment but stopped, as if he had heard something or someone speaking, then pulled away.

"Let's go, boy," he said, motioning for us to move to the town car. "This place never feels quite right this time of the year. Too many ghosts."

International first-class seemed to mean food and wine. It meant hot towels and other things to keep passengers comfortable for a ten-hour direct flight. And I was comfortable, letting the plushness of the seat cradle the parts of me still packed with sand. Part of me was still wishing I would have checked to see whether the creepy mansion had running water for a shower while we rode to the airport. But after take-off, when the man asked me if I preferred red or white blends, the empty manor felt just as far away as the surf, and mattered less.

Now I was three glasses in and unsure which one he'd ordered. I'd gotten too used to the last sips of pina coladas and strawberry daiquiris to remember what decent alcohol tasted like. I was surprised how little I missed the miniature plastic swords speared with half-eaten garnishes, water-logged in the bottom like sunken treasure, now that I had clean glass in front of me. It wasn't that I needed to drink to feel relaxed, but the more the long-stemmed goblets piled up on the tray table, the more I felt myself leaning into his seat. Through it all, one thought dominated my mind, I needed to find my way close to his lips again.

"So, what's your name?" I asked. The sound of my own voice made me purse my lips as I swayed toward him. I was definitely intoxicated.

He laughed just slightly but didn't respond. Instead, he reached into a piece of luggage under his seat and pulled out a plum-colored bag with a golden pull-string. Something tall and firm was inside, and he grasped it with both hands.

"Oh, my boy." The man put his palm on my leg and gave it a light squeeze. "My name depends on what happens after this plane lands."

I didn't understand what he meant, but now my focus was on the bag sitting between his legs. It was big enough to hold a bottle of liquor. Maybe he was doing his best to get me drunker than airplane wine would allow.

If he wanted to get me intoxicated enough to put my head in his lap and blow him on the plane, I was surprised he hadn't realized, I was already there. So much of me wanted to pull up the armrest between us and slip my jeans down far enough to slide him inside of me. If the flight attendants in their buttons and collars saw us, I hoped they would watch.

The last drops of my fourth glass down, he handed me the small bag. I tried to untie the golden string at my seat, but he stopped me. With his hands on mine, he pointed to the bathroom at the front of the plane. "Bring the bag back empty. Don't come out until you've taken it all, boy."

A voice with a thicker French accent than the man had, came over the speakers above us. Despite the static overlay, I could make out that he was saying we were halfway through our trip. There were five hours left until I'd see Europe for the first time, which meant five hours to drink whatever was in this bottle and try not to get alcohol poisoning. That, I figured, would be less than sexy. But if I couldn't have his cock or mouth, I would do my best to please him in any way he asked.

In the tight space of the restroom, I balanced the bag on the counter near the sink and pulled the cinched seal wide until it was fully open. The contents emerged slowly through the ruffled hole. Unlike my expectations, the item wasn't clear or filled with liquid. It wasn't a bottle at all. The inner contents of the mysterious bag was black, solid, and shaped like a tree with a rounded point. Pulling the fabric farther down showed a diameter at the base wider than my own fist. Near the bottom, loose in the bag, was a sample-size packet of lube. This was the biggest butt plug I had ever seen.

I was wishing now he had ordered whiskey instead of wine as I transported the silicone plug to the floor and began unzipping my jeans. Something about whiskey always made me feel bold and ready for a challenge. Luckily, wine at least made me want to get fucked. So, with my ass hovering over the bulbous toy in the jockstrap he'd picked out for me, I tore open the lube pellet with my teeth and lowered down slowly. Bouncing on the slippery tapered shape, I felt my hole open up as I thought about what the man wanted from me.

We hadn't talked about his expectations, or payment, but already I'd gotten a ride in a fancy car, new clothes, and a trip across the ocean. Well, midway so far, at least. In either case, it wasn't terrible for a day I had originally planned to just wake up on the beach and see what I could live off.

Not having a building to call home had become a sort of freedom I learned to enjoy. Wandering into that town, the stars became my blanket and the sand my pillow. But I never planned to stay anywhere forever, and there was no saying where I could wake up tomorrow if I could make the man waiting for me in first class keep smiling.

The squishy pill of lube was bone-dry by the time my hole threatened to stretch over the widest part of the toy. My cock dripped, soaking the jockstrap, but I didn't touch it. I knew if I came it would only make it more difficult to fit the remainder of the firm polyurethane inside of me. It was so big I had to rise again and even thought about giving up. He expected me to bring the bag back empty though, and considering the size of the plug, there was nowhere to hide it on my person. Cher-forbid I stashed it behind the airplane toilet or left it in the bathroom for some poor passenger to find. Either way, I had a feeling he'd know right away if I hadn't complied with his demands, and as far as I could tell, I was on the clock.

I tried again and felt pleased when I got myself pretty far down, but a knock on the door made me stop my momentum. "Just a minute," I said, hands on my thighs, holding my breath with my ass partially swallowing the tapered shape.

"Having trouble in there, boy?" the man asked from the other side of the door. I didn't answer but brought my hands to my knees to boost myself farther onto my feet. My hole tightened instantly knowing he was waiting for me, and before I could answer him, the handle jiggled and the door opened. He stood in the tight space with me, looming again as he had on the beach, standing over me and demanding my sex. He closed the door behind him and pierced with me with an authoritative glare. "All of it, boy," he said.

His words were the motivation I needed to let the rounded tip open my hole again and make me push down. Closer to my body now, his hands on my shoulders from behind pressed just enough.

"Breathe deep, then exhale, boy," he said, reaching down to circle one of my nipples.

I did as I was told, with my hole resting just before the thickest part of the plug. If I could get past it, I knew the thinner part would sit more comfortably. With a deep breath, I felt him rub my chest, and on the long exhale, he pushed down with more force. Enough so the toy thrust its way fully inside.

"There we go. Good job, boy," he said, moving his fingers to where my mouth was wide open and panting.

I felt full, wishing it was his cock but pleased I had proven I could take something so big. Reaching back, all I wanted to do was feel if he was hard, to stroke him in my hand or feel him pushing his length against the back of my throat while I sat on the toy.

But as soon as my hand grazed his dress pants, he again pulled away. He shut the door behind him, and I heard the lock click back in position.

Pulling my jeans over the devoured plug, when I returned to my seat, I could feel everything as I sat down next to him. If I was going to spend five whole hours with this toy inside of me, I hoped that when we landed, I could entice him enough with my open hole to earn his cock.

He had the window seat, but I leaned over enough to see the ocean in what was left of the daylight. It looked different from this height, the colorful shells and shiny creatures smaller than ever.

"I hope you're enjoying my plane, boy," he said and slid the plastic covering on the window closed.

The still nameless man and I were met by a new driver and long black car as the first burst of air of the new climate hit my face. I kept the plug inside of me, but he hadn't mentioned it again since forcing it inside of me in the airplane bathroom. This fresh chauffeur, in his white gloves and Tom of Finland hat, made me wonder if he noticed the precum moistening the front of my jeans as I slid into the backseat. With the toy pushing deeper from the multiple transitions of walking to sitting, if he saw I'd been dripping for almost six hours now, he didn't say anything.

While I sat next to the man in the backseat against new smooth vinyl, the driver looked into the rearview mirror and said, "I hope your trip to the winter estate was satisfactory, Mr. Usher."

The man, Usher, nodded in response, and eyeing me while I wiggled in my seat to adjust the large plug spreading my hole said, "Better than expected," then smiled, just slightly.

We hadn't been driving long when Usher pushed a button on his armrest to raise the partition between us and the driver. "Are you ready to take that toy out, boy?" he asked as the seal closed.

I nodded and felt an unintentional whimper escape me, ready to finally replace the bulbous cone with his cock. He flipped me over and pulled down my jeans, revealing my bare ass framed by the elastic bands of the jockstrap. Pulling at each of the stretchy straps below my cheeks, he let them snap at my upper thighs until the spots began to sting. Then he traced the base of the plug and pushed his finger around my opening until he could force his way past the toy to spread me even more.

Begging for sex had never quite been my style, but I had also never been so completely open. Usher was drawing physical sensations and feelings from me I didn't know existed, a need for his touch and sex. But as I moved my body with the intention of getting his cock near my mouth, he pushed me down. With my face flush to the slick interior, he pulled hard on the toy, attempting to remove it. "Time to give this back, boy," he said as my ass sucked the silicone back in. The resistance felt like quicksand; the harder he pulled, the more my ass swallowed it back up.

When his first few attempts failed, he released for just a moment. "Such a greedy boy," he said and slapped the base of the plug with his flat hand. My cock was dripping again at the sudden impact.

With his other hand still pressing my front-half down, he continued to slap until the skin of either side of my ass burned. Between the snapping of the elastic jockstrap and my cheeks around the toy, I knew my whole backside was red.

I winced at each strike but tried not to whine or whimper under his force. My cock was so hard from the spanking it pushed against his leg. I assumed he could feel it but knew for sure when he asked, "Does it turn you on knowing you already belong to me, boy? That cock, these holes, all of you is mine now."

And while my mouth said "Yes!" without thinking, my body relaxed, and with a swift tug, Usher removed the giant toy from my body. My hole felt wide and exposed to the air. The feeling made me wonder if the windows were as tinted as the other car had been, or if the people on the highways of France could see straight inside of me. His fingers traced my opening again and I felt something warm inside me accompanied by the smacking of Usher's lips. "Swallow that spit up, boy," he said. The warmth dripped deeper in my hole. I had never wanted a man so badly in my life.

When I felt his force release from my neck and back, I used the opportunity to roll until I could get to my feet and straddle him. The movement must have caught him off guard because he allowed me to get far enough to where I could hover my prepared hole over his cock. I grabbed his hands and put them under my shirt, letting him stroke my stomach and chest while I reached down to unbutton his pants. I knew if I could get to his cock and release it, I could have him in me instantly with no resistance from my body.

Usher grabbed me around the hips and gripped hard while his other hand fought me away from his zipper. He hurriedly whispered, "No, boy. We can't." But I wasn't listening. I wasn't paying attention to his commands. Not now, with my cock dripping and hole ready to ride him. I had his button open and zipper half down as he gasped and breathed into my ear, trying to resist me but failing.

It was then the car abruptly braked, and I was flung face-first into the back of the seat in front of me. Cock-out and full of spit on the floor of the town car's shag carpeting. How embarrassing. Usher refastened his pants and didn't help me up from the floor before jumping out of the car. He yelled back at me, "Don't move, boy!" before slamming the door behind him. I could barely see from where I laid in the space picking carpet fibers where they stuck to the lubrication on my skin, but I could hear yelling and sense the glow of fire.

I didn't move, but even if I had pulled my jeans back up to sit into the luxurious bench seats—the ones that totally would have had enough room for us to comfortably fuck on—Usher was quickly back in the car, and were speeding off in a hurry. The partition rolled back down and the driver spoke quickly as Usher ran his hands through his own hair and exhaled nervously. "The hotel?" asked the driver, and Usher nodded with fear in his eyes.

The showers on the boardwalk were always cold, and more often I'd chosen the lukewarm salt water to bathe in when given the option. But in the hotel room, the mirrors were steaming from the heat of the large tub I'd filled over and over. Submerged up to my neck, I wished Usher had stayed with me. That I had been given another opportunity to try to fuck him. Maybe in this jacuzzi tub with built-in jets that was surrounded by mirrors. This was the way to have freaky sex, hands down. Being able to see all the dirty things you do to someone or they do to you reflected back into infinity... this was peak luxury.

Unfortunately, I was alone with the sex tub and had an entire suite full of tufted furniture to myself. The man whose name I had learned only hours before dropped me at the lobby with a key and no further instructions aside from, "To the penthouse, boy. Stay there." He and the driver took off once both of my feet hit the pavement in front of the glass doors. I could only assume they were heading back toward whatever danger and chaos we'd driven away from.

I probably should have been more concerned about what I had gotten myself into, but I was in fucking France with a key to a top-floor hotel room next to people in an elevator who only spoke French and tilted their heads at me when I pushed the "P" button on the lit panel. One man looked down at my jeans, at the wet spot, and shook his head. But I smiled back and nodded to them as they exited to their rooms, all lower than my destination. For once, I was the tourist, and I was enjoying every second of making my vacation memorable.

After cleaning every grain of Beachside from my body in the oversized basin, I ate cheese from a rolling cart that was delivered to the room without my asking. When the bellhop lifted the lid of the silver tray, he said, "*Fromage.*" So I smiled and said back, "*Fromage,*" as if I were saying "yes" or "thank you."

I wasn't certain if the word meant either of the pleasantries I hoped it did, but if he was asking for a tip, I couldn't offer him money. My pockets, although now in a real pair of pants, were still empty. He was cute enough though that if this had been only yesterday, I would have at least offered to blow him through the opening of his tight white uniform. But I didn't.

The bellhop smirked at my terrible French and lowered the top of the tray to the wrinkle-free tablecloth. For a moment, we hung there while he looked me up and down in my robe and moved around the cart to the bed where I was perched. It was nice that French hotels let their staff keep their facial hair, I thought, as he brought his scruffy face close to mine. I could see he was hard under his thin pants, and my cock was threatening to poke its way through one side of the robe where it split at my legs. Our eyes met and the bellhop wet his lips.

When I pushed him away, it wasn't because my body didn't want him. The motion felt instinctual. As though my lust had a particular craving and an awareness I would not be satiated by just any man. The bellhop pulled back politely and adjusted himself in his uniform. "Hmm," he said, pursing his lips.

He followed the sound with words I didn't understand then nodded and smiled at me before exiting the room. Seeing the shape of his ass before he closed the door behind him summoned an unfamiliar feeling. It may have been regret, but more so it was longing. A deep want for the man who had presented me with such extravagance to return. Alone again with only a plate of cheese for my growing appetite, I could only think about Usher.

One thing was certain: it was easier to sleep in the comfort of a plush bed instead of a metal lounge chair. Even if my ceiling was no longer a starlit sky, I could still see the constellations from the large window of the room. The Big Dipper, the Little Dipper—I'd never been much of a size queen and was always happy to see them both on any night.

Taking them in, something felt the same, but the comfort around me was remarkably different. It was funny now, in a way, to think a sandy shore had ever felt like home. That word, home, had meant so many different places over the recent years, but now, I wondered if this new city could become just that. Of course, I'd have a lot more to learn than just the customs of cruising to get by. I'd need to absorb an entire language and discover just how I could meet the expectations of Usher to not only please, but keep him.

I filled the evening by throwing myself around the expansive penthouse. Rummaging through whatever I could find to entertain myself in the solitude until I fell asleep with a large pillow cradling behind me, imagining it was the man pushing into my lower back and ass. In my half-sleeping fantasy, he was keeping me warm and filling me, teaching me new words that all meant sexy things in French. Whispering "boy" at the end of each of his sentences in my ear and telling me all my cum belonged to him until I realized his presence was a dream and had to shift my naked body so my hardness would stop pushing into the mattress.

When I woke in the morning, I was still alone. The same trays materialized at the side of the bed, but this time with fresh bread and orange slices. There was no sign of the attractive bellhop from the night before, and although it seemed I had slept through his presence this time, I thought about what I would have done if he had tried to fuck me again. If I would have had the strength to keep waiting for the man to appear with sexy food dangling in front of me and my appetite turning quickly to starvation.

Figuring the best I could do with my free time was prepare myself for him, I put on the jockstrap he'd selected for me and sprawled across the bed, arching my back anytime I heard the elevator ding. I wanted the first thing the man saw when he reached the room to be my ass in the air waiting for him. But for what felt like hours, I just lay there exposed and rubbing my hardness against the bedsheets, listening for the high-pitched sound.

There weren't other rooms on the floor; the suite took up the entire top portion of the tall building. So when I finally heard the ding, I adjusted the bands of the jockstrap and arched like hell to make sure my ass looked perfect for him. I used the core-strength I had to keep myself in position, holding my breath, then... nothing.

The knob didn't turn and no one came inside. I listened again, wondering if I had imagined the elevator opening onto the floor. There were footsteps shuffling outside.

Even if it was the bellhop coming to deliver me an early lunch, I didn't know why he was lingering outside the entrance. If it was the man, Usher, maybe he was getting himself ready, stroking his cock through the opening in his pants to make himself firm enough to plunge straight into my hole as soon as he saw me. That would be the ideal scenario.

I didn't release my pose, instead closing my eyes and letting the fantasy take me. I'd been avoiding my cock, but now I stroked it lightly. I wanted him to know I was ready for him. Touching the pulsing I'd been saving for him felt so incredible. I felt like I could cum right away and may have had to actively stop myself if my pumping hadn't been interrupted by a knock.

The door creaked open before I could move from my position. "It's time to go," the voice said. It was familiar, but I couldn't place it right away. I just knew it wasn't Usher.

I turned to see the driver who had picked us up at the airport, the man who had probably seen or at least heard Usher filling my gaping ass with his spit in the back of the car. He slid his gloved hand over the frame of the door while I pulled my legs close to my chest on the bed. My cock was still hard and not getting any softer when I took notice of his body.

My robe wasn't far from where he stood, and when he noticed it, he tossed it in my direction, covering my face for just a moment before I slid it down and draped it over myself. "You better put some real clothes on before you get us both in trouble," he said and winked.

I hadn't observed before that not only were we around the same age, but like me, he had trimmed facial hair that connected his mustache and beard around his lips. Perhaps if I hadn't been so fascinated with Usher or had a massive toy expanding my ass, I may have taken the driver in when he'd first picked us up. Maybe I would have noticed the incredibly handsome bearded young man hiding under the shiny black hat and wondered what was underneath his uniform.

As he stood in the doorway smiling at me, I thought about picking up the nearby phone. I thought about calling the hot bellhop for a special request to have both him and the driver pound me into the soft linens currently cradling my bare ass cheeks. It seemed like such a waste for them to have just been slept in and not left in total disarray. The three of us could leave them a nice sticky, sweaty mess. That was the kind of room service I deserved in a place like this.

But somehow, a voice pushed through my dirty thoughts. One that I hadn't heard since the day before in the mansion near the beach. It was the voice from the portrait, and it whispered softly but directly. It told me if I really wanted to be financially satisfied, I would save myself for Usher.

In the car, I could only see the back of the young driver's head, his dark hair sticking out from under his hat, when he said in slightly broken English, "It's usually much prettier here." He was commenting on the trees lining the asphalt stretch we were driving on. They were shades of black and grey and appeared charred as though they had been burned.

His English wasn't bad, better than my French by far, and I was happy to have someone to talk to since the bellboy and I hadn't exchanged many words.

"Was there a fire?" I asked, seeing that we were approaching a gate similar to the one in Beachside. The driver nodded before stopping the car just before the gate.

"Some people in town, they ... think we are wrong. You understand," he said and opened his car door. From the back window, I could see the metal barrier required a key to unlock a large padlock attached to thick chains woven through the iron bars. On either side was a long brick wall that went on endlessly in either direction until it disappeared into dense forest. When we drove through the gate, the driver exited again to close it all behind him and stashed the key in his coat pocket.

In a way, I did understand. People thinking I was "wrong," as the handsome driver described it, was the reason I left the place where I was raised. Not the beach town, but before that in a life when I was chased from my own warm bed for admitting who I was to people who said they loved me. That moment was the start of a long series of moves and searching for a new place to lay my head. And as the mansion came into view on the other end of the long driveway, I noticed how much it matched the Beachside manor, just larger in scale, and I wondered if I could ever call a place so large home.

Arriving at the house, it looked nearly identical to the one he'd shown me across the sea but somehow alive. One difference I noticed immediately as we walked through the front door was the lights worked, but even if they hadn't, there were enough candles lit to illuminate the vast foyer.

Music was coming from a room just beyond the entrance, and a boy in a jockstrap was delicately playing the violin. Other boys sat listening, all in their underwear with their furry chests exposed. But the first eyes that met mine didn't come from any of them. Instead, it was the familiar pair from the portrait in the other house staring back at me. The same picture and set of men, just silent.

The driver took off his hat and caught me inspecting the painting. One of the men, the younger one, was kneeling and something in his face seemed so familiar. "Who is that?" I asked the young handsome driver. In response, he nodded toward the gay concert hall only a few feet from us and put a finger to his lips. "Shh," he said.

I tried to be polite and listen as he led me closer to the candlelit room full of cushy sitting pillows and hairy crossed legs. When the boy stopped playing whatever melodramatic classical piece he had committed to memory, the young men clapped. I saw a boy eye me then whisper into the ear of the handsome driver. Now stripped down to his own backless underwear and nothing else. As if addressing the entire room, the driver said, "Yes, the American."

Whispers in French were all around me accompanied by mischievous smiles. I was the only one still in my clothes, and soon I was surrounded by the young hairy French men. One pulled at my shirt while the others undid my jeans. Hands covered my body until I stood in just my jockstrap like the rest of them.

It was difficult not to notice the similarities in our bodies. We were all different shades of skin, hair, and eyes, but our frames and the body hair from our faces to stomachs were all the same. Otters. Furry young otters.

One boy spoke. It was all French, but his inflection indicated he was asking me a question. And to his inquiry, I responded with the only French word I'd heard: "*Fromage.*"

All the boys laughed around me until a voice said, "I taught him that." It was the bellboy from the hotel who somehow looked even sexier out of uniform. He walked closer and pinched at my nipple. "That's your name now, you know. You are *Fromage*."

I couldn't tell if he was flirting or making fun of me, but it didn't matter when I saw all the boys turn their attention to some place beyond me. A voice boomed as it descended closer to us. "No, his name is boy, like all of you." It was Usher coming down a marble staircase and into the grand foyer, smiling. Near him, standing but attached to a leash by a thick collar, was the other driver. The one from Beachside, before we got on the plane.

Neither spoke while they approached. The room fell silent. But in the candlelight with shirtless men all around me, I didn't feel out of place. I counted the boys where we stood. Including the two drivers, the bellhop, myself, and three more boys I only knew so far by the colors of the underwear—Blue, Green, and a sort of Burgundy—there were seven of us.

As Usher made his entrance, he did little but nod and set a large black whip in the center of the room. The boys seemed well-trained and immediately grabbed colored ropes from a nearby wall. Each boy put his hands behind his back with their rope, and one at a time, they fastened each other in place. The driver from Beachside, still in his collar, approached me with a vibrant orange coil, and without a word, I turned and let him secure me tightly. My cock was rock hard feeling him pull at the cord until he knew I couldn't escape without assistance.

When only one boy remained, the driver in the collar, Usher tied his hands himself and released him into the circle we'd all formed instinctively. We rounded Usher in the dim light and he pulled each boy's underwear to his ankles until all of our cocks were out. The mood was quiet and sinister with the whip sitting in the middle of the polished tile like a threat, and at the sight of my instant firmness, Usher shook his head with disapproval.

I was participating in a game I didn't know the rules to, but as I watched Usher jerk off each boy with spit from his own mouth, I saw them try to fight against the pleasure. They stood in their place and shifted the weight between their feet. They bit at their lips. When they seemed close, he would stop and move onto the next boy, stroking long enough to torment and edge them before taking on the next.

As my turn came around again, I did my best to use their tactics and resist getting excited, but feeling the ropes against my wrist reminded me of when he'd restrained me on the beach. It made me think about how good it felt when he'd jerked me off and opened my hole on the plane. I'd been waiting so long to feel him touch me again, and now, he finally was.

I knew my cock was dripping and watched as Usher tasted my precum and smiled. He whispered, "You're doing well, boy. Just relax," before walking back to the center of the circle to retrieve the whip.

Immediately, the other boys turned their bare asses to their master. They knew the rules, but what they were competing for, I wasn't certain. Usher cracked the long strip against the first boy's hairy nakedness until he glowed on each cheek. I hadn't turned around yet, but when he pierced me with his eyes, I knew I would pay for disobeying him. I flipped my eyes to the wall and offered him my ass, no longer framed by the orange jockstrap he'd selected with intention days before.

I had wanted this then, to have him see my ass prepared and ready for him, but I hadn't imagined it would be like this—with other boys around and sharing his attention. Without warning, the whip thundered against my skin, and each bolt made me consider the reality I found myself in. Around me were endlessly opulent things. A life I could never have had on my own.

A voice whispered, "It can be yours," and I wanted to look at the painting to see if the men in the portrait were speaking to me, but

I was afraid to look anywhere aside from the wall while he snapped the tail at my skin over and over.

The pain came over me like a rolling tide, and for a moment, my mind was clear. Usher had come to Beachside for only one reason: to find me and bring me back here. It had been the house that commanded him to include me in this ritual. Not only did I belong in this castle, I had been summoned here. But I still didn't understand why he had left me in the hotel room for so long.

After I had successfully endured the pain Usher dealt, he seemed tired of controlling the whip and commanded that the boys turn back around. He went back to working their cocks until Blue came, then Green, then the bellhop.

It wasn't pleasant anymore, having him stroke me while I tried to hold the cum inside; it was torture. Something told me if I could just endure it a little longer, I would win Usher's love. If I could outlast the rest of the boys, I could have him all to myself.

Burgundy's cock was the type that pointed toward his belly button, and when he exploded, it dripped down the fur on his stomach. Next was the French chauffeur, who moaned and squirmed in Usher's hand before shooting his load so far it landed halfway to where I stood across from him.

Between the American driver and myself, we were the last, and Usher unexpectedly stopped his stroking and pumping. He untied our hands and pulled us each to the center of the circle by our cocks. The boys still tied and surrounding us watched as Usher moved the driver's hand to my cock and mine to his. This was the last round of the competition it seemed, and it was about to be brutal.

Gripping hard and stroking, I didn't know his background, but I'd had years of practice and was confident in my skills. I flicked at the underside of his foreskin and rubbed his own precum up and down his shaft. When I took some of my own to mix them together, I could feel his arousal reaching a peak. His eyes got wide, like he knew he'd already lost. And despite how good it felt to feel his hand around me, when his warm cum dripped down my closed fist, I knew I had won.

Usher smiled at me, and the boys cheered, jumping in place with their jockstraps still around their ankles. It looked like the master of the house was about to announce something, but in that moment, banging came from the exterior of the mansion. Yellow and red light filled the windows and heat soon followed. Something exploded. Then something else. And soon we were all on the ground showered by broken stained glass and fire.

A mob of what must have been people from the town, the ones the French driver had told me thought men like us were wrong, pushed through the front doors. Just before they surrounded us all, I saw the fear back in Usher's eyes as he yelled, "Run, boy!"

On my feet, I bolted for the other boys and tried to untie them. We jumped over cum and whips and toys, dodging the townspeople who infiltrated our sanctuary. I led the boys up the stairs of the house, but every time I turned back, another boy was missing. It wasn't until I grabbed a door knob on the second floor and locked myself inside that I realized they had all been taken, as if they had vanished into nothing while we ran for safety.

I panted with my soft cock out on the other side of the door, but suddenly everything was silent. Nothing was loud or breaking or burning. When I looked behind me, a large bed sat covered with a dusty sheet. It couldn't be.

Pulling open the door, I saw the cobwebs first, hanging in the darkness. I didn't understand how I had gotten there, but I was in the other house. The one close to Beachside. And everyone was gone.

I called into the dimness of the hallway, "Hello?" and my own voice echoed back. At the end, as it had hung before, was the portrait. Walking slowly, I could see even from halfway down the sheet-covered stretch that something had changed. The young man who had been on his knees was older and in the standing position. I knew why he looked familiar now. And next to him, kneeling, was me.

Leaning in close, I surveyed the image of the men in a way I hadn't been able to before. I traced the deep colors of the faces and details. It seemed to have captured every hair and my body and Usher's eyes, those piercing yet kind eyes, were just as I remembered them.

I'd been naked up until that point, still full of cum from hours of being edged, and knew it was almost out of my control when I began pumping at my cock. Looking deep into Usher's face, the way his body filled the fancy suit he always wore, it took no time at all for my load to spill onto the lush carpet below. I closed my eyes tightly as I came; something had finally released.

When I opened them again, the portrait had changed once more. Instead of two men, there was only one. The Usher I knew was gone, and in his place was the boy from the previous painting. Me, in the fancy suit. There was a nameplate I hadn't noticed before, below the image, and although the man had never asked, if he had, I would have told him my name was Madden.

It was what the small silver plaque said until I looked down to see the imitation was now manifesting in reality. I felt warm and layered. Every part of my hairy body was dressed from head-to-toe in fabric that rubbed against me in a way that felt expensive. The chandeliers and sconces clicked on in the mansion and classical music, like the violin I'd watched the boy in the jockstrap play, cascaded from the linked speakers. All the cobwebs and sheets were gone. Everything inside sparkled.

Looking back at the plaque, my name melted away and replaced itself with five letters spelling out: U-s-h-e-r.

"What do I have to do?" I asked the house, but it said nothing in return. Once again, I was alone in a place not far from water people called the ocean, but never the sea. But as I clicked my shiny shoes through the marble surfaces of what seemed to be my new home, I couldn't shake the feeling that in a world where I had always been the colorful shell creature seeking shelter, the House of Otter had other ideas of who it needed me to become.

THE END

Leo Sparx

Claiming
ALEXANDER

The fall of the *House of Otter* 1

DEDICATION

To Otter Boys
I've loved before

Chapter One

❦

*"His heart is a tightened lute;
as soon as one touches it, it echoes."*

The familiar brick was rough and sandy against the sensitive skin of my fingertips. During my walks to the better side of town, something led me to complete my routine in the woods near a certain house. I'd never understood it, but at my first glimpse of the building, something arose in me alongside my melancholy. The mystery of what lay beyond the wall created a tension beneath the fabric of my jeans that begged for instant release.

It had become a ritual to glide my hand along the length of the grainy brick until I reached the end. Then walk a few paces into the forest until I found a large tree to lean against. The smell of moss and bark filled me as I planted my boots in the soft dirt. I intended to take my time, to let my thumb and index finger find their way under my t-shirt and around my nipples. With my abdomen exposed, the light breeze of the woods tickled while I pinched and swirled around the hard circles.

The line of hair leading into my jeans became a direct trail to my growing stiffness, and I allowed my hand to wander, teasing as I played with the top button of my jeans and slid a single finger between the fabric and my skin. The tightness of the stretchy band moved the delicate flesh of my finger against the bone, back and forth, in and out, begging to be thrust deeper into the warmth building below as dead leaves fell around me.

We didn't have trees that changed to fall colors in Beachside. On this side of town, the timber was as tall as the houses I was too poor to live in. The day had been mostly silent as I passed each mansion, no sound as the autumn leaves drifted just below the canopy before settling to the crunchy ground.

Miles from the shore, these mansions had enough forest acreage to be called manors. Some even had their own names, acting as landmarks to guide me as I continued on my typical path. They were all surrounded by walls and pushed back behind iron gates to keep people like me out.

I often imagined the people living inside to be their own particular shade of happiness: vibrant yellow or burnt orange or maybe some color yet to be discovered or too expensive for someone like me to see outside of a museum. The residents were complete people. They had polished cars, extensive closets, and shiny things only money could buy. What I experienced on my walks over to the better side of town seemed to start with loneliness, but ended with deep longing.

The final exhibit which often ended my tour stood as alone as I felt, nestled between a gloomy forest. Its dark brick and painted wood was framed in a mist, the promise of winter looming in the coming weeks. When I stood at the easement of overgrown hedges and moist grass, I admired the tall pillars and shapes creating the massive structure. It was so incredible in size that I was often moved to call it a castle. Before I'd ventured into the woods, I took notice of the welded metal letters across the rusted front gate. The archway above the locked entrance read, "The House of Otter."

Now leaning against what had become one of my favorite thick trees, I spiraled my fingertip against the clasp of my jeans. The chill of the round button in the breeze sent a delightful rush through my body, making my nipples and cock even harder. My back against the green moss of the broad trunk, I let it carry my weight as I leaned farther back. I released the button and allowed my grasp to move to the bronze zipper. Flicking it back and forth, I mimicked the motions I ached to apply to the pulsing bulge. Just the thought of rubbing the exposed head of my cock made the tension nearly unbearable. I couldn't stop myself from tugging the zipper down, letting the matching teeth open slowly.

Immediately, the crisp autumn air made the precum dripping from me icy. The droplets resembled dew on a furry meadow, viscous and slippery. I used my palm to coat the length of my thickness with the liquid. The temperatures combined into a sensation so pleasurable, I was producing much more natural lubrication than usual—enough that I could bring the taste to my bottom lip with a finger to sample the flavor. Then I took a firmer grasp around my girth.

Finally giving myself permission to stroke, I thought about the House of Otter. I imagined the mysterious man inside I had only heard stories about and wondered if he really did have a house full of hairy boys that were his possessions. Was there a chance it could be true that once he owned them, they were his forever? At the idea of giving myself to a man in that way— trading my body for comfort and security—the pulsing part of me knew I would give anything to live behind those walls.

But the house was empty. Not once on my walks had I seen anyone coming or going. There were no cars in the grand driveway or rolling down the long blacktop. I hadn't noticed any faces through the opaque windows. The aged gate remained padlocked shut. Most likely the legends the people on my side of town had created—the stories of this eccentric millionaire—were intended to amuse themselves. There was no man. No collection of boys for him to play with. And yet, the sight of the house aroused me so much I couldn't help but imagine life inside the manor.

It was often with that thought that I could feel everything that had been building inside me contracting and ready to release. Looking down at my cock, the pubic hair surrounding the mound, dense and slightly curled—I thought of the past. I thought about the boys who had complimented my sex. While I appreciated their admiration—and at certain points their hands and mouths—it had never been more than physical. It was rarely anything other than a form of quick release. Recently, I'd discovered nothing was as satisfying as my walks in the woods where I could be alone with my fantasies of the house.

I parted my lips and let my tongue push out enough saliva to lubricate my strokes. The new liquid created a silky glide that found its way into the foreskin surrounding my bare head. From the base of my pubic bone to my exposed peak, the spit slid back and forth between the hole I'd formed with my fist. Pulling the loosened foreskin over and around the head sent me into a trance that forced me to lose my balance. My boots slipped in the soggy dirt below while my hard cock stood out in the open and my balls hung through my parted jeans.

Steadying myself, sweat formed in the thick hair under my armpits. I moved the hand that had been keeping attention on my nipples to the bottom of my shirt and quickly tucked the material into my mouth. It was doubtful anyone could hear me out this far into the woods. Regardless of the stories I had created in my mind—the ones sending me over the edge—there was probably not a soul dwelling in the adjacent manor or nearby. But still, stuffing the base of my sweat-covered shirt in my mouth gave me access to stroke harder.

The new barrier stifled my moans as I thought about a smirking man tracing the salty residue on my abdomen with his tongue. His fingers in my mouth, holding the fabric of my shirt in place, he told me if I were a good boy, I would cum hard. In my head, his words echoed telling me I would shoot my load for him and give him every drop I had. But I would do it quietly.

By then it was too much, and I felt everything inside of me that day grow into a crescendo. With the grey clouds above and crunching brown leaves below, the sadness I had carried with me the entire walk through the countryside burst to the ground near my boots in a series of quick spurts.

The relief was immediate but temporary. I let the white release settle into the moistened earth as I tucked myself away and re-fastened the zipper to close my jeans. My shirt, dampened from my mouth, now hung slightly misshapen around my waist.

I exhaled and pushed myself from the tree to let my footing normalize. The weight I had been holding in my planted boots redistributed to the rest of my body. I felt dizzy while the autumn chill cooled the sweat on my skin, and the large house through the rigid trunks came back into focus. My walks had become the best part of my day, and now that portion of the day was over.

On my way out of the woods and back to my more humble existence, I looked back at the House of Otter. I thought about the man I had conjured in my imagination just moments before, the one whose fingers in my mouth tasted like money and power.

CHAPTER TWO

B ack home, the wooden shutters had been crumbling since
before I moved in. No one ever bothered locking the door.
Using my evening to walk around the better side of town did
little anymore to help me forget that by nightfall I'd be back where
rain leaked through the brittle roof and buckets caught the water
that eventually spilled over into the stained beige carpet. Tonight—
even though it hadn't rained in days—on the couch between two
full leak receptacles, the first thing I saw was a backpack.

My eyes adjusted through the dim lighting enough to eventually see that the backpack, though seemingly suspended in mid-air
and pumping back and forth, was attached to a male frame. Broad
shoulders and buzzed hair, pants pulled down just enough, as if he
was making a quick stop at the urinal. In front of him was my roommate Darius, balanced on his knees between the sagging cushions.
On all-fours with his elbows over the back of the couch, his furry ass
was facing the stranger. Backward hat in position, he was prepared
for the moment the boy behind him was ready to shoot his load;
assuring the bill wouldn't get in the way of any drops landing in his
mouth when he transitioned to face him.

The sound of the creaking door didn't stop the stranger or my
friend. For a quick moment, Darius's brown eyes were on me, the
side of his face—stubble and half-smile—pressed on the harder part
of the couch, moving in rhythm. He raised his eyebrows, looking

down toward the crotch of my jeans with a sparkle in his eye, an invitation. Whether I'd just spent myself out in the woods or not, the answer had always been, and would always be, "No, thank you."

Free sex had never been difficult for me to come by in this house, if I had wanted it. For Darius and the rest of the boys living here, a fee was only required for an outsider. With the amount of patrons coming and going, there was a reason the front door remained unbolted, why the couch and beds were lumpy and always slightly damp in any season. I couldn't judge the other boys in the house. While I didn't partake in the offers for a free hook-up with any of them, it wasn't because I thought of them as dirty or damaged; they were all cute in their own way and nice enough. To look down on them would be to paint my own portrait with the same materials. Because there was a reason we all ended up here together, and it involved our shared profession.

Flopping on the bed in my room, I found staring at the ceiling did little to facilitate an escape. The peeling wallpaper and patches of mildew in the corners, the hinges on everything rusting and shedding red-brown dust to the floor were constant reminders that I was living in what barely qualified as a house. Certainly not prestigious enough to have its own laid-brick privacy wall, or tall hedges, and definitely not its own name. Not like the House of Otter.

As empty as I was, I could feel myself getting hard again just thinking about being back in the woods near the manor, about the man who had stifled my screams of ecstasy, my moans of pure pleasure. The idea of him had seemed so real in the woods—his fingers and tongue tracing my sweat and skin, his words in my ear with demands so clear, and my eagerness to comply with anything he wanted, my desire to simply please him.

For just a moment, I let myself slide my hands toward the top of my jeans. I couldn't believe just the thought of him was rousing such a reaction from me after having expelled so much from myself already. Yet, I felt full and ready again, prepared to give the man anything he asked for, to shoot any load, as many as he requested. The hardness in my jeans was again becoming unbearable, and I felt my hand moving swiftly to undo the top button—

"That's it man—turn around! Open wide." The sound of the stranger's deep voice echoed through the undecorated house from the living room, the walls reverberating with the sudden growl. Darius and the boy with the backpack may as well have been right outside my door, or next to me in bed, as the volume rose on their climax. I stopped touching myself. My cock went soft. I rolled my eyes and then closed them. If this was my reality, then I'd rather be dreaming.

In the morning, I found my way to the kitchen where Darius was standing in a jockstrap in front of the refrigerator.

"Playing soccer today?" I asked facetiously, leaning over the counter.

"Definitely got some balls on the books," Darius said, finding my eyes and smirking while he bent farther into the refrigerator to push some milk out of the way of the orange juice. He grabbed two mostly-clean glasses from the cabinet and poured us each a few ounces from the carton that undoubtedly had been sucked from by everyone in the house. "We're doing fancy breakfast today."

"What's the occasion?" I asked, searching for the cleanest part of the rim to sip from. Darius dug around for a second before he revealed a wad of cash from the front pouch of his jockstrap, presumably from somewhere tucked behind his sack. Chances were he hadn't taken a shower after last night either.

"You could have had some of this too, if you'd actually work from time to time in this work-house." He put the cash to his nose and gave it a short inhale, smiled, then tucked it away again, his most recent payment now hidden somewhere in the lockbox he had created in his underwear between his collection of money-makers.

He wasn't wrong. I wasn't certain how long it had been since I'd hooked-up with someone, for money or otherwise. If I hadn't been so frugal with the funds I had left, I would have been back on the street months ago. When I did take clients, I was always phoning it in, never present, just going through the motions of letting the other guy have a good time. But then the customers stopped booking, my unspoken language had become a pretty clear "closed for business" sign. I was tired of touching them, and they were tired of the way my body would pull back when they touched me. Long-time hook-ups dwindled to a halt and I never, ever, took walk-ins.

"It's like you hate money almost as much as you hate men." Darius kept speaking but was already done with his orange juice. He turned his attention to the wet spots near the couch and pushed at them with the toe of his sneaker, trying to discern which ones were rain water and which were something more slippery. "Not that I blame you. They do certainly make a mess."

Bundled up on the couch was one of our other roommates, Sonny, whom I rarely saw awake at all. He seemed to move from room to room like a pet, trying to find a new comfy place to settle in. In the time I'd lived here, I'd seen him go a solid eighteen hours curled in a ball. Loud music, parties, customers coming in and out—nothing seemed to bother his expert level sleep schedule. Darius grabbed a ratty sleeping bag from the floor, smelled it, and shrugged. Deeming it clean enough, he spread it over Sonny's nakedness and patted his head lovingly.

Tracing the glass circle at the top of my beverage, I knew Darius didn't expect a reply or extended conversation on the topic that had been presented. Like Sonny, I paid my portion of the rent on time for now, and that was all anyone in the house needed to know. But Darius was aware, as much as I was, that my money was running out. With the lack of jobs available in Beachside, this really was the only reasonable profession for boys like us.

"A letter came for you. Like a real letter, on paper. I didn't even know we could get mail here, but I guess they just slipped it under the door." Darius grabbed a sealed envelope from the corner of the front room. Slightly wet, like everything else in the house, the ink on the front said my full name in dripping black letters.

Careful not to destroy the contents, I used the saturation to open the envelope at the top with a single finger. Unfolding the paper inside, I saw the note was short and had an address in the center. Below that, the signature was large and filled most of the paper. It read, "Roderick."

"Who's Roderick?" Darius asked, grabbing my empty glass from me as he peaked over my shoulder. The memories flooded back quickly, but the question wasn't easy to answer. Who was Roderick? Before my life here, he was everything.

CHAPTER THREE

A s a kid, I'd often found myself collecting things. It's a reflex when you have very little to hoard the things you do, especially free things, items I could acquire from the earth. Gathering shells into an empty cup one day, I saw Roderick's shadow on the sand before I heard him speak. A summer sun beat down, and we were both standing shirtless with the waves rolling in to cover our bare feet. I'd seen him before but was always too shy to say hello, having learned to keep to myself while staying out of the house, where I'd often woke to the sound of objects being thrown against walls.

Rising, with my heap of sea treasures spilling from my styrofoam container, Roderick spoke first. "You want to make some money?" he asked.

Through the blinding sun, I nodded to his silhouette, and we were quickly picking through my collection all afternoon to find the largest pieces. We sat crossed-legged on top of a deteriorating picnic table near the beach playground, carefully selecting shells to receive a full coat of a designated color and a hastily scribbled green dollar sign.

Blue was worth the least, then purple, but it was the yellows we made the most profit from. Selling them to other poor neighborhood kids, our "shell dollars" were marked-up several-hundred percent, considering paint was easy enough to steal from people's sheds or the hobby store in town.

Our schemes evolved as we grew taller and could focus on adults with actual money, learning over time we shared as much of an appreciation for making quick money as we did for men. The teamwork was essential because Roderick knew how to pick them, but only I could carry it through. It was easy to rip a guy off, to pretend you were going to blow him and then run off with his wallet instead. But it became a game after a while to see how far either one of us would take a situation.

One particular evening, on the cusp of adulthood, we'd been living in an alley between a pizza place and sushi restaurant. Only one was a reasonable place for scraps, and we'd been living on garlic crust for weeks. A man invited me to his apartment, and inside it was all clear glass vases with little bubbles in them. It was countless mirrors that made the rooms look even bigger than they were. Something about the interior made me the most erect I'd ever been at that point in my life.

In most situations, I'd find the money and escape as quickly as possible. But tonight, I'd made the first move and kissed the man. I liked feeling his beard against my skin, letting him hold me in his arms in his silky sheets while Roderick waited downstairs, expecting me to run out with the goods and be ready for a quick getaway. I must have been up there for a couple hours but when I finally did make my way downstairs, Roderick was still leaning on a railing outside the swanky apartment building.

"I seriously thought you were dead up there," he said, trying to keep his tone level, but his face was full of an emotion I couldn't place. Was it anger, concern...jealousy? "Where's the money?" I held out the modest amount the man had given me in exchange for our encounter. Not only the first blowjob I'd ever given, but the first everything.

"Okay." He seemed displeased. The money in hand was an affirmation I had gone through with the original proposition that granted me entrance. "Where's the wallet though?"

The truth was, I hadn't gotten it. I'd been so overwhelmed by the experience, I hadn't even thought to grab it. I was happy to have been paid for something I actually enjoyed.

Roderick sighed and pushed himself off the railing. "So he likes them young, huh? Alright, let's hope he's rested up." He started toward the lobby entrance of the apartment building.

"You're going up there?" I asked, surprised.

"I'm not leaving without the wallet," he responded, already pushing through the door.

It was an hour later when he finally returned, wallet and payment bulging in his pocket, a satisfied smile on his face matching my own. As strong as our bond had been since meeting that day on the beach and becoming partners, something unbreakable started with the experience of losing our virginity on the same night, even if it hadn't been to each other.

There wasn't much in the letter, just the address in town not far from the alley where we used to sleep side-by-side on cold pavement together. The scrawled message simply said, "I need you." Regardless of how we left things before going our separate ways from sharing body heat in chilled alleys and undersides of bridges, I had meant it when I told him if he ever asked, I would be there.

As impressed as I was that Roderick was living in a home at all, the outside of the apartment was expectedly rough; empty bottles on the front stoop and paper bags blowing in the sea air. There were perks to living in a harbor community—edible plants and cheap ocean showers—until the natural sodium in the air began to degrade every piece of metal and make the exterior wood swell. Seagulls pecking at trash and leaving food remnants in a trail leading from the buildings to the sea, sediment and burnt oil always hanging in the air combined with the thick of something fried and salty; realistically, life there, was the worst scented candle, ever.

Six flights later, I was standing in front of a door with a crooked number barely hanging on the textured plaster. Dirt handprints marked the bordering walls, and vinyl flooring was peeling back around the doorframe. A dump equal to my own, but still a giant leap from the places we'd called home in the past. It seemed, alone, we were doing quite well for ourselves. Perhaps I was right when I had told him the last night we were together that I didn't need him anymore.

I was still catching my breath from the climb up the steel steps when Roderick answered my knock. He wore a wide open multi-colored housecoat and track shorts with a less than three-inch inseam. How he was balancing each ball on either side of the stitching was a mystery. But it was a look he was definitely pulling off.

"Alexander!" He instantly wrapped his arms around me, the soft fabric of his housecoat draping around my shoulders, holding us together in a furry, partially-closed cocoon for just a moment. I had forgotten how warm it felt to be against him.

From the doorway, over his shoulder, I could already see the interior of his quarters were small, but like his costume, a sort of boho-chic: tapestries on the walls, kitschy knick-knacks in every direction, and a hanging fruit basket full of ripe produce hanging in a doll-sized kitchen.

"I'm glad you got my note. I knew you wouldn't have a phone, so I didn't even bother asking around for a number," Roderick said, releasing my body to close the door and lead me to a sitting area covered in scarves and cushy floor poufs.

"Oh, and you do?" I assumed I already knew the answer as I was asking the question. He'd never had a reliable phone either. But taking in the remainder of the apartment I hadn't seen revealed a huge television on the wall, a computer, and an impressive collection of camera equipment. The lens pointed toward one of the tapestry-covered walls.

"I do now." He took out the newest possible phone from a pocket I didn't imagine his housecoat would have, the phone I'd been told people had just been waiting in line for a week before. Never the shy one, Roderick put his device down next to us on the couch and smiled. Holding my hand in his, he said, "Do you want to make some money?"

Chapter Four

"A millionaire?" I asked, looking through the lens of the camera fixed to the top of a tripod. A black image stared back at me.

"No, BILLIONAIRE," Roderick corrected, removing the cap from the front of the camera with a quick motion to reveal the framing of the tapestry and more rainbow-colored floor poufs. I hadn't noticed the array of sex toys sitting on the side tables until now, the different sizes and shapes, butt plugs and dildos. Some housed batteries and probably vibrated, others had bright jewels or thick rubber tails at the end, the kind that wiggled when they were inside a tight hole.

He didn't spare me the details of what he'd been up to since we'd parted ways. The mysterious man tipping him the moment he entered his cam room, the gifts that started appearing at his door followed by the nightly private shows and sudden sponsorship of upgraded broadcasting equipment. The way he found new hairs on his ass by seeing it in full high-definition, and how he had learned to love each one.

"You don't know what a joy it is to pay rent and still have money left over, to not feel like you're being cheated out of your income just sending a check for your electric bill." Roderick spoke as he moved dildos around the set, cleaning them off with a spray and wipes, then stacking them on their bases in a line according to size. "Sure, he's demanding. He requires my full attention. But there's nothing like casually saying you're in the mood for pizza, having one just show up within thirty minutes, and getting paid to let him watch you enjoy it. It's full-time, but some of the easiest work I've ever done."

"So, what's the con?" I asked, not certain how much longer I was going to be able to listen to stories about his bliss knowing at some point I'd be going back home to my leaky roof and stained pillows. I stood up from my bent position where I had been looking through the camera lens to the cinematic version of Roderick. Unfiltered and back in reality, he was just as handsome as I remembered thinking he was the day we met on the beach.

He stopped arranging the silicone and polyurethane. Lifting an industrial-sized bottle of lube to slide back under the table, he said, "Well, I've been invited for something more... physical, let's say. Our mysterious billionaire friend would like me to come to his residence for the evening."

"Hopefully longer, if he's as rich as you're saying." I meant to sound optimistic, but I'm certain I sounded jealous.

"Hmm." Roderick paused for a moment, thinking something over before he spoke again. "I need you to be there tonight because I intend to grab a few things on my way out."

I had questions about why he would sabotage a good situation and steady source of income to mop a few extra bucks or wallet full of credit cards that would eventually just get cancelled. Why rip off a billionaire to take some unique dinnerware or a couple handfuls of expensive toiletries, when you could keep the checks rolling in instead? But over all of that, my immediate question was, "Tonight?"

"We have a few hours to prepare, and understand, I also intend to stay on payroll after this. My concern is the sustainability of this situation. Getting too comfortable is death. Plus, he just seems a bit..." Roderick struggled for the word. It didn't seem like he was searching for the right one as much as deciding how honest he should be with me.

"A bit what?" I asked, letting myself fall ass-first onto one of the woven tweed poufs that seemed to cover at least half of the flooring in his apartment. I leaned back on my hands, spreading my knees with my feet facing toward him. I couldn't see if he was looking, but I could feel his gaze burning into my jeans, the same ones I'd been wearing the day before and were probably still stained with salty droplets.

"Intense. Yeah, let's go with intense." He cleared his throat. "Like, I don't know. He's some dude I met on the internet, and I've never seen his face. So there's that, but he's also just very particular, and I want to have a back-up plan if things get weird."

"So I'm your backup plan then?"

Instead of responding, Roderick wandered into the tiny kitchen to pull a turquoise kettle from a cabinet. "Tea?" he asked, but I knew he planned to prepare it regardless of my answer.

I nodded. He just wanted me there for security. That was it. No new con, no recreating the wheel. We were going to pull the same shit we'd been doing since we were kids, the same set-up that never seemed to get us ahead before, but—according to Roderick—was suddenly the answer to all our problems. At least I wouldn't have to get my dick out or touch anyone else's to make some money.

With two mismatched cups and saucers, Roderick joined me on one of the nearby pieces of pseudo-furniture. As comfortable as I felt, it was hard to remember we hadn't seen each other in over a year. It was even more difficult to remember the exact reason why we had stopped talking, the specific incident that had made me believe we could never be part of each other's lives again.

The tea was too hot for my mouth, but Roderick was already drinking it down, placing the cup on the saucer with a clink only to pick it right back up and continue sipping. His lips red and slightly swollen from the heat, moist and velvety from the herbs—he didn't have the kind of mouth that made it easy for men to say no.

"How dangerous is this going to be?" I asked, setting my cup on the coffee table. I wanted the truth, but I already knew I wouldn't get it.

Roderick quietly set his tea down near mine and retrieved his phone from the couch cushions where we'd been sitting before. He put it in my hand and nodded to the various forms of new technology around his place, to the endless pizza boxes he'd stacked into a shrine to his own accomplishment and formed into some sort of art installation, to the twenty-some-odd probably overpriced bohemian bean bags he'd decided to spend his money on, the nest he'd earned himself and built piece-by-piece.

"How badly do you want to get out of that rat hole you're calling a house?" he asked.

CHAPTER FIVE

I had told Roderick in the past that just because something was black didn't mean it was still indistinguishable from the darkness once it had sequins added to it. But here I was, creeping from his wrought-iron fire escape in faux-leather pants so tight they squeezed my ass cheeks and a mesh tank-top studded with glittering rhinestones along the collar.

"It's the only black I have!" Roderick had said, throwing it at me while we were changing. There was no way that was true, but compared to the sheer catsuit he had prepared for himself, mine was definitely the more solid option. My only concern as the sun began to set and the streetlights buzzed alive, was leaving my dirty jeans at his apartment in case something went wrong and the police somehow ended up scrubbing the place for DNA evidence. Our cons had never gone that wrong, but there was always a chance they could.

From the height of the fire-escape, the sea breeze was cooling. The salty smell was almost pleasurable compared to my typical association of the ocean with poverty. Living seaside, being a beach creature, you may as well live under the ocean to anyone dwelling a few miles west. Which was exactly where we were heading in our carefully constructed attire, to the manors on the countryside where the rich people lived.

Roderick's heels clicked on the pavement in front of me, leading the way. The transparent fabric on his body allowed the breeze to flow through, pushing the hair on his chest with the direction of the gusts. Even his dark beard and the peach fuzz on his ass seemed to sway with the briny air.

"Why are you wearing black, though? He knows you're coming." I was already loud-whispering, hoping my voice would carry over the light howl of the wind. We had been walking for a few miles before it occurred to me that I was the only one needing to be camouflaged during this caper.

"I look fucking cute in this," Roderick said over his shoulder. Fair enough. He did. "I have to show off my fur; it's his favorite part of me." He did a full turn in my direction as he finished speaking to run a single finger down the deep v-neck of the catsuit through the lush forest on his chest and stomach, stopping just short of where the tight backless briefs hugged below his belly button. I tried to remember how far the hair went down, but he turned back around before the image materialized.

Beachside was far away by the time we crossed over the train tracks. Gravel thick under our feet, I was glad I was still in my boots. At some point, we started to merge with my usual daily walk, passing the large houses and gates, the ones pushed back so only their balconies and roofs were in view from the path. I wanted to tell Roderick about my walks, about the sadness that had gotten so thick, at times it felt like I was drowning, about not being able to keep working or touch anyone, that something happened to me after we stopped relying on each other. But I said nothing, worried our codependency would return if I ever hinted at how much I needed him.

"He said to go through the woods on the side and then around the back," Roderick said, pushing himself on his hands to attempt a peek over a wall. I'd been so in my head I hadn't realized I was touching the familiar brick, that my hand had been tracing it instinctively. We had arrived at the laid stone wall with the archway and locked gate, The House of Otter.

"Are you serious? No one lives here. This place has been empty forever. Someone is playing you," I said, but Roderick was already at the end of the wall and heading into the woods. I wanted to turn around, to go back and get my jeans, take off these ridiculously tight pants, and go home. I whisper-yelled after him, "Are you in a hurry to get murdered? What if this is some sort of set-up? We don't even have flashlights!"

From the edge of the woods, Roderick pulled out his fancy phone and hit a button that created a light bright enough to guide us through the moss and roots. He smiled at me and kept walking, disappearing into the foliage.

Just being there in such close proximity to the house with the moonlight shining down made me half-hard, but also fully-terrified. And for some reason seeing Roderick take charge of the situation—telling me where to go, how, and when—was making it difficult to walk. At first, I was worried he would notice, that he would brush against me and ask me why I had a boner. But feeling him so close made me wonder what would happen if I stopped and asked him to feel it, to release me from the tightness of the pants he'd all but forced me to wear. Maybe that was the reason we were really out here.

"This house is one-hundred percent haunted. If there's anyone in there they're a ghost. They're a ghost with a ghost dick," I said, uncertain why I always felt the need to turn to humor when I was nervous.

"As long as they don't have a ghost bank account, I'm not worried," Roderick said, linking his arm in mine.

I was putting Roderick in place of the forceful man I had imagined because he was here next to me in a place I associated with being horny. It wasn't him; it was skin on my skin, something familiar mixed with my only current source of happiness. But it was also being told what to do.

"This way," he said as he continued, fearlessly leading me forward as though he had taken the route countless times. We took a sudden turn to the left and navigated a narrow dirt path only wide enough for one of us at a time. Behind him, I could see the dark curly fuzz through the fabric of his flowy catsuit, the way his round ass shifted back and forth as he pulled his heels out of the dirt with every step.

Unable to wrap himself around me, Roderick reached his hand back into mine to make sure I wouldn't lose my way as we arrived at a large courtyard. From the ray of the phone light, all I could make out at first were the large cut stones, artistry below our feet set in an array of carefully placed spirals. Then as he pointed the phone toward the structure, a covered area leading to a set of large French doors.

Following the path toward the door, Roderick flipped the phone around unexpectedly to what appeared to be a tall silhouette of a man. I jumped back, a small scream escaping my lips. Roderick's hand was immediately over my mouth.

"Chill your nips," he said calmly as he walked the beam of light closer to the figure to reveal a chiseled statue of pure musculature. Tufts of pebbled hair covered the male form and some sort of harness was around the upper portion of his frame and shoulders. Even in the dim lighting, the craftsmanship was clear; this piece was worth more than I had ever seen in my life. Whoever had once, or now did, live here—they appreciated the finer things.

Roderick handed me the phone as we got closer to the French doors, then dusted himself off from the woods. A few leaves fell out as he ran his fingers through his hair and licked his lips to make them glisten.

"What if something goes wrong and you don't have a phone?" I asked, shining the light in his direction.

"Would you rather stay out here alone in the dark?" He laughed. "Besides, who would I call?"

I shrugged. It was hard to say if Roderick had made any friends since we had stopped talking, if he had evolved in any way aside from financially since the period of time when we were all the other had in the world. He owned enough seating in his house for a tea party, that was for sure, but possibly had no one to share it with; no one to offer steeped herbs and a rainbow floor cushion.

"If I'm not back in two hours, find me," he said. I looked down at the time on the phone: 12 a.m.

"Don't you want to wait like five minutes? You cannot enter a spooky poorly-lit house at exactly midnight. There are rules for these things. Some hook-up handbook about not letting a friend be involved with your homicide?" My whisper-shouting ineffective, Roderick put a finger to his lips, telling me to stop talking.

"Funny. Normally this would be the other way around." He smiled and turned the knob. White flowing drapes flapped from the interior of the door in the autumn breeze, circling around him for just a moment until the door was closed, and he was gone.

With the drapes settled, I thought about what he'd said. This was the first time I'd found myself playing bodyguard for him. I couldn't imagine what Roderick had done all those times I'd gone upstairs and taken hours longer than I should have. But with him inside, I settled into the darkness alone with my new best friend— the super hot stone guy in the courtyard.

CHAPTER SIX

❦

L iving in luxury meant feeling dew form on the grass, without the humidity of living near sand. It meant being able to build a house made of heavy material minus the fear of it sinking too far below sea-level and being swallowed by a sinkhole. It was lush greenery and trees with thick trunks; leaves that didn't feel like they had been spawned from bay water. But most importantly, flowers, real flowers—not just weeds that budded. Out in the courtyard, all around me, there were colorful blossoms.

Aside from the perennials, one of the best things I discovered while exploring the grounds outside with the phone flashlight was there were virtually no bugs at all, no mosquitos or horseflies, even though we were only miles from the shore. Which was good because over an hour had passed since Roderick had entered the house, and if we had been closer to home, I would have been devoured.

So far, I hadn't seen any lights from the windows or heard any sounds escape. Everything still seemed dark and uninhabited. I wondered for a while if there was a chance Roderick had gotten lost without the light, that perhaps he was stuck just inside the back entrance, feeling around for the doorknob to find his way back to the courtyard. There was still a strong possibility that this whole thing had been some sort of set-up. I hadn't thought to ask Roderick before agreeing to this if he had made any enemies recently. What if they had gotten him inside this abandoned house and were hurting him? He could be lying in the middle of the floor waiting for me to rescue him while I was out here admiring topiaries.

The darkness allowed my mind to fill with anxiety and panic. Circling past the stone man as I paced around, revealed more silhouettes in the distance. I discovered another man in a harness, but smaller, less muscle-bound, and on his knees. Furry but thin, the statue had something in his mouth, some sort of rounded ball attached to a strap that fastened around the back of his head. His hands were tied behind him. The artist had taken great detail in the expression of his eyes, a mix of surprise, excitement, and fear.

It was nearly 2 a.m. and the phone battery was drained from having the light on the entire time. At this rate, we'd have nothing left for the walk back through the woods and to the apartment. I hadn't thought of using the phone as anything aside from a light and truthfully didn't really know how it worked even if I did want to snoop. The cell phones I'd used, when I'd found the money to afford them, had been the type that only received calls and the variety of texts that had to be typed-out using the number pad. Luckily, Roderick had left the flashlight controls up for me. I found a spot near the door, leaned against the smooth stone of the exterior wall, and in an attempt to conserve our resources clicked the "OFF" button on my only reprieve from the darkness.

My other senses heightened from the lack of sight, I could smell the flowers in the night air, the wet dirt and thick grass. I could hear the chirps of crickets and croak of something in the distance. I'd never found water in the woods during my walks, but I had also never been this far out. It hadn't crossed my mind to venture this deep, to see if there was a way into the house. Before now, the structure had stood as impenetrable and only to be admired from a distance. Being this close, sitting just outside what only yesterday was the source of my arousal, I could feel myself tightening in the black pants again.

Growing thicker, I laughed at myself. The two hour mark was close, and I needed to develop a rescue plan, not jerk-off outside some old house like I had a fetish for architecture. It was then my sense of touch was activated. Something brushed against my leg, gliding over the faux-leather pants. I shifted my weight and scooted a few inches away from the sensation, assuming it was a gust of wind or a fallen tree branch with leaves pointing toward me, something I hadn't seen before I sat. But the sensation returned, and this time, it was directly on my half-hard cock, rubbing lightly over the zipper and tugging at the button above it.

I jumped quickly, but my body was blocked against something firm and directly in front of me. It pushed on my shoulder, landing me back against the wall. A voice said, with force, "Sit down boy," and continued to unbutton my pants. I could feel his breath close to me as he spoke. Fumbling for the phone, I struggled for light as he kept his firm hold on me.

The phone leapt from my hands and directly to the stone ground with a terrible crash that made us both jolt. In that quick moment, I rolled to the side and out from under him. Feeling around for the phone but finding the door knob instead, I turned it and let myself fall inside. The white drapes fluttered as I jumped up to close the door behind me. Unsure whether the person would follow, I looked rapidly around the interior for an escape. One red light was in the distance, and I ran straight for it, my boots heavy against what felt like slippery tile.

With little illumination, I kept my pace down a hallway that seemed to stretch on forever, putting the red light farther and farther from my reach. There seemed to be no other light inside, so this had to be where Roderick was. I called for him through my panting with no response. My own voice echoed back at me against the flooring. As I yelled, I tripped and fell through the doorframe of the room I had been attempting to reach. From behind me, heavy footsteps approached, then stopped. I struggled from the floor, attempting to get to my feet, but his hands were already around my ankles. My face and hands slid across the tile as he dragged me.

His strength surpassed my own, which made an easy task of pulling off the mesh tank-top I had been wearing to blend in with the night and wrapping it around my wrists. In the red light, I could see a giant X bathed in crimson and adorned with straps on each end. He lifted and heaved me to the structure, parting my legs and fastening them to either side. From behind, he removed the tank-top rope only to grab each one of my hands to complete the X and put them in their own buckles, velvety but tight around my wrists with what felt like a metal clasp joining the material.

Coming out of what must have been shock, I began screaming again for Roderick, for help, the total nonsense people yell when they are terrified. With my mouth wide-open in mid plea of, "Who are you? What are you doing? Let me go!" I felt the mesh tank-top go straight inside, forcing my tongue flat in my mouth so I couldn't push the fabric out. I was muted and completely immobile.

Without me struggling, he took his time undoing the metal button of the pants I had borrowed from Roderick. He circled his finger around the hair just above the band, slipping one finger through where a belt would normally be just to feel the tightness. Then he let both his hands slide around to grab at each of my ass cheeks and give them a squeeze. The zipper came down last, and as he brushed the hair around my cock, I was hard again.

My saliva soaking the shirt, I didn't want to moan when he started stroking me, but I knew he could hear me through the mesh. The precum leaked out, creating a smoothness between his fingertip and my foreskin, and I should have been trying more desperately to get loose. But my cock disagreed, and as he continued teasing and pumping with the liquid dripping out of me, I was getting firmer.

I couldn't see his face, but the voice was the same. It was his words that made it impossible not to finally release. Slowly, with a tight fist around me, he said, "Do it, boy. Give me that load. Now."

Chapter Six

My entire body shuddered as I came, my hands balled into fists and toes arched off the safety of the small platforms I had been braced on below the straps. Everything went black.

CHAPTER SEVEN

It was my hearing that came back first, the sound of Roderick's voice saying, "Are you okay?"

The man had just left me there, suspended and tied down. At least Roderick found me in the house. Maybe there was still a chance we could get out if the man had released him, or better, never found him at all.

"Where's the phone?" he asked. "It's so dark."

The next of my senses to return was touch, and more specifically, one side of the French door smacking against the back of my head as Roderick forced it farther open to scramble around on the ground searching for a source of light. I was back outside but had no memory of how I had gotten there.

Roderick was fumbling with the phone against the stone, and after a few seconds, the beam was being cast over my closed eyes. I opened them slowly. Roderick was above me, looking exactly the same as when he had entered the house.

"Stellar bodyguard you are. Did you seriously fall asleep out here?" he asked. I didn't even know how to answer the question.

"What time is it?" I managed to get out instead. Roderick looked at the clock on the phone.

"I could've been dead in there. It's twenty after two." He sounded reasonably agitated. "Not that it matters. He didn't even touch me. But I got the money." He lowered a stack of bills in my direction on the ground and shook them like a fan. I was still blinking my eyes, unsure of how it could possibly be just after two in the morning when my time with the man had felt endless.

"Let's go before this battery runs out," he said, reaching out his hand for mine. I wanted to tell him everything, about the man and the giant X, being dragged across the floor by my ankles, and more importantly, completely ruining the crotch region of his favorite black pants by cumming all over them. But back in the courtyard with the stone statues and flowers, the hum of late night turning into early morning, it all seemed less real now.

With Roderick there and unaffected, my shirt still in place; nothing seemed different from right before the moment I had felt the man's presence near me in front of the door. Aside from the sense of relief in my body and the relaxation that usually came paired with an extended walk in the woods, it was pretty apparent I had never actually been in the house at all.

We were halfway through the woods before I was awake enough to start asking questions, but Roderick began filling me in from the second we were out of earshot of the house. He told me about the kind of information you can get out of a man depending on what you show him you can fit in your mouth. About the replicated array of toys matching the set-up in his own house, that had been displayed in perfect order and prepared for him to use. And that the room he was directed to stay in was almost identical to the start of the dream apartment he had constructed. He told me that, all-in-all, it had felt like being in a cam session, just with the man in the actual room to instruct him.

"I still have no idea what he looks like, but he honestly sounds kind of hot." He nearly tripped over a root as he spoke. Side-shuffling into some ground-cover, it wrapped around his heel before he shook it off, and we found our way back to the main path.

"The money was just laying there ready on a dresser before I even started taking off my clothes." He didn't have pockets but had shoved stacks of bills into the piece of long black ribbon he'd turned into a makeshift belt to create a waistline.

"He knows the money gets me hard, so he told me the entire dresser was full of cash. It definitely worked." He sounded like he was smiling. I was still reeling from rejoining reality after how vivid my dream felt, but this world was starting to get just as strange. I had figured, knowing Roderick, he was going to grab some stupid tablecloth or jewelry to sell. I hadn't imagined he'd be bold enough to grab the guy's wallet like we had pulled in the past or mop real money from the guy he'd self-described as "intense."

"Okay, so I may have taken a little more than he told me to," he admitted. This was a one-sided conversation. "But he told me the money was all going to be mine eventually anyway."

"Alright, okay." He was reacting to my silence. "I took a lot more than he told me to, but it's not the same as stealing if it was already mine!" He wasn't trying to convince me. "You know, just because you're not talking doesn't mean you're not coming off as bitchy."

We didn't speak again until we reached the edge of the woods and the brick wall was in view. This time, I didn't run my hand along it as we walked. I didn't look toward the arches of the top of the house to admire them. We were edging closer to the main road when the phone died and the light went out, around the same time I decided I would have to find a new place to take my walks after tonight.

"Well, that's fucking great." I had obviously struck a nerve in Roderick. Tension was high, but I knew we needed to talk through the darkness, use the sound of each other's voices like sonar to figure out where we were going.

"What if he notices how much you took? Aren't you worried at all that this guy knows where you live?" I finally asked the question I should have asked before we left Roderick's apartment to pull off this ill-conceived heist.

"He's never been there." He said this with such nonchalance as we encroached closer to the railroad tracks that it made me stop where I stood. I kept in place until he turned around, alerted by the suddenness of the sound of my footsteps no longer following behind him.

"If he's sent you a pizza, he knows your address." Even in the moonlight, I couldn't see his reaction, but his stillness matching mine made it apparent; now he was worried too.

Our pace continued forward, the sea breeze getting thicker and the sounds of the ocean becoming more distinct. The toe of my boot stubbed against something solid, and in the same moment, Roderick screamed and fell to the pebble near me. We'd found the train tracks.

"I tripped," he said matter-of-factly, with a slight whine. He'd honestly had quite a night already, and I knew I was being tough on him. Shuffling my way toward the sound of his voice, I helped him up, and together we navigated the blackness of the night over the metal railings. My arm wrapped around his back and his around my shoulder, our bodies were pressed together at the side with the friction of our outfits creating warmth between as we made our way toward the coast.

The streetlights became more luminous as we approached the outskirts of town. In the distance, the moon still hung high, but the sun seemed to be considering rising over the sea, tempted to begin its journey to create a new day. Bathed in faded hues of orange and blue light, we climbed the fire escape to the backdoor of his apartment. Changing out of our caper costumes, I grabbed up my jeans and forced a leg inside.

Roderick stood next to me, the other pant leg around my ankle and shirt barely over my head. "Can you stay the night?" he asked.

"You mean the morning?" I wasn't sure if I was trying to be funny, but I knew he was being sincere with his question, that he was actually afraid the man may clock the missing money and come after him.

"Just in case?" He hadn't finished dressing either, and while I should have been looking at his eyes, instead I was staring at his chest and nipples. My focus pulled to the moist hair covering him and how it rose and fell with his breath, the sweaty fur as dark and thick as the beard and mustache framing his lips.

His heart seemed to be beating quickly, either from the fear he had brought upon himself or the fact that he had forced us both on our exit and entrance to use the fire escape instead of the front door in the off-chance someone in his building was questioned about whether or not he had left that night. As if the cops would make it a priority to ask them if he'd had the opportunity to rob the eccentric billionaire down the road that no one actually believed existed.

I had already decided that after tonight, I would never tell a soul there was someone actually living in that house. Even though I couldn't convince Roderick, something in me knew the wealthy man he'd connected with was not the type to get involved with the law. If I were in Roderick's position, it wouldn't have been the police I was worried about finding me anyway.

I wanted him to be safe, to know for sure that the next time we saw each other wouldn't be at his memorial service. But staying to keep watch over him would mean falling back into old habits and a full day of trying to avoid looking at his body with the sun shining. I wasn't sure when I would see him again, but I knew if I stayed, I would never want to leave.

"I can't," I finally managed to get out, forcing myself to break my gaze and look at his face. "I just ... can't." With my share of the money shoved in my pocket, I finished putting on my pants and allowed the varying shades of dawn to guide me home.

Chapter Eight

Three in the afternoon often felt like breakfast time, not just for me, but for the entire house. Not that breakfast was more than a shared pot of black coffee and a few cigarettes for most of the boys, all bent over the high-top counter and gossiping about the men they had seen the night before, elbows on formica and dirty coffee mugs. There were rarely names during the conversation, just dollar amounts and endless dishing about how a quick handjob became Mr. Fries and a Shake or how something more intimate or lengthy was Mr. Utilities Bill. For the rare overnight stay, a trick could even be named Mr. This Month's Rent, especially if he was into fetishy stuff he could never ask his partner to do with him.

"I'll ride any face for a new comforter and set of pillows at this point," Darius said, spinning a spoon around his coffee, as if we had milk or sugar in the house to mix into the liquid. He pulled it up and licked the metal clean, letting it slide down his tongue. It was a reflex of the job, always being sexy, always being on. "They're getting empty and flat, and I know it's about to get cold again."

"Beachside winters are not even winters though. You don't need a blanket. You need a hammock and some coconuts," Brent said, swishing around what was left of the carton of orange juice Darius and I had just about killed the day before. He looked directly at me in a way that said, *I know you drank this*, but didn't say it out loud.

Instead, he took the last swig, crushed the cardboard in his fist, and threw it in the trash.

Marco watched him and added, "Then Alexander can move outside to the hammock since we know he's about to miss his rent."

Why the brothers had decided to move this far south after growing up in a place north enough to have real seasons, I had never understood. But Brent and Marco seemed to love it here. Despite being so broke they shared a room and twin mattress on the floor, they maintained the tanning was better and so were the tricks. They had this idea that *season*, meaning the time period when it's snowing everywhere else so the daddies bring their families to Beachside for vacation, was going to be peak money.

There was a knock at the door, and immediately Marco popped up. "The bleach is here," he said, running through the front room.

"Am I the only one that isn't getting mail here?" Darius said, throwing up his hands. "I thought they said it was too *dangerous* out here for that." I shrugged in acknowledgement. He said "dangerous" like he was mocking the type of people that were afraid to be out this way. Beachside was considered the bad area of the county we shared with all the rich folk and their mansions, but we were living in the worse side of the bad part of town.

Marco turned back from the door, looking at Brent. "How much did you order? We only need to dye it once." We all walked to the door to see the front stoop full of cardboard boxes. None of them had labels, but unless those idiots had accidentally ordered a few palettes-worth, it definitely wasn't hair dye. There didn't seem to be a delivery truck or person nearby, just a folded paper on the closest box. Brent reached down and unfolded it.

"They're for you," he said, looking at me. This was the first time I had ever seen him read. Before that moment, I wasn't certain he could.

"Whoa, who you been fucking?" Marco said, poking me in the ribs with his brawny elbow. He always smelled like lemon juice, the kind with preservatives added. Darius was still the only one who knew the answer to Marco's question was: *no one.*

None of us had changed into real clothes. We'd been brunching in underwear and jockstraps, and most days that was the nearest any of us got to an outfit inside the house. But with no hesitation, everyone was out on the porch helping me load the boxes inside, giving the neighbors an unobstructed view of whatever we had worn to bed the night before. Even Sonny, who had been curled into a blanket full of holes on the dirty couch, got up and wrapped the blanket around his waist like a long towel. He let it fall off his hips as he lifted something heavy to his chest and continued dick-and-ass-out all the way into the house. His contribution being complete, Sonny gave us all a tired smile and snuggled back up into his cozy spot.

"Like having a cat who pays bills," Darius said, running his fingers through Sonny's long brown hair. He was already lightly snoring.

"The note said to open the biggest one first," Brent said, like he was the leader in the escape room that had become my mysterious delivery.

"Did it say who it was from at all?" I asked. He shook his head while Marco identified and pointed at the biggest box.

Slicing open the packing tape, another folded note appeared at the top of layers of foam packing peanuts. The message was handwritten and said,

> *Follow these instructions exactly.*
> *Assemble everything and turn it on.*
> *I'm waiting.*

I couldn't remember the last time I had received a gift, and the anonymity of the sender made the entire thing even stranger. Digging farther into the box, I found cables and a little farther down, what seemed to be a small camera. Marco opened a long, thin box. "It's a tripod," he said, pulling it out with a storm of spongy pellets. "And I think that's a webcam." He motioned toward what I had unboxed.

They were passing around an old steak knife now, taking turns opening the boxes closest to them. "Dude, there's a whole computer in here." Brent had gotten one of the larger boxes.

"Oh girl, this camera is brand-new!" Darius was already attaching the strap and putting it around his neck.

Technology was never among my talents, but eventually with the help of the boys we were able to connect everything to the specifications and instructions we found in the boxes with the equipment. Luckily, we were still able to steal a signal from the house next door to get online. With all the right lights blinking, we powered on the computer. A window with a single video file opened first, titled, "Watch Alone."

"Wow, okay." Darius was personally offended after having spent the entire afternoon helping me connect all the correct cords and blinking boxes together.

"But for real, you have no idea who this sugar daddy is that sent you all this stuff?" Marco asked. I had told them over and over I didn't know where it came from. I didn't have a sugar daddy. I'd never had a sugar daddy. But I shook my head again to answer the question.

"Well let me know if Daddy is looking for some more underprivileged youth to sponsor, because damn," Brent said, his hands on his hips, taking in everything we'd put together. "I guess this means you won't need that hammock."

Darius seemed more concerned than the other boys, and while he shuffled them out to leave me to it, he said, "Is there a chance this could be from your parents? A peace offering?"

I wanted the answer to his question to be yes, to think there was a shot my family was trying to reconnect, that someone had hit the Beachside Lottery and decided to use the opportunity to reach out to me via pricey gifts. But I knew the chances of that were slim after so many years.

Darius shut the door behind him as I played the video file and heard the recorded voice instructing me on my next steps. I didn't know how it was possible, but I suddenly knew exactly who had sent the gifts.

CHAPTER NINE

ello?" I had opened the software and followed the directions the voice had given me but still, the screen was black.

"Good job, boy." A familiar voice was live and coming out of the speakers.

"Who is this?" I asked, as if I hadn't heard the same voice the night before while I was waiting for Roderick to finish inside the house. The voice didn't respond. "How did you know where I live?"

A short inhale from the speakers. "You're asking a lot of questions when you should be saying thank you."

I stopped talking. The math had already been done by the boys during the set-up on exactly how much I could make off this stuff. Resale, pawn-shop, store credit return: I had options after this interaction. My privacy had been violated, and I wanted answers.

"You're a very private boy, aren't you?" It seemed like he was going to keep talking. The black screen on the window didn't change, but I could hear him moving around. Sounds of metal clinking together, rubber or straps sliding, like the noises I'd heard when I dreamt I was attached to the giant wooden X. "Perhaps you prefer: independent?" he said with a jingle of some hardware.

"What do you want me to do with all this stuff?" I asked, ignoring his question.

"It's yours to do with as you wish. It's a line of communication for us, no strings attached after this conversation. Everything, like the money you stole from me the other night, is yours to keep."

"I didn't take your money."

"Don't misunderstand, boy. I'm not upset. I expected your friend to take more than was instructed. I'm just glad he had the sense to share it with you. I wasn't certain I could trust him to do that."

"Is this what you did when you met him? Sent him all this stuff to get his attention?"

"Do I have yours?"

I shifted on the bed, forgetting that even though I couldn't see him, he could still see me. It hadn't crossed my mind to change out of my underwear or to put on a shirt before opening the video. I hadn't realized the webcam was going to turn on.

I'd been acting annoyed with his gifts. As if he were inconveniencing me. But from the second he began speaking, my mind wandered to what my imagination had created, our time together in the house and the seemingly now real myth of the owner of the mansion I'd made into the object of so much affection. Before I'd learned he actually existed, I wanted so badly to know what he desired, to understand what he did inside that house and who, if anyone, kept him company.

Even if our session had never actually happened, I'd gotten the voice right. The deep rich sound of his tone from across the internet connection may as well have been whispering in my ear in that dark red-lit room. I shifted again, trying to hide the firmness building under the flimsy white briefs I'd been wearing since yesterday.

"Take out your cock, boy."

Even as I was doing it, I didn't understand why I was listening to him, what turned me on about him demanding things from me, buying my time and attention. But I wanted to obey. I wanted to know my body and time were worth more than I had ever gotten handed to me for a quick pound on a dirty mattress. I was harder now, leaning my head on my hand. My weight was balanced on my side, facing the camera as I let my cock slide out of the top of the elastic keeping it against my abdomen, almost making it look like an accident as I stared directly into the camera lens above the computer screen.

"Very nice, boy," he said from the other side of the black window. I could hear more shuffling around and from just his inflection, I could tell he was smiling. Licking a broad stroke across my palm, I rubbed the saliva over my head and a little of the shaft. My finger slid up my stomach to my nipples and circled each one, letting my hand grasp more firmly against the pulsing sensation that was building.

"Stroke, now," he directed. I obeyed and began rubbing furiously. My own spit and dripping precum mixed into a perfect lubricant. It was rare for me to reach this point so quickly, but knowing he was watching, that he was demanding this show, I already wanted to cum. Just not until he asked me to.

"You're going to hold it until I want it," he said as if he could read my mind. "You're going to shoot even harder than the last time."

I wasn't sure what last time he was talking about, but I didn't have blood left in my brain to process the possibilities. Every ounce of my blood seemed to be in my cock, making me rock hard. Still stroking furiously, pinching my nipples harder and feeling my balls so full they were ready to explode, I needed his permission.

"Now, boy. Give me that load. It's mine. It belongs to me. Do it."

The release was instantaneous to his command, and I shot hard all over my chest. Droplets reached my neck and chin. I wasn't certain how good the resolution was on his end, if he could see the cum all over my body and face.

"Show me how good you taste, boy," the black screen demanded. I scooped a smaller dot from my chin and pushed into my mouth. Sucking it hard and swallowing the salty but sweet flavor of myself, I imagined he was forcing it on my tongue, this man I had never seen but was already so real in my head.

Still covered in my own cum, he said, "You're coming back tomorrow."

I was out of breath when I asked him, "What about Roderick?"

"He can't be trusted."

It wasn't my first instinct to take Roderick's job, but it sounded like he had lost it on his own. I thought about Roderick's apartment and everything in it. The new outfits and tea kettle and stupid little tweed poufs all over the hardwood floor. I thought about the things I deserved in exchange for my time. If Roderick was going to lose the income whether I took the job or not, maybe it was my turn to have something good happen.

As I considered the proposition, there was a quick knock on my door. Before I could say to enter, Darius was there clicking a glass of orange juice against his nails and whispering, "Dinner?" like a real question. Someone must have run out for more while I was interacting with the man. It felt like only a few minutes, but I could see through my window that night had fallen.

Noticing me lying there covered in my own cum, Darius covered his mouth and in full-volume said, "Oh, oh, okay," then shut the door behind him. He didn't know he was in view of the camera standing in the doorway. I was immediately worried I had violated some sort of protocol or instruction, that my opportunity was over before it had begun. A few seconds of agonizing silence followed.

"You're such a good boy," the voice finally said. "I could never spoil a boy like that one, decent beard potential, but not enough fur. The boys you're living with right now, they'll give it to anyone with a half-stuffed money clip. You're not like them; you're special."

There was a short silence again, but during this one, I smiled. I made sure he could see how happy he had already made me. "Tomorrow," he said. "You know where to go."

Then the black box was gone.

CHAPTER TEN

❧

Something that had been proven the other night: it was easier to navigate the walk during the day. The man hadn't specified a time, so I left the house as if I was just going for my typical stroll. The duration of the journey allowed me to drift in and out of excitement crossfaded with concern. I had already decided that going forward with the man's requests was not a direct betrayal to Roderick. It was uncertain to me why I hadn't been put through the same trial, why the man had invited me to meet him in person directly after our first interaction. He had said he saw something in me. Perhaps he didn't feel the need to test me any further. Yet, I worried how much my former partner-in-crime had told him, if I'd ever come up during their cam sessions. There was still a chance the man knew; if this had been just a couple years ago, Roderick and I would have worked as a team to take him for every cent.

In the daylight, the house appeared less sinister than it had in the darkness. Much less *abandoned Victorian estate with a horrifying backstory* and more *potentially hot rich guy that enjoys his privacy*. The wall leading to the wooded area seemed once again inviting enough for me to reach out and run my fingers across, if only for a moment. In the safety of the canopy, I could pick out the different trees I had used to lean my back against so many times, before I knew the wonders that lived only a few hundred more feet into the depth. The journey to the courtyard was lined with crusted spots in the dirt that still wore the mark of my visits. The indent of my boots were still prints in the soil, spread in a wide-stance to frame the splatter pattern.

Curving around to the left, the path to the back of the house wasn't as easy to find as Roderick had made it seem. Somehow despite not having a map or clear lighting, he had instinctively known the way. Eventually I located the small dirt path, just wide enough for a single person, with tall hedges on either side. Sun barely shined through the denseness of the forest onto the loose sentiment below as I let my hands grab onto the tight brush surrounding me. The labyrinth wound in a disorienting zig-zag until it eventually spit me out into a clearing full of stone men. I hadn't seen all of them last night, the dozens that stood, kneeled, or lay in the grassy open garden. The flowers surrounded each one like a shrine and all had harnesses or straps, leather and latex depicted in earthen detail, beards and scruff expertly chiseled into the polished rock.

Part of me wanted to stay and admire them, give my attention to their individual uniqueness, but behind me, the back French doors were already open. The sheer white curtains, blowing in the wind. From inside, music; something classical, violins and wooden instruments, beckoning me to enter. I didn't want to keep him waiting.

Following the music, I crossed the threshold I'd fallen asleep on the evening before, still unsure if I had dreamed or actually been part of the encounter in the red room. Inside, I looked to my right toward the long hallway I had run through, the one that seemed to stretch endlessly as I ran for the light. To my surprise, in place of the hallway from my dream, there was a wall. No hallway, no door. Below me was the same flooring I could still feel a burn on my cheek from being dragged across, but a few feet from where I stood, meeting at a sharp edge with the tile, there was just a flat wall with a long table pushed against it. I was sure now: I had absolutely imagined the entire thing.

Walking toward the table, I saw it was full of fresh magenta and gold flowers with long thick stems. Well-hydrated and obviously looked after with care, they were displayed in tall transparent vases on either side. Between them on the table lay a beautifully hand-written note in the center that read:

> *Your room is on the second floor.*
> *Make yourself comfortable.*

The marble stairs began wide and welcoming at the ground level and split after about thirty steps. Taking the fork right and climbing to the second floor of the house, I tried every door until one finally opened. Everything else had been locked, and even when I knocked, there was no reply. As strange as it seemed to be in the house at all, it was more odd to be completely alone, to hear my own knock and voice accompanied by nothing more than the constant soundtrack in every hallway and staircase. He hadn't been there to welcome me when I arrived, but this orchestrated scavenger hunt through his home made me wonder if he would eventually be the prize.

My first observation of the only unlocked room was saturation of color inside, the array of hues which flooded the variety of cushiony spaces: a four-poster king-sized bed with a canopy in bright blue, a sitting area with couches and chairs in maroon, a bathroom with a walk-in shower with detailed gold tiles, and a purple clawfoot tub. The bathroom alone felt bigger than the whole floor plan of any house I had lived in my entire life.

Another hand-written note on the bed said:

> *You can have anything you wish.*
> *Pick up the phone and simply ask.*

The phone on the bedside table was cream and corded. An earpiece and receiver with gold accents completed the vintage style, not because it was old, but because it was classy as fuck, like everything else in this house. Vibrant and colorful. Elegance sitting somewhere just before tacky. Balance mixed with extravagance.

I didn't know when he would arrive, but my first instinct was to get in the bathtub, to be clean and ready for him. The basin was deep and took a few minutes to fill. Pulling with my big toe at the gold chain leading to the drain plug, I knew what I was missing. I hopped out, wet and naked, to pick-up the vintage phone.

"Hello?" I said with some hesitation. No one replied, but I could hear breathing. "Um... could I please have some bubbles?"

Immediately, there was a knock on the door as if my request had been anticipated. I opened it up to find a glass container of something tinted light purple sitting on a silver tray, corked and curved, with a single loop handle, like a genie bottle from cartoons I'd seen as a kid. But I didn't see anyone. "Thank you!" I yelled down either side of the abandoned hallway. My own voice echoed back with the violins supporting it.

Thick suds came fast under the running water and smelled like the blossoms outside in the courtyard. Lavender, peony, something fuchsia or plum, small and delicate. As if they'd been crushed between stones for hours to create the subtle aroma of the soap, but paired with something more, something rough and masculine, like sawdust and chopped wood. I let the expertly-crafted musk engulf my senses while the hot water and foam swallowed me inside. Sighing a long deep exhale, I realized I'd been smiling since the moment I walked into the house.

After my bath, I'd figured I would towel off and put on the same jeans and shirt I'd been wearing for days, but picking up the heap of them now, they were malodorous and offensive compared to the fragrance sticking to my skin and body hair.

Naked for a while, I opened a large wooden wardrobe across from the bed to find a lovely black robe, soft and soothing, like a blanket with arm holes. Opposite the hanging robe, shirts hung organized by color, collared and casual, in all shades. Below them in drawers lay the fit of jeans I liked, the kind that grabbed my ass in the right places. All brand new.

Other drawers were full of backless underwear, all in my size, some cloth, some made of neoprene or shining plastic. Trying on a collection of them, I worried I was invading someone's curated apparel, that perhaps all of this was not intended for me to have a fashion show. I was, after all, a guest in this house. But seeing my reflection in the oblong mirror standing in the corner, the way my ass was framed in every jockstrap perfectly, I knew he had picked out everything just for me, like he knew my taste better than I knew my own. He had bought me everything I would have picked out for myself if I'd had the money to spend.

Positioned off to the side of the large bed, a television so big I questioned its stability was mounted to the exposed brick. Using the variety of controls in the bedside table, I picked a movie and settled into my robe—my body scented like a husky lumberjack with a flower tucked behind his ear. I waited for the man to come, to smell me, to take my holes in this huge bed. So much of me wanted to try, to allow someone inside after so long. But he never came.

My hair was already dry, and my stomach was empty. I hadn't stayed long enough into the afternoon to take in the usual coffee breakfast with my housemates. It had been at least two days since I'd consumed much at all. Now I was here, and I was going to take advantage of the amenities.

I picked up the cream and gold phone again. "Could I have a sandwich please?" Breathing on the other end of the phone then a click. After a few minutes, another knock on the door and on a silver tray, the most gigantic sandwich I'd ever seen. Layers of fresh soft bread and sauces, delicately cut vegetables paired with warm tea in a detailed cup with a floral pattern and matching cream pitcher. Taking it inside, I wondered if this was the type of treatment Roderick had been only days from accepting as his own, that perhaps this had all been prepared for him initially, and the fact that he'd stolen the money had allowed me to take his place. He had put in the time, but I was living his reward.

Despite the opulence of my surroundings, Roderick seemed to find his way into my thoughts. I wasn't sure what I would say to him the next time we met, if we ever did meet again. Perhaps I had something I needed to apologize for, taking this right out from under him. But the items in the room were obviously arranged for me, not him, and I allowed this thought to soothe me as the warm tea coated my insides. I convinced myself I was as special as the decor and clothing was letting me believe until my sandwich was just crumbs on the silver tray, and I fell asleep.

CHAPTER ELEVEN

ꗃ

ays passed in what seemed like an endless cycle of movies, delicious food, and glorious bubble baths. As far as I knew, no rules were in place to keep me inside the room, but I still didn't want to push any boundaries. After mornings of soft biscuits with preserves and nights with chocolate cherries, I figured it would be nice to at least thank the people preparing my meals, so I used that as my excuse for the occasional walks I took around the mansion. My exploration revealed no workers or servants—no other people at all. No one was visibly maintaining the house or courtyard. As I had observed while I was surveying the house from afar, not a soul seemed to come or go, but they had to be living here, somewhere.

The majority of doors remained sealed, aside from my own and some entrances to larger portions of the house. Every wing unveiled more hallways leading to the occasional open library full of paintings or sculptures. I was learning about the man before even meeting him by wandering his chosen antiquities, his collected art and unique pieces, the items he decided to surround himself with in this household. It occurred to me at some point, with no new handwritten notes appearing, that the man was probably rarely there at all. To have billions of dollars meant to never have to call one place home. It meant having the means to create a space like this in every part of the world.

I felt a longing to hear his voice again and craved his attention, to let him know how much I appreciated the gifts and to apologize for my attitude when we had spoken over the camera. His home had made me understand his deep need for happiness, and my sudden urgency to fill that space. I found myself suddenly in lust with the idea of an endlessly wealthy man seeking fulfillment, his collection telling me that sex was a hole in his life he longed to satisfy. I made it my mission to find clues, to learn his questions and become his answer.

The library provided information, the sort of literature a lonely man would collect for himself. Further inspection of the cabinet in my room filled with harnesses, collars, and leashes provided more. I would become this object of affection, his favorite toy. It would be my quest to earn everything he had already given to me and more.

I was in a deep sleep when I was awoken by a knock on the door. Outside, on another silver tray, lay a folded note:

Mr. Usher requests the blue harness
and your presence in this location.

Below the words was a hand-drawn map of a section of the house and a marked path leading to a room with a huge red X over it.

The man had never told me his name, and I hadn't asked. There had been nothing penned with his first nor last name around the expansive house. If he had family or the type of surname that should be well-known, it had been kept from this place intentionally. This altar to his more personal life held no indications of who he could be anywhere else. Perhaps that's where he had been all this time while I was here alone, somewhere handling whatever business afforded him this luxury.

He hadn't specified, but I wondered if that's what I should call him when we finally did meet in person. *Mr. Usher. Mr. Usher, Sir? Mr. Usher, Keeper of Bubbles and Fancy Sandwiches.* The winning golden ticket I found on the floor of my former best friend's life. It was difficult to understand how this mysterious man had become my entire world so quickly when I hadn't even been given his name before this moment. I wondered if Roderick knew it, if he had gotten that far. So much of me wanted to know if his experience had been at all similar to mine before Usher decided to cut him off.

The color-coding made it easy to find the requested gear: a harness with two loops on the back and a ring in the center on both sides, and a jockstrap to match with a zipper on the front for easy access. I wanted to at least appear modest while I walked through the house, not bore him with my nudity. In honesty, as much of me wanted to offer him payment for everything I had been given, there was so much more of me that was still worried about being touched. The months that had passed since a man had put his hands on me, since a hand that wasn't my own had allowed me to climax—I wasn't certain I could do it again. But I wanted to. I wanted to try—for him.

There was a satin robe matching the fluffier one in the closet, black with a ribbon to tie around my waist. It covered my ass just below the cheeks, leaving my upper-chest exposed. I intended to be a dish he had to uncover, for him to picture me as one of the silver trays my food and gifts appeared on with a matching cover ready to be lifted at any pace he desired.

I walked the house in the darkness. The typical piano or violin music was absent and only low ominous tones replaced it. Everything on the first floor was bathed in the familiar red light, the one I was certain I had created with my imagination. The tones too seemed unreal after hearing the relaxing classical instrumentations throughout the days and nights. They made me nervous and full of anxiety, as if the sense of leisure I'd achieved had never happened at all.

It seemed odd though, that even in this sudden haunted vibe of the house, I should feel he meant me any harm, as if the comfort he'd offered me was intended as misdirection for the hurt he was about to inflict. I paused in the dim hallway to breathe, resting my hand against a burgundy painted wall. I was manifesting scenarios in the darkness, allowing my imagination to run wild, the way I had the first night while leaning on the stone wall before falling into my dream.

With the constant, potentially false, reminder floating in my head that I was safe, I drifted barefoot down the staircase ascending into the main foyer of the mansion. The French doors opening to the courtyard were now closed in front of me. It was the first time I realized I had never in my wandering found another entrance in or out of the house nor revisited this one. I hadn't wanted to leave. Not since the moment I had arrived had I worried about anything outside. It hadn't seemed important to tell anyone where I was going, and now at least a week had elapsed.

Standing not far from the marked X, the map said to turn left—which put me facing a total dead end. The wall that I had once imagined as a long hallway leading into a room was now directly in front of me. From the wall, the lined dots creating the path on the map extended through it.

As I got closer, a booming voice said, "Robe off, boy." He was here, and he could see me. His low and direct tone echoed off the tile floor as if it was coming out of the speakers that had been playing such calming music when I'd arrived. His voice mixed with the dramatic sounds that now played in the music's place. My breathing was getting shallow.

At first, I wanted to respond. I wanted to explain myself and not remove the robe, tell him, "I'm a fancy dish," and hope he'd understand, that he would appreciate my modesty. But this was his house, and I had already decided in exchange for the extravagance I had been given, I would play by his rules. Sliding it off my arms, the robe fell in a ball near my feet to the cold ceramic. My shoulders felt frigid in the places the harness didn't cover my skin.

I wasn't sure what to do next. It seemed less than sexy that my first words to him since our first interaction would be asking him how he expected me to teleport through a solid wall. Maybe there was some instruction missing or some wrong turn I'd taken. There was a chance he was watching me stand in front of an actual wall like an idiot who didn't know how to read a map. He was most likely poised behind his camera monitor wondering how he had chosen such a stupid boy.

Sweating with anticipation, I was trembling between the building anxiety inside of me combined with the coolness of the floor against the bare soles of my feet. The chill of the air on my body and my ass out in the open made my nipples firm. I felt a familiar brush upon me. From behind, a body pushed against mine. I didn't move while I allowed him to caress my back, run his fingers around the curve of my ass and thighs. It had been so long since I felt a man's touch, at first my body wanted to recoil. I wanted to pull away. But this was the most I had ever been paid for anything, and I was going to play the part I had been assigned. I wanted him to be the one to finally break me.

His arms were above my head, then something was lowered in front of my face. "Open, boy," he said, his whisper tickling my ear. I opened my mouth to feel something round pass my lips and fix itself behind my teeth, a rubber ball, blocking me from speaking, attached to two straps that he fastened together with care behind my head. Running a hand through my hair then grabbing it hard with force, he pulled my head back toward him. I could already feel my spit gathering behind the ball, watering at the thought of what it would be like to kiss him. But instead, my mouth was already full, and I knew it would stay that way as long as he wanted.

He pulled both my hands behind me and coated rope was quickly around my wrists, holding them together. Bringing his fingers back to my hair, he used his grasp to move me around as he wished, marching me forward to the table sitting against the wall with the vases full of flowers. I hadn't noticed before they had been replaced with fresh ones from the gardens in the courtyard, different from the blooms that had been there when I'd arrived.

Above the table was a horizontal mirror just high enough for me to see myself. At the right angle for me to get an unobstructed view of the ball gag in my mouth, the image of me submitting to this man was reflected back through the darkness. Behind me, with his head a few inches above my own, his large hand full of my hair, was Mr. Usher. Dark eyes and hair, a sinister smirk told me he was happy to finally have me where he wanted me.

"Hello, boy," he said and pulled me back roughly toward his body in a way that made me swell.

Chapter Twelve

"Why don't you want men to touch you?" he asked, holding the whip in front of my face. I was on my knees now in a room so dimly lit I was only able to see what he allowed me to.

There had been a device for the wall under one of the vases on the table. He'd said, "You didn't think to check the credenza," while he pushed the hidden silver button. If I hadn't been gagged already, I may have said, "What the fuck is a credenza?"

"I have a prediction that you need this. I'm glad you've taken the opportunity to relax and enjoy yourself. For what you are about to endure here, I needed your body clean and ready to submit, to be fixed before it could be broken."

He was looking down at me, drool forming around the edges of the sphere in my mouth, my legs spread apart at the knee in front of him. His hair was nearly black and fell effortlessly in place aside from a single wisp on his forehead. Mustache and scruffy face, the stubble on his defined chin gave way to a fully buttoned collared shirt. Like his fitted slacks held with a polished belt buckle, everything on his body was tailored and flawless; he was letting me take it all in, allowing me from my kneeling position to get a full view from his eyes to his boots; both made me feel more naked. It was difficult to understand how a man this attractive would ever pay for sex.

"Someone has to give you permission to be happy, and I'm going to allow you that happiness at a price." He dropped the tip of the whip toward my spread knees. My bare legs opened like the top of an arrow pointing its way to the more delicate parts being cradled inside the pouch of the jockstrap.

His tool was different compared to any sort of whip I'd seen used for sexual purposes, the handle was long and thin with just one single snapping tail. He let the strand dangle near my inner thighs, tracing the sides and lightly hitting them with the tip of the rod. The sting was light at first, but as it continued over the same patches of skin, it developed into a searing pain. Using his polished boot, he kicked my right knee, then my left.

"Wider" he said, and my body fell where he wanted it, my stance now open enough to feel the air finding its way inside the pouch.

Bringing his boot up, he brought it down slowly to rest it on my cock, knowing I was hard inside. He let the rough sole press more firmly, just enough to create discomfort. Then using the tip of his boot gave the underside a light tap. My body shuddered and I winced, the spit I'd been trying so hard to contain behind the ball was now flowing in light streams down my chin. I wanted to bring my legs together and fall on my side, allow myself to recover, but I let the discomfort well-up inside me instead. Tears met the spit on my chin.

He laughed, hovering the boot back over my cock, leaving it suspended while his eyes fixed on mine with intensity. Initially, I'd been concerned about being sexy, about being this perfect object for his desire, but now, wet-faced and eyes tightened in strain, I didn't feel desirable. As he lowered his boot again and pressed down hard, I realized he wasn't paying for my sex at all. This was the game of torment he had to purchase; it was physical and psychological warfare.

"Understand, I can buy anything boy. I won't buy your body, but you will give it to me," he said, finally releasing my cock from under his boot. Walking backward, he put the whip away, trading it for a different instrument I couldn't quite make out in the lack of light.

"Up," he said rubbing the new tool between his hands. It was something thicker than the whip, but still black. With my hands tied, I wasn't certain how I was going to stand without something to grab onto. I could roll over onto the floor and try to wiggle to a standing position, but I wasn't sure that was what he wanted, if it would please him to have me look like a fish on the floor, gasping for air. Some part of me couldn't commit to looking so helpless. Instead, I rocked back quickly, letting my ass touch my heels before using the momentum to thrust myself up on my feet. I nearly fell forward into him but was able to steady my body—which was lucky because he didn't reach out to catch me.

"Alright, on to the bench, face down." He was still holding the object which now that I was closer looked to be made of the same material as the ball gag, just more cone-shaped, with rounded edges. It was black paired with red accents, like most of the decor in the room.

I turned around to face the area he was pointing toward as I moved closer to something resembling a converted weight bench. It welcomed me to squat down and throw my stomach on top, letting my face hang over the front edge. Just behind it, I could see the giant X—the wooden structure I remembered from my dream.

He saw me looking. "The Saint Andrew's Cross, yes. Perhaps another time. I have plenty more to show you in here before we get back to that."

With my legs slightly bent and spread apart with my ass in the air, I knew he had a clear view of my hole. Before I could think much more about what he meant by *back to that*, I felt his legs press against mine. Still safely clothed in his pants, the expensive fabric on my bareness felt smooth as high-thread sheets. But as I watched the drool from the gag drip to the cement floor below me, I could only focus on my sudden craving for his skin.

CHAPTER THIRTEEN

～⊰⊱～

Knowing I couldn't respond, he asked anyway, "What if I opened your hole right now, boy?"

I started to murmur behind the ball gag, not that I was even certain what I was trying to say.

Pleased enough with my inability to have an opinion of his proposed actions, he continued. "Have I earned your trust, boy? Have I shown you that all I want is your happiness? If I shove this plug in your hole, will that make you happy?"

He was treating me the way he had treated Roderick, letting the toys do the work for him. The gear, the whips, the restraints. It was all so elaborate that it finally hit me—he was afraid to fuck me. He wasn't going to penetrate me at all, not with his body, not without something between us. Usher had been telling me I needed him to give me permission to experience pleasure, as if he were going to free me from something. But there was a chance he needed me just as much as I needed him. Aside from our tax brackets, perhaps he and I weren't so different at all.

I did my best to push the gag out of my mouth, but it wouldn't budge. Fearing the whip or a swift boot to my balls as punishment, I wiggled my ass anyway to gain momentum. Straightening the bend in my knees, I stood, straddling the bench and attempting to flip myself around. His flat palm was immediately on my back as he growled, "What are you doing, boy?"

Continuing to move, his force was greater than mine, and his hand was soon around my neck, bracing it hard. My air restricted, he continued to push his weight against me to get my body face-down on the bench and returned to position. I lowered my chin to tuck one of the fingers he had near my throat between the strap of the gag and gave a quick tug. The spit-covered ball slipped down my bottom lip, and I wasted no time to say everything I wanted to say. "Please kiss me, give me your cock, let me feel you. Please touch me!"

I was begging for everything I had been avoiding for so long.

His hold on my neck and back released, leaving me straddling the bench and still restrained. I didn't move; I was too terrified. I knew I had made a mistake and that at best I was about to be beaten mercilessly. It was too scary to imagine a worse option. For a moment, it was quiet, until I could hear the sound of his boots stepping backward slowly on the cement.

"No," he said, "that's not what we do."

"Please, let me see you." I had already gone this far and just wanted to look into his eyes. I wanted to know what he was thinking, to see for sure how badly I had just messed everything up.

His footsteps inched closer to my ass again, and I prepared for the whip. I steadied myself for the large toy he had prepped to be shoved inside of me without warning. Instead, his hands found my wrists and untied the smooth rope. He braced me by the shoulders as he lifted and spun me around. My ass now on the bench and sitting, our eyes met. I wanted him. I needed him. Something was there now, something I hadn't seen before, a sparkle from deep behind his stare as he leaned in close to me.

His lips against mine in that moment would have made me cum instantly, but instead he pushed me onto my back and unbuckled his pants. My harness pushed into my shoulder blades from the firmness of the bench. The view from my back was limited, but I could see him taking out his cock, feel him edging closer to my hole. He leaned down and over me, our lips close to touching. "Say it again," he said. It was demanding but sincere. I knew exactly what he needed to hear.

"Please," I said, "touch me." His fingers wrapped around the front of the harness, and he pulled it in sync with the moment his cock pushed inside of me. We were intertwined on the bench, his hands occasionally lifting my legs to bury the full-length of himself in my depths. There was raw passion but no subtlety in the motions; we had both waited too long for nuance. He grabbed around my hair, yanking with force as I opened his shirt and wrapped my arms around his back, feeling his sweat from pumping in and out of me, his bare skin against mine.

"Is this what you wanted, boy?" His voice came from somewhere uncontrolled, from a place I could only assume he hadn't let himself go with a boy before. It was pleasure mixed with anger and terror. His palm came down hard and flat across my face, the other occasionally hitting my ass or outer thighs with a smacking sound or a hard tug on my nipples, a pull on my bottom lip, the vulnerability he was experiencing manifesting as pain he had to share. I was happy to take it all, to ride the sensation with him.

His hand eventually landed in my mouth, and I sucked his fingers hard, imagining they were his cock fucking my face at the same time as it was filling my ass. His eyes were back on mine as he took the spit from my mouth and brought it down past my chest and stomach, reaching the band of the jockstrap and sliding his fingers under. I was so wet between my leaking precum and the spit, I knew it wouldn't take much to get me there.

"Tell me who your cum belongs to," he said.

I didn't hesitate. "You," I said as he thrust himself harder and faster into me. He flicked at the head of my dick, stroking it occasionally with force, using the wetness building under the pouch.

"Is your body mine?" I could feel he was just as close as I was.

"Yes!" I yelled into the cement room, my words bouncing from the floor and walls.

"Cum, right now." On his demand, I came on the wide hand stroking me. The spurts shot hard and fast, coating the inside of the jockstrap. At that same moment, he burst in me, screaming and moaning as the eruptions filled deep into my hole. Our collective sounds mixed with the haunting tones in the red room.

Still within me, he reached his hand from under the jockstrap and up to my mouth. He pushed my own liquid through my lips, and I sucked then swallowed the flavor. I wanted him to offer his cock near my mouth and allow me to lick it clean, let me taste us both, but I didn't ask.

With my legs beginning to relax, I felt him pull out of me. My eyes closed and my head rested on the bench with relief. I wanted to kiss him; if I couldn't have more of his cock then I at least wanted his lips. But the next sound after the moans of our simultaneous climax was a door slamming closed. He hadn't kissed me, even once.

Whatever passion I had raised in him was limited and stopped the moment he released. I was alone in the room, his cum dripping out of me.

Chapter Fourteen

❦

I didn't call after him to stay. Instead, I remained sprawled on the bench wondering how long I was supposed to wait, whether he'd be coming back or if there was some acceptable amount of time I should keep in position. I laid there long enough for the warmth he had left in me to turn cold in his absence. What had felt like an antidote to my loneliness just moments before felt like venom in me now. I knew I had likely just ruined everything he had built for us by being so insistent, by not playing by his rules.

I needed a bath. Tip-toeing in the darkness, I saw that the lights were already on outside the steel door. The music had been returned to the classical soundtrack, even in the hallway. I took it slowly, still sweaty and wet, my skin and face burning from where his hands had made contact. When I exited through the open space where the wall and table had once been, it slid closed behind me. The vases and flowers remained unbothered. Either the house was smart enough to sense motion or someone was still watching me.

My room had been cleaned, everything turned over and made, satin pajamas laid out on the bed, and a hot bath with flowery bubbles already drawn. My first concern was pulling the damp jockstrap and harness off me; my second was how these people I never saw always seemed to know exactly when and what I needed so precisely. If I hadn't been so sticky, I may have picked up the phone to simply say, "Thank you." Something about knowing they wouldn't respond made me feel empty.

Letting myself disappear under the bubbles, I thought about Usher, about how I had expected him to be a dirty or disfigured old man from the black box of his video chat, that despite his kinks, he was not only handsome but charismatic. We were not so different in age, although he was still a Daddy type. It didn't matter to me either way, but I assumed his hair was naturally more grey than the jet black he presented, that if he allowed it to be natural he'd have a distinguished salt and pepper look. My mouth submerged under the surface, I breathed through my nose and fantasized that if we had met outside of this situation, we could have been something more than a financial exchange.

Suds clinging to my torso when I climbed out of the tub, I could see in the surrounding mirrors that my body was raw and already starting to bruise from our encounter. Even though the warm water had soothed me, he had left my hole sore and well-used. I'd come to associate that feeling with guilt and shame. Not because of the sex, but for letting them have me for so little. This felt different, even if I hadn't experienced passion with Usher, the price tag was finally right. If I could build a tolerance to the more physical portions of our sessions, I could do it for as long as he would have me. Assuming he still would.

A quick knock on the door and another silver tray outside, this time with a grilled sandwich and tomato soup—comfort food, the type of meal Roderick and I would describe to each other after our parents had kicked us out around the same time. When meals like that ended and we were instead eating anything that could be punctured with a can opener in a tent, we'd say, "Remember warm soup?" and feed each other unseasoned beans or mushy spinach with a shared spoon.

The bath and soup helped, and although I still had Usher on my mind, his smile and intensity—I mostly wondered when I would see him again, or if he would leave the house right away. Tucked under satin sheets, I could almost sense him entering my room. In my half-asleep vision, he held me close and asked how I was feeling, massaged me gently in the places I told him hurt, ran his fingers through my hair and did everything he could to heal the wounds he had inflicted on my body for his enjoyment.

But the pleasant thoughts quickly clashed with images of him bending me over hard and fast, hitting me over and over again, and forcing any object of his choosing inside my hole—the impersonal side of his need in high-contrast with the moment we had shared together. A moment I worried we would never have the opportunity to replicate, nor the chance to smooth over, to show him that I accepted and craved his vulnerability. That he could kiss me.

Otherwise, I slept soundly for the remainder of the evening and let myself stay in bed the next day. I told myself unless I was summoned, I wouldn't wander. I wouldn't go looking for more information. Three meals came and went, delivered swiftly with extra treats: strawberry truffles, raspberry cookies, and dainty cakes. A note with a request for laundry put me in a strange position to set the dirty blue jockstrap outside the door only to have it returned clean and folded on its own silver tray. I assumed it was nothing the workers here hadn't seen before.

I kept my mind occupied with movies and binge-watched everything I could, never knowing when my time could be up, if at some point the next knock on the door was going to be a note telling me to go home, to return to squalor. I was uncertain if I'd done a good enough job pleasing him to secure my placement, if that's what he even wanted, a live-in play toy. Best case scenario, that was what I had become.

My anxiety was getting to me again. The thought of having gone too far with Usher always pecked at my brain. I needed something to focus on, a game, like the mindless ones people had on their phones. Usher had bought one for Roderick. If he had given him one, there was a chance I had been good enough to earn one as well.

I picked up the receiver, "Could I get a phone please? Like a cell phone? The kind with games on it?" I heard the breathing and then the click, the sounds I had learned to associate with a request about to be filled. But nothing came. No knock on the door or silver trays, nothing. I hadn't been good enough.

The sadness of my first request being denied stayed with me through the evening and into the next day. I thought about Darius and how I hadn't even told the boys where I was going or left a note. In fairness, I hadn't figured I would be gone for more than a few hours, but here I was over a week later—I had to find a way to tell them I was okay, that I was safe, relatively.

The phone I'd been using to request things had a dial on the front, something I had only seen in old movies, but I understood enough how to work. I put my finger in and spun it to the first number of Darius's cell phone, the only phone number I knew by heart anymore. Letting each number spin and click back to me one at a time, I finished dialing. Then, nothing, no trilling to assure me it was calling to anywhere outside the house. I didn't have much experience with landlines, but after hanging up then putting the receiver to my ear again, I should have noticed before there had never been a dial tone. This phone was strictly internal—for use within the manor only.

My quest for a real phone began in the morning. The sounds of woodwind instruments greeted me as I walked through the wings and floors of the house. My bruises had begun to turn different colors, but most were starting to fade and no longer hurt when I moved. I searched from room to room, finding mostly locked doors but also some spaces I had never seen before, rooms filled with more books and paintings, high-backed velvet furniture and carved boys. Every time I found another fancy phone, I'd pick it up only to hear the same breathing and click. The even breath eventually turned into a sigh, some poor person intended to wait on me undoubtedly exhausted by my relentless mission.

Once, to the sigh, I said, "Please, I'm just trying to call my friend." The line clicked off immediately. I hadn't been given any rules, and I wasn't doing anything aside from sitting in bed all day getting fat off snacks and watching movies. So I put on a fresh pair of jeans and boots from the wardrobe and took off for the backdoor. If I couldn't call, then I'd just take a walk, a short one to let Darius and the boys know I was alive. Then I'd come right back.

When I reached the double-doors, it was dusk. It had been hard to tell the other night from the inside, but looking through the panes of glass, I could see the doors had been locked from the inside. I turned the locks and pushed. Correction: the doors had been locked from both sides. Chains rattled against the wooden doors and glass. Something large and metal, like the storm shutters my parents had used during hurricanes, blocked the windows and what was left of the daylight from coming through. It was no longer a door. I hadn't thought to check before, but running to every window I had found in the rooms I could access revealed the same metal sheeting over the glass.

I picked up the closest phone. "Am I not allowed to leave? I just want to tell my friend I'm alright." No answer. I was beginning to panic. Out of pure desperation, I tried something else. "Is that you... Sir?" I was still unsure what to call him but didn't dare use his name. The line clicked again, making it clear no one that could help was listening. Of course it wasn't him. He probably wasn't even here anymore. Whoever was keeping me locked inside was just doing their job.

As a last effort, I ran down the stairs and past the locked double-doors. On what I now knew was called a credenza, I lifted the left vase and pushed the silver button below it, the way I had seen Usher do during our night together. The wall slid open like a panel, the long table following with it as a single unit, revealing the long hallway. I walked through slowly, unsure if the wall would close behind me. If it did, I had no idea how to get out. Toward the door, silhouetted in red, the hallway seemed as long as it had in my dream, different somehow than when I had been marched down it by my hair with Usher.

It was the sounds that drew me in closer; the ominous tones coming from behind the door made it impossible to turn back around. Then the screams, the moans, the cracking of a whip and a voice that said, "More, boy. You're going to give me more."

Another crack and scream, then a familiar voice muffled and yelling, "Please, I can't! I'm sorry! I won't do it again!" The voice sounded like Roderick.

CHAPTER FIFTEEN

I retreated immediately back down the hallway. This time the panel didn't close behind me, and I had to push the button under the vase to let it slide closed again. I fled up the stairs to the second floor, back to the relative safety of my room where I let myself become a ball under the covers and cry. While the sheets and blankets absorbed my tears, it was uncertain how much time elapsed. When I finally took a normal breath again, my face was swollen and wet, my lips tasted salty.

It was hard to pinpoint the exact reason I was so upset and overwhelmed, why I had let my emotions spill over as if I'd been holding them in forever. I couldn't even remember the last time I had cried. Not when I was living on the street. Not when I was about to get kicked out of my house. Not even when my stomach was so empty it hurt and I didn't know where my next meal was coming from.

Today, maybe it was knowing I was trapped in a house or being in a quasi-relationship I had no control over. This realization that I wasn't the only boy in the house, that I wasn't special, sat like a boulder in the pit of my stomach. To top it off, if my ears hadn't deceived me—if I wasn't just making a bad situation worse to drive myself over the edge—the other boy here was Roderick. I was crying because I was certain now, at least one man had been lying to me.

Usher didn't ask for me after my tears dried. No notes were paired with the food that arrived at my door. I spent two days staring outside the bedroom window through the small opening in the metal sheeting overlooking the woods and the large trees, the same scenery I had once found so calming. But in my solitude and contemplation, I still couldn't decide that if given the opportunity, I'd even leave.

Lunch arrived, another pressed sandwich with warm soup, something I could have used after spending half a day sobbing into my pillows, but it was better late than not at all. I slipped the tray inside and lifted it to the bed. Picking up the napkin to tuck into my lap, I found something underneath: a phone. A real phone. One with a touch-screen and everything. I unlocked it immediately, expecting it to be disconnected from the outside world. Maybe Usher felt bad enough for leaving me in the room neglected for so long, he was offering me the form of entertainment I had requested.

To my surprise, the numbers made sounds when I pressed them, and when I hit the green button to make the call to Darius, the line trilled. A sleepy voice on the other end said, "Hello?" It was Sonny.

"Sonny! Praise Cher, I need you to put Darius on."

"Did you get locked out?" As usual, he sounded exhausted and three rips deep.

"What? No, I'm not even there. I'm—just give the phone to Darius," I said, knowing it would be less than useful to explain anything that was going on to Sonny. My best chance was to hope he could stay awake long enough to bring the phone to someone who could form sentences.

There was silence, followed by a long yawn, then Sonny yelling, "Darius! Your phone was in the couch cushions again, and Alexander wants to talk to you." Somehow, he seriously had no idea I hadn't been there for almost two weeks. I wish I possessed the ability to sleep that well.

The change in tone was immediate. "Bitch, where are you?" It was Darius. I felt myself smiling just hearing his voice but realized right away I didn't know how to answer the question. If I told him everything, he'd want to call the police. Even if I could convince him to come here and help me, I didn't want to put him in danger. More so, I wasn't certain yet if I wanted to leave.

"Hello? Are you okay?" He sounded genuinely concerned.

"I'm okay," I said, trying to stay calm and contain my excitement.

"So you were just gonna take off and not tell anyone? Are you coming back? Don't think you don't owe rent just because your body isn't in there. All your shit, all that computer equipment and whatever, is still taking up space." He was asking all the right questions, but I couldn't give him the answers. Not yet. Just the memory of my old room, the damp smell and chipping paint, the small bed and empty refrigerator, helped me make up my mind quickly. I needed to stay here. I wanted to stay.

"Do you have a pen? I'll get you the rent money and more." On the other end of the phone, there was a sigh. I understood his hesitation, not knowing what kind of bullshit I was about to drag him into.

"Alright girl, go ahead." Darius was a better friend than I gave him credit for. I just hoped I wasn't putting him in a bad situation by giving him the address.

It was uncertain how long it was going to take for him to reach the location, but I made sure the volume was turned off and the phone was set to only vibrate for when he called back to let me know he had arrived. Hours passed but still nothing. The worry was constant, my mind cycling through the possibility that receiving the phone had been an elaborate trick, Usher testing my submission, that without explicitly telling me I was to have no communication with anyone else, I still should have known.

There was a chance that by calling Darius, I had failed, that at any moment I would be escorted out of the house. Punishment I could take, and at this point, welcomed. If misbehaving would get me close to him again, if I could somehow get Usher's attention— it would be worth any amount of abuse he felt he needed to inflict upon me. I could endure everything as long as I didn't lose my place here, the comfort, the luxury, but more importantly, his affection.

A vibration purred near my head, a familiar number on the screen. "Hello?" I was whispering now, just in case.

"I'm here," Darius said on the other end, "but it's empty."

"What do you mean? Are you sure you went to the right place?" I asked, confused.

"I went to the address you gave me, but no one lives here anymore." He said this with certainty.

"Did you do the special knock?" It seemed like a stupid question to ask since I had made it so clear during our first call. Three knocks, two knocks, one knock. The system Roderick and I had developed to give the *okay* during a con. Over time it had become a shorthand for so many things. All good, I need you, please help me—it was the audible code of our friendship and the only thing I could offer to Darius to try in case Roderick was on the other side of his apartment door worried Usher was coming to get him for more chastising.

I sent him there with the promise of reimbursement, knowing Roderick had plenty to hand over, and would, for me. I'd already decided I would find a way to pay him back once I figured out how. There was still a chance he had never been here at all, that other than the night we came together, Roderick was not involved with Usher anymore. He could be totally safe with his weird furniture and the money he'd gotten away with. Maybe I'd let myself believe I heard his voice the other night only to hurt my own feelings, the house and the solitude getting to me, making me create stories.

"I did the knock; I even opened the door. When I say empty, I mean EMPTY, girl. There's not a person or teacup in this place. "I'm not sure who this friend is, but it looks like they cleared out with whatever money they had of yours with the quickness."

Roderick was gone. Something had happened. There was no way he had left that palace he built for himself on his own. A strange feeling trickled down my neck, and my blood rushed.

"So what now?" Darius was still on the other end, waiting for my instruction. As I began to speak, the phone buzzed; it was going to power down. Whoever had given me the phone hadn't provided a way to charge it.

"Go back to the house, sell everything in my room and use it for whatever the boys need." I still didn't know when my time here would expire, if I was setting myself up for disaster when I'd inevitably come home completely penniless. There was a chance that equipment would be my only saving grace for when Usher released me, but I couldn't let the boys suffer because of my choices.

Before he could reply, the phone was dead. At least Darius knew I was safe. Something about that felt like a win for the day. I hid the useless phone in the back of one of the drawers in the wardrobe behind rolled balls of clean white briefs. Then I let myself bask in the thin slit of sun peeking through the layered metal against the window until it faded away and turned to night.

CHAPTER SIXTEEN

I heard it first on the door: three knocks, two knocks, one knock. Waking up slowly from the first deep sleep I'd had in days, it seemed early for breakfast. I didn't bother to get dressed since no one was ever outside when I opened the door for the trays. From the lack of light showing through, it seemed like it could still be dark outside.

Naked and kneeling in the hallway in front of my door, I found a single empty glass, upside down, the rim resting in the lush carpet. What a terrible snack. If imagining my drinks was a new game, I wasn't awake enough to appreciate it yet. But I thought of orange juice and iced tea. I didn't typically drink much alcohol but at this point a mimosa or bloody mary seemed necessary.

Maybe it was a message from Usher, his own indirect way of telling me this is where it all stopped, the beginning of the end for the food and fancy drinks. All this cushy stuff, the bubbles and the blankets, was coming to a close. I was right, it had been a test, and I had not done what he wanted. I'd called someone on the outside and given him a reason to doubt my commitment to him and this life, our life, together.

It was difficult to understand why I was so heartbroken over a man I had only met once and the rapidity in which his hold on me had become so strong. I knew I would miss the stuff. Admittedly, the service I'd been aching to provide him did just so happen to come paired with surroundings I would never be able to afford on my own. But it wasn't just the payment. It was his eyes, his hands on me. It was thinking I would never see or feel him again, never feel his thickness inside of me. I'd wanted the opportunity to make it grow, to let our relationship continue to develop, but now—it was over.

I took the glass inside and stared at it for a while, this crystal symbol of the end. Leaving it on the nightstand, I figured with my stay to be complete at any moment, I may as well use what was left in the bottle of suds, let myself bathe and submerge myself in the grand tub before I was dragged through the house and thrown out in the dirty clothes I had arrived in.

Under the water, I let my mouth blow into the flat surface of the water as I had so many times in the two weeks. I breathed only through my nose in a way that felt close to drowning, the way it feels when the ocean is warm and calm and you're just floating there letting the current take you wherever it decides, contemplating letting go of your control and becoming one with the sea.

Thinking about the vastness of the ocean, about Beachside, I heard it again: three knocks, two knocks, one knock. I let my ears perk up out of the water; the knocks were coming from outside the bathroom. Jumping from the tub, dick-out, I walked in circles around the room attempting to locate the sound. It wasn't emanating from the bedroom door. Water pooled in my fur and dripped down my body, soaking the thick carpet below. The knocks were coming from the wardrobe.

Flinging both doors aside, I pushed the hanging clothes and harnesses out of the way then smushed my face to the back panel. The knocking continued in the rhythmic pattern, but it was getting softer, as if the person on the other side of the sound was giving up. But I could hear something else now with my ear so close, a muffled voice. I couldn't make out what they were saying, but I replied anyway, "Don't stop talking. I'm coming! Hold on!"

Running to the nightstand, my balls bounced lightly against the top of my thighs as I grabbed the empty glass and hopped back to the wardrobe. Pressing the rim of glass to the flat wood and my ear on the smaller end, I finally heard him. "I'm on the other side. Are you there?" I could only make out some of the words, but it was Roderick. He was here and he was looking for me.

Pressing my lips as close as I could to the barrier and still speak, I said, "I can hear you! I can hear you! You're here! I'm coming out to find you!"

"No!" the voice said back with urgency, loud enough that I could hear it without the glass. I stopped and put the rim back against the panel.

"He's watching us." His voice sounded like he could be trembling on the other side. "Is your friend coming?"

My heart sank. Somehow, he'd snuck me a phone, and I had totally messed it up. I wanted to thank him and to ask him so many things, to tell him about my last two weeks, but with my lips at the back of the wardrobe again, I could feel my breath pushing back toward my face while I simply asked, "Are you safe?"

The glass back on the dark wood, his response was delayed, probably with disappointment that I hadn't told him that help was on the way. Eventually, his voice returned, "I'm so sorry Alexander, I—"

A loud bang on the other side of the boundary silenced Roderick's voice. I whisper-yelled his name to the panel until my lips were flat against the smoothness of the wardrobe and moved the glass around to different spots trying to hear what was going on, but nothing. He was gone.

After having drizzled a line and series of spirals around the room in water and soap, I finally grabbed a towel to dry myself off. Roderick had gone through so much trouble just to let me know he was okay, but I didn't understand why he had apologized.

As I pulled the gold chain from the tub and watched the foamy water drain, I wondered if Usher had been watching me since I'd arrived, if he'd seen me pacing in my room and eating cookies naked in bed. Even from outside the house, he seemed to have a way of controlling everything we did, the food I'd been given being the only exception. Roderick had discovered a way to send me messages; I just hadn't been listening. Every sandwich and warm cup of soup, every snack arriving at just the right moment I needed comfort: it was Roderick saying, "I'm here and I love you."

I kept the glass close in case his voice returned, hugging it close against my skin as if it were Roderick, and we were back in that tent, depending on each other. The place we found ourselves in now was so different, and yet it all seemed so familiar. With the glass tucked into my chest, I held it tight knowing sleep would be elusive as thoughts spiraled around my mind.

I'd slept on my fair share of uncomfortable beds or worse, concrete, in the past. Relaxation was impossible in the constantly waking, always in half-dream state that felt like being suspended between two worlds. I never felt truly awake or asleep with the sounds of the city by my ear or roommates grunting from neighboring rooms with thin walls. Here, it had been different. But now, I could feel everything looming. I knew I would be summoned by Usher soon, and for the first time, my fear went deeper than eviction from my new lifestyle.

A hard knock on my door jolted me. I didn't feel like I had rested, but the sliver of light seemed to be shining through. Still holding the glass with me, the expected note read:

> *Mr. Usher requests your presence at dinner.*
> *Your preference for wine is required.*

If this was his way of breaking-up with me, it was pretty classy. I wasn't even sure I had a preference for wine. Aside from the type that came from a box, with that pink hue that seemed to be the run-off from everything else being bottled, I didn't have much experience. I had to ask myself what Julia Roberts would choose. If she would fill her long-stemmed goblet that was deep but never totally full, with something white or red before tipping it far enough back to take in a generous sip.

I tried to sound certain in my decision when I picked up the phone. "Red," I said without hesitation. Although I was still unsure if the person on the other end was employed or if somehow Usher had orchestrated this entire operation on his own, I knew the time for pleasantries was over.

It seemed clear now that either way, someone had always been watching, that I was being monitored, nothing had been accidental. He had seen me watch movies with my chest covered in cake crumbs and shake my ass in the mirror covered in soapy bubbles. It must have been amusing for him to see how happy I was in his home. Surprisingly, the only embarrassing thing I hadn't done in the room was jerk-off, which had been such a ritual before my stay here. In fact, it had been my only form of release for so long and yet, I hadn't even thought about touching myself. I wanted to hate him for keeping me here, for lying to me and doing whatever he had to Roderick, but I couldn't deny how much I still craved him, this wealthy older man who had become my keeper: Mr. Usher.

Chapter Seventeen

The harness and matching red jockstrap requested in the next note wasn't comfortable under the fancy suit, but I imagined there was a chance that was the intention. I'd never been the type to dress-up, having never really had a reason. I could remember though, before losing contact with my family, my mother telling me that a man gets his first real suit for his wedding. But I figured out at an early age if I did tell my parents I was attracted to men, more likely my first suit would be for my own funeral.

Additionally, it was still uncertain to me that today was not that day. My funeral. At the very least, tonight was most likely the death of the strangest, but still arguably best, thing that had ever happened to me. Now I was dressed right for the news. I supposed his insistence in the second note, that I wear gear beneath the formal attire, should have been an indication that he intended to do more than show me my way out tonight, but I had learned not to take anything at face value in this house.

The new map with a familiar X over a room that had been paired with the note told me to arrive in the dining room by nightfall. In my exploration, I'd never found anything resembling an eating space. I had taken every meal in my bedroom, surrounded by soft pillows and empty silver trays full of food scraps. This place was as full of secrets as it was rules, and I always felt like I was three steps behind in learning them.

As I followed the map down the stairs and toward a side of the house that had always been a dead end, I found it to be surprisingly open today, another wall turned door that led me to expansive rooms with vaulted ceilings. It wasn't to say the house didn't always look incredibly huge from the exterior, but being inside made the maze feel boundless. The music I'd gotten used to seemed more somber and dark somehow and only got louder as I continued along the dotted line on the map and closer to the giant X. If anything was certain, my host had a flair for the dramatic. He knew how to set a scene.

Usher was already seated at one end of a long table when I entered the final room, tapping his fingernail on a wine glass. The globe produced a high-pitched ting sound, an audible twinkle that reflected off the walls of the massive room. Surrounding the table were too many chairs, at least ten on either side. For a man who seemed to value his privacy so much, I couldn't imagine what sort of twenty-two person dinner parties he was intending to emcee. It seemed like something only a person with money to burn would do, filling every room in their house with furniture because they could. Not out of necessity, not because they were going to use the house to entertain or crowd it with as many bodies as the space would allow—just because.

"Sit." The sound of his voice replaced the reverberation from the glass. I took my place at the opposite end of the table, closest to the door I had entered from, where a full wine glass had already been set out. The rings of the harness hit the back of the tall wooden chair and prevented me from resting my back entirely. I thought about the bruises he had left on me the last time, how painful they would be right now against the straps and rings he'd instructed me to wear between my skin and the layers making up the suit.

"As expected, you Beachside boys do clean-up nicely." He said it like a compliment, but his tone reminded me of the time the owner of the house I grew-up in came by to tell my parents he was raising their rent, the way he introduced himself by saying, "I'm your Slumlord."

"Thank you," I said immediately, certain my memory was misplaced in this context. He was trying to calm me, to let me know this dinner was just that: dinner. He wanted me here, and I was excited to see him again. Already the moths were back in my stomach and making their way down my abdomen. I had to shift in the chair as I swelled from just the sound of his voice. If I had been upset before, I couldn't remember why now.

"I apologize for my absence during your stay so far. I had business away from here." He paused, looking at the wine in front of me. "Please, drink," he said.

Picking it up by scooping the round part and letting my fingers part around the stem in a V shape, I felt like I was handling the fancy object incorrectly. I watched Usher pick-up his own wine glass by pinching the stem between his index finger and thumb. I followed, using my other hand to brace it as I switched my grip around. He was looking at me adjusting my placement when he smiled and said, "That way the wine doesn't get too warm."

The red liquid was thicker than I remembered the light rose-colored wine I'd had before to be, with a flavor that was rich and sweet enough to lick off my lips while I set the glass back on the dark wooden table. There were candles I hadn't seen when I'd first entered. Large candelabras that stood on either side of us, illuminating the room. Down the vibrant red table runner, white tapered candles made one long row, a line of fire leading from me to him as he continued to talk.

"I'm not angry with you. In fact, I'm quite impressed with your devotion. It seems to be in your nature to please."

"I want to please you." The words came out quickly, like a programmed response. I hadn't thought about it, hadn't processed what he was saying. I just knew I needed him to know I wanted to continue to serve him.

"As I'm sure you always have in your line of work," he said, tipping his wine glass back to let the liquid pass his lips. His mustache and scruff seemed lighter than they had before; he was letting the specks of grey I had assumed were there show through. It looked incredibly hot. The half of me that wanted to crawl on top of the table and weave my way through the candles on my hands and knees to sit in his lap and kiss him was fighting against the side of me that knew what he still thought of me—that I was just Beachside trash. I would never be good enough to be more than a toy he hid away, if I was good enough to stay here at all.

I didn't have the words to confront him about the moment we had shared, to tell him that everything he had let go of while we were together that first time, I'd abandoned just as much. I had shed a part of myself I had been holding onto for so long I wasn't sure if it was part of my skin. He'd let himself do the same. I'd felt it between us like a blaze, but only the amount we could both give for now. I wanted to tell him that I still ached for his kiss, that I enjoyed the luxury I had found myself living in at his expense, but that I wasn't just here for the money. I was here for him, even if he didn't believe it, even if that was the reason he had held back and left so suddenly after our connection. That if he was scared, I understood. But I couldn't say any of that.

All of that in my head, instead I asked, "Where do you go?"

"This is not my only estate. I have many houses to fill, boys to meet and train." My gaze on him moved to the flatness of the table, to the polished wood. I pushed my finger at the base of the wine glass, letting my fingernail create its own ting sound. "Did you think it was just you? Silly boy."

Now my face was hot, I didn't dare to look back up. I had always known there was a chance other houses just like this were out there, and I knew now for sure there had been at least one other boy, but hearing him admit it, to say the words so casually, was painful. The moths in my stomach burned like fireballs. I was embarrassed by how much I had given to this man, how I had stayed in the house just longing for his touch and approval without understanding the rules to his games.

"As a matter of fact, this house used to be full of boys. It will be again, soon enough. With your help." I ignored the last part of what he said, concentrating on the fact that there was a reason the Beachside townspeople had created the stories they passed around about this place. They were true. For decades, this house had been used for this purpose. For his boys. According to him, not unlike so many other houses of his around the world that probably had their own legends in the surrounding cities.

I had let myself grow quiet, still avoiding his eyes, concentrating on finishing my wine instead. It was my hope that by the time he demanded I face him, he would pass my red face off as flush from the drink, that he wouldn't know the pain I was feeling in my guts and heart. He filled the air with more information than I expected, about furnishing all the empty rooms I had found, about how gracious he was to let his boys rest in comfort before using them again, why he had to have a variety in order to satisfy him or risk exhausting a boy too quickly.

As he detailed his exploits to me so nonchalantly, I suddenly felt bold. I felt angry. Looking him in the face, I asked, "What happened to all the boys that used to be here?"

He seemed surprised by my intrusion on his explanation and paused for just a moment before he spoke. Usher didn't want to think of me as his equal, as someone he could have a real conversation with. "I'm not sure what part of that is your concern."

My eyes lowered back to the table. He was going cold again. The wicks of the candles sizzled and popped. I hadn't noticed before that they were giving off an aroma, more crushed flowers mixed with cut wood, a scent that had become branded to my duration in the house, a priceless perfume without a name.

"It won't happen again." He was answering the question I hadn't asked. But I knew what he was referencing. Our intimacy had scared him. Leaving me for days alone after our encounter with no contact had indeed been a test. Even if he had been away from the house, he watched to see if I would stay, if I wanted him the way he wanted me.

"I will make you happy, boy. I will give you everything you desire. That has been my intention since the first time I saw you. But as much as you will love what I provide for you, I do not ask for nor require your love. Know that I will never love you."

Usher wasn't looking for a boyfriend. There was no need to fulfill in his life that required a toy with more than moving parts. I could want him endlessly, and it would make no difference. My desire was complementary and unnecessary. His words said he needed me to commit to the role he was asking me to play or not be here at all. But my heart still heard the longing in his voice.

"I did mean it when I told you I found you special. When I saw you, stroking that lovely cock on my property, as if you were drawn to me... you knew what I was, what this house could do for you, and you wanted it. Don't ever forget that while I may have instructed Roderick to guide you here, it was you who sought me out, boy."

The words I didn't want to hear, a truth I hadn't allowed myself to even ponder: Roderick had conned me. He had used everything we learned together against his own partner in crime. I wondered what he had been promised in exchange for my imprisonment, if he was in some new apartment with his feet up on his ugly beanbags, drinking his scalding hot tea and enjoying everything he had exchanged for my freedom.

"I have a present for you," Usher said, "or rather a reward. Something I know you're too afraid to ask for yourself. But you must promise me that you will do anything I ask of you from this moment forward."

His gaze burrowing into me, it didn't feel like a choice when I nodded. Smiling in return, he let himself take a long sip before he spoke again, "Your wine is empty. Red, wasn't it?" Usher rang a small bell sitting next to his thick fingers. A swinging door behind his seat opened slowly. Roderick was there, shirtless and holding a silver tray with a full glass decanter balanced in the center. A collar was wrapped around his neck and a leash hung at his bent arm, ready to be commanded and pulled. I noticed his jockstrap first because it matched the one I was instructed to wear this evening. But it was his body, badly bruised and red in certain spots, that held my attention.

I had been angry only seconds before with this idea of him profiting from my misery. But now, I wanted to run to him. I wanted to inspect his skin and make sure he was alright, instead I stayed in place and quiet, afraid again.

He didn't speak either as he approached my empty glass and refilled it. I wanted him to look down at me, even from the corner of his eye just to give me a look that said he was okay. But he didn't dare break his attention from Usher, who watched his every movement as he spoke.

"It's a shame he hasn't had a chance to rest from his punishment which, I'm sure he would agree, was well-deserved. But as I said, tonight, is a reward. I'm going to give you both something you've always desired."

Chapter Eighteen

Usher rose and grabbed something from a table near him, carrying it in our direction. When he was near, making a triangle with me in my seated position between each man, he said, "Stand up, boy." I wanted to down the freshly poured wine first, but I found myself on my feet before my brain could assess what was happening.

"Undress him." He was talking to Roderick now who set down his tray and without hesitation obeyed his master. It was clear to me now that Roderick had been Usher's pet for quite some time before I had arrived, that he had lived in the house and learned far more secrets than I knew.

Our eyes didn't meet as his fingers slowly undid the pearl buttons of the white shirt that had been issued to me, one of the garments I'm sure was expensive and fitted perfectly to my body. His breath was getting shallow, and the first time his skin brushed mine—his palm, seemingly accidentally, touching my chest—I wanted to touch him back. I wanted to place my hand flat near his nipple to see if his heart was beating rapidly in time with my own.

Usher watched the process, the delicate way Roderick removed my clothes and folded them on the table, but it was difficult to say if he was pleased. When I was disrobed down to nothing more than the harness and jockstrap, Usher finally smiled. He lifted my chin, and in a single motion so my eyes were on him, fastened me with a collar matching Roderick's. Grabbing the metal chain acting as a leash, he pulled Roderick closer to us both. Then, using a hook on the bottom end, he attached it to my new collar, a single line now created between our necks so he could pull us both at once.

"On the ground, boys," he said, tugging at the metal links as we both knelt and found our way farther down until our hands were flush with the floor. He walked us back to the other side of the table near his chair where he made us stay on the ground while he poured and finished more wine. There had been no actual food during our meeting and it seemed now, dinner was about to be a very different sort of feast.

There were so many questions I wanted to ask Roderick, with the predominant one being, "What the fuck is even going on right now?" But there was little I could do to make him risk even a non-verbal interaction with me without permission.

As we crawled across the various types of flooring through the house, our knees took a beating from the tile while Usher brought us past the French doors to what seemed to be his favorite location. With Usher a few steps ahead, I tried over and over to steal a glance from Roderick, but he remained obedient, and we continued to move forward.

Down the long hallway and into the familiar red light, the ominous tones had begun. It was something I still hadn't figured out, whether Usher had some sort of remote control in his pocket he could access to make it look like a magic trick, or if there was help somewhere in the mansion assisting in the soundtrack to his sexual madness. From an aerial view, if I hadn't been the one with a collar on entering a sex dungeon, the execution and planning of it all would have been impressive. Usher didn't just want submission; he wanted a full sensory experience to be achieved for all participants, and it was.

The door at the end of the hallway closed behind us and locked shut on its own. Taking a half-seated position on one of the taller benches, Usher brought his hand up in a way that made Roderick rise to his knees, instinctively. I followed his lead, in no hurry to disappoint or earn myself the type of punishment that had been so recently inflicted on Roderick's frame.

"Mouth open, boys." There was no hesitation from Roderick to part his mouth wide and welcoming to whatever Usher wanted to put inside. Again, knowing I had agreed to obey his every demand, I followed Roderick's movements. I was being trained by example.

"Are you mine to do with as I want?" Usher asked. Mouth still spread and ready, Roderick forced out, "Yes, Sir."

Usher looked at me, expecting the same. I was uncertain how to form the words without closing my mouth, but using my throat let the sounds of something like "*Ess Sear*" find their way out. He smiled, almost laughing at my need to please, my intention to follow instructions even when they weren't explicitly given.

"Very good," he said and leaned over our still accessible orifices. He pursed his lips and let a droplet of his spit glide out until it landed on Roderick's tongue. It sat there, visible from my peripheral vision where I knelt next to him. Moving a step over closer to me, Usher prepared another full droplet of spit inside his mouth, taking the time to guarantee it would be equal or greater to the previous one. He didn't ask for it, but I kept eye contact with him as the spit fell to my mouth, his taste taking over my own. The wine and saltiness of him sitting on my tongue was as close to kissing him as I had gotten and his saliva mixing with mine was making me rise inside the jockstrap.

"Swallow," he instructed, and Roderick immediately closed his mouth and let Usher's spit run down his throat. This was his way of demonstrating his power, a reminder: he owned us. Our bodies, every part of them, were his. I had yet to close my mouth; Usher looked down at me, commanding my compliance.

More than when he'd asked me before, I felt like this was my first real decision, the moment I would decide if I was giving myself to him, if I would not only be his and stay in this house, but carry out his demands in every way. His spit in my mouth felt like royalty; it felt like freedom from the life I had known before and never going back. I swallowed. My stomach felt full of some part of him now, and I wanted more.

"Now, because you are so fond of each other and have been, for the most part, such good boys." He looked at Roderick while he said *for the most part*. I had come to assume that, although I was still uncertain how he had pulled it off, sneaking me the phone was among the protocols Roderick had violated on my behalf. The signals he'd offered me knowing he was risking punishment, the exact meal I wanted while I was recovering from Usher's abuse, and finding a way to communicate through the wardrobe: they'd all been found out.

It was that level of detail to my needs that had made me leave so long ago, abandon the home we'd created together. The night he had told me he loved me, that he wanted us to be something more than friends sleeping on the ground together, I couldn't be sure if what I felt was more than a codependence we'd formed from necessity. I didn't leave because I didn't love him back; I left because I wasn't certain how to tell if the love was real.

"Kiss," Usher said, still looming over us. "It's okay. You have permission. I'm giving you each other as a gift."

For the first time since I'd left him standing alone in his apartment—told him I couldn't stay for the second time in our lives—Roderick looked into my eyes, deep and passionate, as if he'd been waiting for this moment since the day we met on the beach. Because as many times as we'd gotten this close, we'd never actually kissed. We'd never had sex or touched each other for more than warmth at all.

Usher laughed at our hesitation, seeming to be just as surprised as we were that we had never hooked-up. From what he had gathered by our interaction and concern for each other, I'm sure he was certain we had always been lovers.

"This is not a request," he said, still amused. "Kiss," he repeated. Now that it was an order, there was little to consider and our lips met in the middle. We filled the space Usher had been keeping between us quickly, and his mouth on mine felt like home. It felt like years of longing satiated. My sadness that had felt like deep hunger for so long finally satisfied by the kiss I didn't know I needed, sitting like comfort food and taking over the space I thought I had reserved for Usher in my stomach.

He watched us from the bench for a while, releasing the metal leashes for just a moment while we rolled on the ground together kissing and sucking each other. Our hands firm around each other's cocks, sharing the taste of Usher's spit in our mouths, our collars clinked together as we fiercely caressed each other's bodies.

"Enough," Usher said, quickly done with our show. I didn't want to release my grasp on him or feel Roderick take his skin off mine. Even a few more minutes to feel him inside of me or me inside of him, to continue exploring this place I had forced myself to avoid for so long, was all I needed. But on Usher's command, Roderick released my cock from his hand immediately and was back on his knees in front of him. I followed with less enthusiasm, our cocks both out and hard near his boots.

During our tussle, I hadn't noticed Usher take out his own cock. But now he stroked it slowly and looked at me, then Roderick. It was the first time I had seen it up close, thick and long, bulging through the open fly of his fitted pants. If I couldn't touch Roderick, then I needed Usher in my mouth immediately. I thought about violating orders, about inching closer and taking my tongue to him without permission, to see if he would allow it considering how hard and displayed he was in the moment.

But as I imagined my saliva dripping from the tip of him, he raised his hand up and with a swift motion brought it across

Roderick's face. The quick smack cracked like thunder against the cement walls and ceiling. Roderick was on his side, heaped on the cold floor, moaning with pain. I was too surprised to move, to check on him, to speak.

Disconnecting the chain line keeping us together, Usher pulled me to my feet by my collar and forced me over the bench he had been sitting on. With my jockstrap still in place, he forced himself inside of my hole. Pulling out just for a second to spit onto my ass, he thrust himself back inside and pumped hard, grabbing my hair.

"Tell me you're only mine," he demanded.

"I'm yours!" I yelled back, knowing Roderick could see everything that was happening from where he lay on the floor. There was pain, but something so confusing within me was incredibly turned on by Usher's inability to follow his own rules, that I somehow had the ability to get more than his whips and toys. I was different, no matter what he said. He did want me.

If I had been drawn to him, he had been just as drawn to me. There could be a million bearded, hairy boys saying they were his in the world, countless houses and furry holes for him to fill, but there was still something we could give each other that no one else had been able to provide.

With Roderick still on the floor, I knew his eyes were fixated, his cheek probably burning with agony while he dealt with the confusion of Usher doing something to me they had never done together. He was going to have more questions for me than I would for him after this night.

Usher came hard and quick inside me, his warmth leaking from the space he had opened so quickly. The silence that followed was telling; he was not proud of the emotion he had let overcome him once again, that he had shown his vulnerability not only to me, but to Roderick. He had put our secret on display, if only to demonstrate to another man offering me affection that they could never have me. I was his.

Pulling backward, Usher withdrew directly, as he had done the first time. I couldn't see Roderick from my position on the bench, but I imagined his shock, the array of emotions he may be experiencing seeing me so willingly claimed. Not moving, I wondered if observing Usher's cum dripping out made Roderick consider whether I shared the desire Usher seemed to have for me.

Catching his breath from the quickness and force of his action, I could hear Usher fasten his pants and grab Roderick roughly by his leash, "Back to your room, boy!" he yelled. Then to both of us, "I expect to be thanked for this gift. Make no mistake. You will never touch again without my permission."

I was up on my elbows on the bench now just enough to see Usher dragging Roderick out the door by his collar. He slammed it behind them, leaving me in solitude but still full of his spit and cum. In the glow of the red light, with his mark inside my body, I wondered if that feeling was the closest I would get to his love.

Chapter Nineteen

❧

Through the thin slit between the shutters outside my bedroom window, I could see the trees outside had now fully undressed for winter. I couldn't open the glass or part the metal farther on the other side, but if I hadn't been sealed in, I imagined the air would feel refreshingly chilled. Not freezing yet, but cold enough to know a real change was occurring, that the plants outside were dormant only in preparation for their rebirth.

I wasn't surprised I hadn't seen Usher after that night. What did surprise me was my door remaining locked from the exterior unless a silver tray was resting on the carpet. Without fail, once I took whatever was being given to me inside my room, a few moments later I would hear the lock turned again. Usher was keeping me where he wanted me and making it clear, regardless of our intimacy, I did not have his trust.

It took a few days longer than was typical to heal my body from our unexpected three-way encounter, and during that time, I often found myself thinking about Roderick, wondering if the old and new marks Usher had left on him were starting to turn back to his normal shade of skin, if he had been punished further for our lips finally touching, even if it had been at Usher's command.

After what must have been a week of sunrises and sunsets peeking through the naked canopy of woods, I began to wonder if Roderick was still in the house at all. I found myself often with my ear pressed against the back panel of the wardrobe, moving the empty glass I had stashed away, hoping to hear even a murmur of his voice in one of the corners. Nothing came.

A quick knock on the door and the click of the lock being released, I dropped the glass to retrieve my afternoon meal. Instead, outside on a tray, was a ring of keys. I really would have preferred a sandwich, or anything edible, but I pulled the collection inside letting the metal of the keys scrape as they slid across the surface. The variety of aged blades and teeth were heavy in my hand. Most were long with only a few spokes at the end; it was difficult to imagine the type of locks the odd grooves would fit into. Even with my quick response to open the door, as usual, there was no one in the hallway. The door was finally open, and I was still hungry.

Whether the keys were one of Usher's games or a signal from Roderick, I couldn't be sure. Tossing and catching the keys in my palm, I took them as a sign either way—it was time to leave my room. Perhaps they were a reward, Usher demonstrating to me I had further proven I was worthy and had earned new privileges in the house. Still, more than wanting to secure my home with Usher, I hoped that whatever door the keys opened, I would find Roderick waiting on the other side.

Racing back to the wardrobe, I pushed garments aside looking for something all-occasion. If I was going on an adventure, I wanted to be ready, to have something aside from underwear on for the first time in weeks. Settling on some jeans and boots with a plain t-shirt, something caught my eye behind the now empty hangers. It was hard to believe I hadn't noticed it before, but in the upper left corner where the dark wood met was a lock. As if it had just appeared, pressed in the corner of the back panel of the wardrobe, a strange latch met a loop threaded with a thick padlock and keyhole.

The ring twinkled glamorously around my wrist while I tried each of the strange keys I had been given. Then, success in the form of the lock releasing and the back panel turning into a squeaking door which opened into a large stone passage. Roderick hadn't been talking to me from another room when he'd made contact with me before; this was something else. There were no other doors that I could see, just a cold and drafty tunnel beckoning me to explore. Looking back to the unlatched door of my room, I couldn't be sure this new passage would lead to food, but I took my first step in anyway and let my boot rest on the smooth rock floor.

Beyond the safety of the wardrobe, it was tall enough inside the passage for me to stand in, just barely. Reaching out my hands, I could touch either side with my fingertips if I didn't bend my elbows. My breath was now blended with the sound of my wristlet of keys chiming against themselves and echoing from the surrounding stone as I walked farther through what became a winding path. The music I'd gotten accustomed to was now silent with no violins or spooky piano vibes penetrating the rock to act as a score to my adventure. While the distance from the artificial light of my room grew, the dimness took over, and I was forced to rely on my sense of touch combined with a slight glow that felt like sunlight and guided me forward. The smell of pine and earth wafted through the chill, and I kept course for the daylight until the stone tunnel ended in what felt like another dead end, like so many in this house.

If I'd learned anything from my stay here, it was that the manor was nothing if not exactly the opposite of what it seemed from the outside. Weeks ago, I would have sat on the ground defeated and hoping I could feel my way back to the safety of my room, but instead I pushed and felt around for latches and buttons, secret things that would reveal the next step. My hands discovered something carved from the stone, a heavy door with a rectangular hole letting the scents and rays find their way inside.

I pushed and slid it aside, and as my eyes adjusted to the new light, I found that this entire time, my room had led straight to my favorite spot on the property. The keys had to be a gift from Usher to show me he had always been watching. Even when I would come to enjoy his woods, I had always belonged to him.

Something glittered from the base of a large tree, one that I had often used during my walks. On the ground, near dried splatters still shining from the dirt, color: blues, purples, and golds. I couldn't believe it until I was holding them in my hands, feeling the grit and sand—shell dollars. I'd always assumed they were gone forever, that when Roderick and I had found ourselves without a home, we'd left behind the last of them. But he had saved them, somehow, all this time and he had brought them here. Like always, he had found a way.

This was a message from Roderick, my first contact with him since the night we'd rolled and kissed on the floor of the red room. The keys had appeared to tell me: he was safe. Out here now, letting the cold winter air penetrate my skin after weeks of being locked indoors, the shells gathered in my hands were a postscript, Roderick's nonverbal message to make sure I knew: even if we couldn't see each other for fear we would be punished worse than ever before, Usher would never break our bond.

Leaning against the tree, the sudden sense of calm and relief was so overwhelming it got me half-hard. The shells slowly dropping to my feet, I imagined Roderick's lips near mine. I stroked over my jeans thinking of the ways I wanted to continue to explore his body, put my tongue on the tip of his cock and lick the underside while I looked into his eyes, flip him over so I could move my tongue to the fur between his ass, but most importantly kiss him hard and cum together. Maybe it was too late. In this world, in this house, we were owned. We'd given our lives and bodies to Usher. They belonged to him, and he had made it known that Roderick and I could never be together in this house.

But outside with the colored shells surrounding my boots, my soles grinding deeper into the dirt as I pulled the hardness from my jeans and began to stroke, I knew Usher did not control my mind or fantasies. Pressed on the tree and ready to shoot toward piles of thick fallen leaves, I could pretend I had told Roderick when he'd asked the first time that I did want to be with him, that we would find our way through anything with our love for each other.

The thought quickly turned to my association with our partnership, the way it was paired with lack and poverty, sleeping on cement in the rain during nights I wasn't able to romanticize our very real financial struggle. The truth was, even when the bruises on my body were grey, or purple, or some shade of blackish blue, I was happy: orange happy, yellow happy, shades I could see now that I hadn't been able to before. I was where I wanted to be and felt close to gaining Usher's confidence. Admitting my feelings for Roderick would only complicate my effort to work toward Usher's affection. I had felt it twice now, his resistance to show me the intimacy he craved. Already, Usher had given so many material things I had wanted in my life and assuming they would continue, in exchange, I would give him my body and dedication. I would help him achieve the physical relationship with a man he denied himself.

My cock standing long and thick from the fly of my jeans, precum dripping like an icicle, in my mind, Roderick's presence transformed into Usher. The thought of giving myself so completely, of being a kept boy in such an extravagant household, used to get me hard in the woods. Now, the mysterious man I'd only heard about in rumors wore the very real face of Usher, and the whisper of his commands for my cum still sent me close to the edge. I was finally on the right side of the iron gates and wanted to stay there. Imagining his breath in my ear again and voice commanding me to shoot, my body convulsed against the rough bark. Spurts fired one after the other as they found their way to the earth, and with my bottom lip under my front teeth and eyes closed tight riding the sensation, a phone rang.

My orgasm nearly ruined, I stumbled quickly to redistribute my weight and let the blood find its way back to my brain. Shoving myself back into my pants, I hastily attempted to fasten the zipper and button, certain I was about to see Usher behind me with a perverse tool, something that could do more than bruise my skin. For this offense, I expected him to draw blood and pull me by my hair back to my room, toss me inside and leave me in confinement for as long as he decided. But, struggling to catch my breath, I looked in every direction around the dense trees and I saw no one.

Among the logs and shrubs close to frozen in the gusts of early winter, it was the first time I noticed my breath visible in front of me. The phone was still ringing. I turned toward the sound and followed it until I was on my knees at the base of a nearby tree not far from where I had just spilled my load. Still bulging and partially unbuttoned, I grabbed up the phone from the base of the trunk where it met the icy ground. It was the same phone Roderick had snuck to me weeks ago. The one that had died, and I'd stashed with my clean underwear. On the display was a familiar phone number scrolling over and over.

"Hello?" I said, putting the phone to my ear. I was still pulsing below my pants with a mix of terror and release, but the former was winning the moment I heard his voice on the other end.

"Where's the door to this place, girl?" Darius asked. I knew I hadn't contacted him or told him to come, but somehow, he was here.

THE END

Leo Sparx

Taming
ALEXANDER

The fall of the *House of Otter* 2

Dedication

Fur Bryan

No otter boys combear!

CHAPTER ONE

O ver a year ago, on the night I'd left Roderick in the rain, I didn't know where I was going. I only knew that if I was going to survive on my own, I needed to work. The boat launch became my new home. Near the brackish water, the boat launch was in a park where men would sit in their cars and wait for each other. Where they'd cruise from the safety of their silver four-door sedans or baby-blue SUVs until they saw someone they liked and ventured into the brush.

I'd tried the bathhouse before that, loitering near the exterior of a place that marketed itself as a men-only gym, but didn't have any workout equipment inside. The pretense of waiting for my workout buddy in hopes a customer would invite me in to share his rented room was exhausting, but it was the only way inside without paying my own admission. Even getting a locker for a few hours was out of my price-point as an initial investment to make a sale.

Pacing circles at the boat launch park and weaving through the used condoms in the sand near where the mangroves met with the bay water had a much lower overhead. I could spiral from there to the parking lot half a dozen times pretending I'd just arrived before a Daddy would notice and follow me through the long green and brown shoots and stems. Once we found an open spot, I'd ask him if he was feeling *generous* with doe-like eyes and a smile before I got to my knees in the wet sediment or bent over a pile of salty driftwood.

He had to know the code first. That being *generous* meant he was willing to pay for quality head or sex from a professional. But once the formalities were out of the way—regardless of how the low tax of the park often matched the general look of the clientele—it was typically worth the constant charade to finally score a paying customer.

Darius told me later, after I'd been in his house for a few months, that his approaching me at the boat launch hadn't been entirely selfless. Apparently, multiple men had complained about me lifting their wallets while they had their pants on the ground and word traveled fast. He wasn't angry when he pulled me aside that summer evening in the park, but he was direct in letting me know I was giving the boys doing legitimate sex work in town a bad name and cutting into his business. I was lucky to encounter him before anyone else who wanted to point out my mistake. Instead of creating an enemy, Darius offered me a room and a job. He gave me a place to stay and a safe space to turn tricks.

As I got to know my new roommates, Brent and Marco—the bleach-blonde brothers from the north—and Sonny—the kid with the long wavy hair who only stayed awake long enough to take dick and paper money—I realized we had more in common than we didn't. We all had different stories for how we ended up in the house Darius had somehow acquired. Even if the structure was falling apart and so filthy it could never be truly clean, it was more than most of us had ever had as a shelter once we'd become adults.

The stark contrast of my present surroundings in The House of Otter from my previous dwellings didn't escape me, even if the pleasantries from Usher seemed to be dwindling more with each passing day. When I'd received his most recent note, it was difficult to determine if he was angry with me:

White briefs.
Downstairs.
Now.

If this had been just a few afternoons before, and especially after using the secret passage without explicit permission, I would have been filled with anxiety that this sudden request would mean my dismissal from the house, but after the experience with the three of us together—bound to Roderick and taking Usher's spit inside of me—I felt more secure. Even if the notion was a coping mechanism on my part, it had all been so ceremonial. Something about the encounter made things seem more official, as if part of a ritual had been completed.

Usher didn't have many words this evening. Upon my arrival in the room, he kept his back toward me, simply instructing that I sit on a black metal block and remove the briefs I had just been told to put on. *Make up your mind*, I thought, but didn't speak. My balls and bare ass were frosty upon the block as I watched him gather toys and whips on a table, then wheel the giant wooden X, the one he had called a Saint Andrew's Cross, into the center of the room.

I was seated to the side of the structure in a section of the room which gave me an unobstructed view of his preparation, and I held my breath as I watched him give each whip a snap against the table, choosing the perfect weapon. There didn't seem to be a way to physically prepare for the pain, but I exhaled and hugged my knees to my chest trying to convince myself that whatever he was about to inflict upon my skin would only be temporary. I let myself hope there was always a chance I could find his eyes and convince him to handle me with more care. Even if part of me was still confused by the ebb and flow of our intimacy—not to mention the physical anger he consistently showed toward Roderick, and the way he was keeping us separated from each other—my craving for his cock and touch seemed to outweigh my anger and confusion anytime I was in his presence.

When Usher seemed pleased with his selections, he walked toward me and said, "Don't move, boy."

I nodded before he ran his sprawling palm through my hair, letting his fingers wrap around to give a light tug while he used his other hand to push my legs back into a position to leave me exposed. The motions made me close my eyes and bite my lip. I waited, trying to anticipate his next move, the punishment I hadn't yet received for venturing into the woods and attempting to contact Darius.

When I'd used the keys to open the wardrobe which led to the passage, I didn't know who had provided them. It wasn't until I found the phone and colored shells strategically placed in the trees that I knew Roderick had been the one orchestrating my first peek at an alternative exit from the manor. There was an endless list of actions Usher could decide were violations at any time, even if I hadn't known the acts were against the rules while committing them.

The keeper of the house I'd chosen seemed to adhere to a policy I'd first discovered while handcuffed in the back of a police car. When three cops surrounded me with their dicks out at the boat ramp, and I'd been tasked to give the blowbang of my life in exchange for my freedom. I thought about the imaginary itemized missteps I'd made since accepting my place as his boy: enjoying Roderick's body, using the hidden passage without permission, and leading Darius to the house. As if Usher had said them himself, the cop's words from the experience before my life here echoed in my mind: "Ignorance of the law is not an excuse."

Usher released my hair, and for a few seconds, I lingered in the expectation of a slap or a tail snapping at my nakedness, but instead, when I opened my eyes again, he was gone. The brighter lights in the room were off, and the corner I was in had turned mostly to darkness. He had closed the door behind him, and the ominous low tones I hadn't realized were missing before were suddenly cued-up and playing.

It seemed colder now. The white briefs I had worn were still balled up on the cement near my feet. I was high enough that my soles didn't touch the ground, and as I waited, I let my heels tap rhythmically against the hollow block with nervous tension. So many of the sexual games Usher orchestrated seemed to be about the waiting, demonstrating submission through patience. It reminded me of clients other boys had told me about who liked to be kept in confinement more than engage in a physical encounter. I'd always wondered what those men thought about in their cages, if they could reach a state of meditative euphoria from simply being left alone. Solitude I could manage, and previous to this life, often needed. But I was still uncertain whether I found the idea of being a kept object as arousing as being financially secure.

A bang came from outside, then another. I stopped swinging my heels as the metal of the chamber door rattled in response to the exterior noise. Following the series of sounds and joining in the haunting chorus of spooky Halloween tones was a constant screaming of indistinguishable words. They were the peaks and valleys of a voice I'd gotten very familiar with over the last year, one that had woken me for late lunches and early dinners of mostly juice concentrate, someone who had given me shelter when I was in desperate need.

Now here he was being dragged through the door with Usher's firm grip around his socks at the ankle, pulled the same way I had in what I still tried to convince myself had been a dream. Usher was busy forcing Darius's body, which I could see now was clothed in something tight and black, through the door, but he took just a moment to acknowledge me in the corner. Seeing how I observed the scene, he pierced me with his eyes in a way that made his last words reverberate through me, "Don't move, boy."

CHAPTER TWO

I wanted to trust Usher, to assume that he had my happiness in mind no matter what, but watching him hoist Darius toward the giant X made me want to leap toward them both. Instead, I stayed paralyzed while Usher secured each of Darius's feet and hands away from each other. He had forced Darius's shirt inside his mouth as a gag. From where I sat, I could see everything, including Usher's smirk as he ran his fingers through the furry body hair that seemed longer and thicker than I remembered it being on my former roommate's body. His typically smooth face was now covered in a longer stubble that Usher took the time to vigorously stroke. Darius didn't have a view of me and my inaction, but his stifled screams made me shiver.

Thinking back to the night I'd sat outside the French doors waiting for Roderick inside this house, my mind filled in some blanks I hadn't let myself think about before. Roderick had known exactly what he was doing, leading me to Usher's home and within his grasp, letting me believe I was somehow safe outside while he probably helped Usher with the elaborate setup in this very room. I'd worried about him then, concerned that someone inside the house was harming him and I may need to come to his rescue. In reality, he was the one who could have chosen to save me before I officially began the process of becoming one of Usher's toys. Instead, he'd remained quiet while he heard my screams and pleading for release.

Roderick had sat naked in this spot and watched Usher administer the first steps. He'd known the whole time we dressed together in his fake apartment that I was going to cum on his favorite pair of black pants.

I'd seen Darius's cock and balls so many times they were nearly committed to my memory. He'd always been attractive to me in a traditional sort of way, like how I would appreciate a tree with perfect branches or a beautiful scent. That's not to say we haven't fucked before. Shortly after I moved into the house, we'd absolutely fooled around. Neither one of us hinted at our interest in each other, but I was thankful for his hospitality, and as I had learned to do in life, demonstrated my gratitude in a physical manner.

It wasn't that it wasn't good or enjoyable for us both, but as much as we flirted after that night, we never messed around again. Our relationship became brotherly. Darius was my family and meant more to me as a mature sibling I could rely on for advice and understanding than a convenient fuck buddy. He'd continuously defended me to the other boys in the house when I was short on rent, and now he was further demonstrating his reliability by showing up here. I hadn't sent for him nor asked him to come, but I had made contact with him. I'd put him in a position to find out where I was and worry about saving me. Still, I was uncertain if that was the reason he showed up at the manor looking for a door or if his invitation had come from Usher himself.

Even considering my familiarity with the perfection of Darius's setup, seeing his thick cock released through the zipper of the dark pants he wore by Usher's large hand made my breath quake. From where I sat motionless, I couldn't take my eyes off of either of them. As Usher began stroking Darius's firmness, I wasn't able to hide that between my spread legs over the corner of the block, my own cock rose and dripped precum down my shaft. I tried not to draw attention, not to touch myself or look at how quickly I was growing. There was no way to hide my reaction, no throw pillows or blankets. The minimalist nature of Usher's favorite room left little to the imagination, and my nakedness only added to the aesthetic's lack of nuance.

Usher stroked Darius with a tight lubricated fist, occasionally taunting him with the whips on the table but never making contact with his skin. With his hand pushing the saliva-covered shirt deeper into Darius's mouth, Usher made eye contact with me, then looked immediately at my hard cock. I hadn't noticed when I'd been in Darius's place on the giant X whether or not Usher had been looking off to the side or behind where I was fastened in place, but if Roderick had been there the whole time observing the domination, it had been for the same reason I was here now. This was another test.

Usher's face displayed disappointment with my erectness, complete betrayal at the moistness building up below my foreskin and pushing its way out to trickle down between my hairy thighs and to the metal block. But he raised his eyebrows—not just with permission, but insistence—a non-verbal command to touch and stroke myself. My first instinct was to resist, and still, I worried his approval was yet another layer of his game, the tests he so often administered with the hope I would fail. He didn't need a reason to punish me, but he seemed to enjoy making me feel as if I'd forced his hand. In certain ways, I suppose I did as well, since defying him often meant more of his attention.

Ignoring the pulsing, which continued as I heard Darius approaching climax, was unbearable. I knew his sounds from the time I'd swallowed him, but also the countless encounters he'd had inside our house with customers. From his expression, I couldn't tell if he was aroused in spite of himself or if he truly wanted Usher to force out and claim his cum. His eyes widened, and his breath quickened in rhythm with my own. I wanted us to shoot at the same time, but it wasn't just him turning me on. It was the domination; it was Usher and his commanding presence. I wasn't jealous about him touching other boys the way I assumed I would be when he'd told me about his various estates. Observing the way he worked, the commitment to allowing a new boy to have a full experience, only made me want him more.

Pumping at my cock now with the tips of my fingers first and then my whole closed fist, I knew it wasn't going to take much for me to expel my load. Usher was staring into Darius's eyes, the way he had when I'd been the new boy restrained and at his mercy. He was commanding him to cum, and Darius complied as more spit dripped from the sides of the drenched fabric gag. While his last spurt ran down the open fly of his pants, Usher's eyes moved to mine with a similar demand, and I shot hard, trying my best not to make a sound. I was compliant in his game. Not only had I watched the entire thing, I'd enjoyed it.

Staring at the cement floor, I wondered who was tasked with cleaning up the mess every time it was covered in cum. Darius seemed to be motionless now, his body relaxed and his head resting on his chest. After taking a small taste from his finger, Usher wiped the cum and lube from his hands then removed the restraints from Darius's wrists and ankles. He cleaned him up, fastened his pants, hoisted Darius's full weight onto his shoulder, and carried him in my direction. Before exiting through the metal door, Usher looked at my soft cock and the release I'd left on the forest of hair covering my pubic bone. He shook his head with disapproval before disappearing through the door toward the hallway. I'd done exactly as he'd commanded, and yet, I had still somehow failed his test.

CHAPTER THREE

Several minutes elapsed before I could hear Usher's heavy footsteps approaching the entrance again. If the music had stopped, I would have assumed it was time for me to return to my room, but it still chimed with mysterious bells and electronic rhythms. I hadn't moved at all in the short amount of time he was gone, even to wipe myself off, and I was thankful to learn I had finally made a correct decision when he saw me still in place and said, "Good boy. I'm not done with you yet."

It felt good to hear kind words, even if I could sense punishment looming in the air. He'd hardly used the whips laid out at all, and I worried that every tool he had chosen was intended especially for me.

My guess was that he'd returned Darius to the porch in the courtyard with the stone men, that the French doors were again bolted shut, and he'd be leaving him out there until Darius came directly to him—as I had. It was speculation on my part, but there did seem to be a pattern, some sort of method to the ritual our keeper coordinated for each of us.

"You shouldn't have cum," Usher said, tracing his hand over one of the longer paddles he had on the table. "This is all going to hurt a lot more now." His back was to me as he analyzed the tools and toys he'd collected.

Often he stayed in his fancy clothes: a suit, sometimes a tie, like today. He hadn't even removed his navy jacket while he'd played with Darius. But now he did and left it hanging over one arm of the Saint Andrew's Cross. He loosened his slim matching tie and unbuttoned the top button of his crisp white shirt. His formal attire so often felt like an intentional division between us, a wealthy man in contrast to my lower-class status, his hidden body to my near constant nudity. From my perspective, the fitted suit was the sigil of man who took his business seriously, but even more so, it was a symbol of his power over me.

Perhaps it was the relaxation that came with ejaculation, but before I could overthink what I was saying, the question slipped from my lips. "What did I do?"

Usher cracked the side of his mouth in a half-smile while he removed the silver cufflinks from his shirt. "I had hoped you would be different, boy," he said, rolling up his sleeves. "But just like your friend, you've disappointed me. I offer you gifts and you use them to show me you cannot be trusted."

He turned his eyes to the spot where I'd rolled around with Roderick while he watched just a few nights before. It felt like so much time had passed between then and now, from the last evening I'd touched Roderick or had even seen him physically. I wondered what it had been like for him, to observe from the corner I was seated in now, while I'd been the one secured to the wooden structure. With the straps around my wrists and legs while Usher's hand tugged at my cock, I imagined he must have seen everything. From the moment Roderick had left me alone in the dark courtyard until I'd been dragged back unconscious and returned to the cold stone, I could only assume he'd witnessed it all as I had tonight with Darius.

So much of my interpretation of what Usher said relied on what he didn't say between his carefully chosen words, but one recently vocalized selection stuck out to me: *disappointed*. If he was comparing me to Roderick then I had replicated something he'd done in the same position. Recalling the way Usher had punished him immediately after that first initiation, I wanted to understand how I had just potentially earned the same treatment for myself.

"Perhaps this new boy will make up for your short-comings." Usher traced his fingertips over the sweat Darius had left behind on the wood. Rolling the wetness between his fingers and thumb, he brought the moisture to his mouth, dragged the salty liquid across his bottom lip, and smiled. While his tongue curled around his lips to taste the residue, my blood ran scalding hot then immediately ice cold. I should have been happy Darius would be in the house with me soon, but I sensed that Usher wasn't bringing him in for me to have a companion; he was using him to challenge me further.

"Why him?" I asked and inhaled deeply, my anger forcing itself past my better judgement to question a man within reach of a full selection of disciplinary objects. Usher caressed the handle of a whip wrapped in dark ribbons of coarse black material before raising his eyes to mine.

"Afraid of temptation?" He curled his fist around something but kept it behind his back and out of my view. The choice had been made.

"Temptation?" I wasn't certain what he was talking about, but as a reply to my confusion, he nodded to the sticky droplets drying on my stomach and his floor. The metal block still housed small translucent domes sitting between my bare legs and soft cock. As he pointed toward them it became more clear: he thought I wanted to fuck Darius. That had been the test I'd failed. He wanted to know if he could trust me around his newest addition to the mansion. And like Roderick must have done when he'd been my ambassador to the lifestyle within the manor, I'd gotten hard from the display of Usher asserting his power over a boy.

I didn't have the words to explain right away, to tell Usher that as sexy as Darius was, he hadn't been the one I was looking at while I came. Usher had commanded my nakedness and vulnerability, he'd provided an atmosphere of sexual dominance. Observing him commanding a load from Darius's body as he had from me the first time I'd felt his grasp around my cock—that was what had brought me to such a state of arousal, and it was only his insistence that led me to believe I should shoot. It had been for him.

As much as I'd been thinking about Roderick since I'd felt his lips on mine, I couldn't deny the craving I still had for Usher's body. At times, it was even stronger than my need for his approval. But I didn't know how to tell him. While I'd watched him demonstrating his power, it was him I wanted, to be back in that place and restrained with my cock exposed for Usher's enjoyment, responding to his demands. If not being aroused by his interaction with Darius had been the test, I hadn't failed exactly. Not in the way he was insinuating.

But with Usher approaching where I sat with the mysterious whip concealed behind his back, I couldn't plead my case before I felt several hard stings across my chest. Now revealed, the weapon he'd decided upon had more tails than I'd seen before and twisted knots at the end. My skin burned as he pushed his free hand into my open mouth to force me on my back. He tasted like salt and coins. It was Darius's sweat mixed with the metal surfaces of the red room Usher had been arranging when I'd initially arrived for the evening's event.

My back now flat on the coldness of the block, Usher grabbed both my ankles and took the knotted tails to my ass and thighs. I screamed out from the slashing pain while I used my hands on either side of the surface to steady myself in place, making an active effort not to resist. Usher had somehow managed to palm both my feet together and knowing he could do so with one hand made me bite my lower lip, fighting a smile. Something felt right about being at his mercy again. Being restrained while he paused for just a moment from the lashings to poke the base of the whip at my balls and soft cock, felt even better.

CHAPTER FOUR

"Y ou're going to regret not leaving any loads in there for me, boy," Usher said, using the cylinder of the handle to give the thin hairy skin hanging between my legs a few lights taps. I struggled to keep in place and attempted to wiggle away from the sensation. He released his hold and allowed me to lay on my side for only a moment to breathe before pulling my legs out straight to force me to my stomach.

With my ass in the air, I heard the object he'd been using to beat me hit the cement somewhere near my drying cum and underwear. He pulled me by my waist with a quick motion to bring me to my hands and knees, then pushed my face toward the block until my cheek was flush with the metal, letting my ass spread open enough to expose my hole. At first I worried he would retreat to the table for a toy or something else to force inside me, but instead, I felt the familiar fabric of his suit on the back of my thighs. With his pants brushing against the areas he had hit with the tails, my skin felt raw and singed.

The only pleasure came when I felt the hardness of him behind the fly of his pants pushing against me. Despite the delicate state of my backside, I thrust back and wiggled my ass over his firmness, hoping my body would reassure him he was desired. A reward came swiftly as his belt buckle clinked against itself. I could feel the warmth of his cock pulsing against my hole and within seconds even warmer spit from his mouth dropping to the tightness.

"It's going to hurt, boy," he said, using his cockhead to spiral the saliva around my opening. I was mentally aroused from feeling him so close to the precipice of fucking me, but wasn't getting hard. It hadn't been enough time since I'd spilled my load to be ready to offer another. Usher was right. Having him fuck me was going to be painful, but any opportunity I had to feel him inside was an opportunity I was going to take.

"Tell me, boy." I could feel his head forcing its way inside already, just teasing and pulling back out, making the pucker between my furry cheeks open and close around his girth. The silkiness of his precum slowly dripped beyond the threshold of my hole, and I imagined it going deeper. I wanted it to slide inside me while I waited for his cock and cum to follow. Curving my hands around the top of the hard surface in preparation, I nodded in response to his request.

"No. Say it, boy," he commanded. I hadn't noticed before that water had pooled in my eyes from the beating, but now the tears ran salty and warm to the block along with perspiration from my chest, armpits, and hair.

"Please fuck me!" I yelled out. "I need you to feel you!" With no further teasing or hesitation, he pushed his hips forward and plunged the entire length of himself past the entrance of my ass. I gasped with a rush of pain and stiffened my grip on the side of the block. He grabbed me by the hips and propelled his cock in a solid rhythm, never missing a chance to feed me every inch of himself after pulling out halfway.

There was something different about being fucked after I'd gotten off. It wasn't the first time, but it was the only time I'd known the discomfort was inevitable and had asked for it directly. Not experiencing the physical act for my own enjoyment as much as just being accessed for someone else's wasn't a new sensation, but having Usher use me as a hole for his satisfaction felt like a victory.

My own precum drizzled from my foreskin again at the realization, adding to the collection of liquids under my body.

"Know that you won't have any of them without my permission, boy," he said, grabbing my hair from behind and making me crane my neck upward.

"I only want you!" Again the words escaped before I processed their full meaning, but in that moment, it didn't feel like I was lying. It wasn't my intention to give him lip-service just to earn his cum, but with immediacy, a familiar moan resonated between the surfaces of the room and his release was within me.

Unlike the previous times he'd defied his own rules, Usher didn't take the opportunity to leave directly after he came. Instead, he stayed buried in my depths and along with the temperature I'd become accustomed to, his cock remained where he had finished. I could feel him growing softer as we both basked in the warmth, but his hand moved from the back of my hair to my lower back, where his fingers caressed my skin, tracing lines and words I couldn't understand. My fur bristled under the unanticipated gentle touch, and it took all of me to stay in place, to not turn around and sneak a kiss somewhere above his beard but below his dark mustache.

I thought about his lips but knew any sudden movement would make him slip out of me. I intended to savor the uncharacteristic gesture as long as possible. If I did turn to face him and dared put my mouth on his, the whip and collection of unused paddles were still within his reach. Pushing his boundaries had worked before to gain some form of his affection, but our encounters were so few and far between that when I gained the opportunity to interact with him, I didn't want to risk tainting it.

A satisfied moan escaped me, something animalistic and unplanned. I ached for more of him, and I wondered if he knew. Almost in response from behind me, Usher grunted with a tone I could only recognize as guilt and immediately withdrew himself from me.

"You've ruined me, boy," he said, refastening his belt. My ass and chest both burned from the fury he had inflicted with the tails upon my skin. I didn't want to sit on my tender thighs to turn toward him, but I needed to see his face. Balancing on my palms, I spun slowly until I could rest on my knees. My cock was still dripping, and with my ass now hovering over my ankles, my hole was so open Usher's cum leaked out to add to the mess I'd left on the block.

He looked down at my cock, still not fully erect but obviously affected, and smirked. I couldn't believe he was still in the room with me at all, but I searched for the right words to ask him what had made him stay. My mind cycled through the combination of letters I could use to ask him what he meant when he said I had *ruined* him, but my body kept the blood it needed for deep thoughts in my pulsing cock. Nothing in my brain was processing correctly. I felt dizzy and knew I was only seconds away from losing his attention.

Before my better judgement could kick in, my mouth put it simply. "How did I ruin you?" It wasn't my most articulate turn of phrase, but with my body in such a state, I was impressed that some part of me had managed to form words at all.

Usher gathered his cufflinks and jacket. As he reassembled his more familiar polished facade, he sighed. "You'll find a phone in your room when you return, boy. Not the one you and your friend have been using to deceive me. When you receive my messages, do only as you're told."

He was by the door when he reached into his pocket, and the music stopped. The magic trick revealed in some capacity that as I had imagined, Usher did control the tones from some remote device on his person. That explained how the lights and atmosphere timed so well to any action performed inside the manor. In a certain way, I was disappointed to see behind the curtain, as if he'd decided I was no longer worth the illusion, smoke, and mirrors, that I didn't deserve his show.

"Your other friend will be among us shortly I'm sure. Make him comfortable, and understand boy, I have moved the world for you. Do not disappoint me." His words were stern as the door to the red room slid open into the hallway. Before he disappeared into the grandness of the house, he turned toward me one last time.

"This is not how we do things here. Be assured, when I return, this will not happen again." The overhead lights lit the room at full-power, bringing my attention to the ceiling. The brightness revealed more of the room than I had ever seen before, and it felt like being in an empty theme park directly after sunrise. I hadn't seen him push any new buttons or reach into his pocket to turn the lights on. When I looked back to the doorway, he was gone.

I smiled and let my wrecked body relax onto the semen-covered block. Perhaps he did still have magic left for me after all.

CHAPTER FIVE

ooking had never been among my talents. I can suck a
dick like a downspout in a category five hurricane, but
gathering ingredients and following a recipe? The text
Usher had sent telling me it was time to make lunch may as well
have been asking me to teach advanced calculus or translate Latin
poetry. It was the chopping that seemed impossible from the start.
I couldn't figure out the right knife in the kitchen I'd gained access
to that would cut the vegetables well enough to throw in one of the
hanging pots or pans. There were just too many options.

When the map I'd received over my new piece of technology
led me to the library not far from my room, I wasn't expecting further instructions to lead me to a solid bookcase pressed against
a wall. Below the map Usher had sent was the title of a book I'd
never heard of before and had definitely never read. When I pulled
the textured cover from the spot it sat sandwiched between other
bound books, the bookcase slid to the side. After the incident with
the credenza on my first real night with Usher and my discovery
in my own room, seeing the stone passage was less surprising, but
after following the tunnel and having it eventually open up into a
giant industrial kitchen on the first floor and finding a skimpy apron
with "boy" embroidered on it waiting, I had to admit there was
no way to get used to the endless mystery of the house. Every day

new secrets—whether strange, wonderful, or terrifying—seemed to reveal themselves.

Usher, of course, requested in a new text that I wear the apron—only the apron—while I cooked. This sounded sexy in theory, especially after spotting the cameras in every corner of the massive room and knowing he would be watching while I did my best imitation of a chef. In reality, once the blades were out to trim the tips from thick carrots and everything was heated to boiling temperatures or spitting oil, with the ties of the apron hanging from the knot and slipping into the crack of my ass, I felt more like a walking safety violation than the seductive star of *Cooking With Otters*. My assumption was the fantasy show, of course, was somehow being broadcast directly to Usher. If anyone else could see me mostly naked and on my tip toes trying to reach a large pot without it falling directly on my head, I wasn't certain.

What I did know for sure was Darius had made it inside the house. My initial hint that things had gone well after Usher left me alone in the red room was the first text on my new phone asking me what sort of food I thought Darius may enjoy. The truth was I had rarely seen him eat. I knew he preferred wintergreen-flavored condoms and had an affinity for a particular brand of cherry lubricant that dyed his white sheets pink at one point, but otherwise, extra money in the home I'd shared with the boys infrequently went toward groceries. Anything that didn't come from a value menu or gas station rotisserie was crunchy crumbs in an aluminum bag or some bright liquid in a paper carton. In our lives, hunger was rarely a culinary opportunity as much as an inconvenience.

Darius had told me before about the dishes his grandmother used to prepare for him before he moved away. Once when he was feeling nostalgic for home and had hit a particularly large payday with a client, he came home with brown paper bags full of non-processed ingredients. He laid out a rainbow of vegetables and cooked them among infused oils and fresh garlic. With the entire house of boys, he shared a piece of himself that we knew he missed terribly. He served what he told us was a stew with rice on paper plates. That night was the most at home I had ever felt with the boys, all sitting in our underwear on the dirty carpet because we didn't have a table, but smiling and moaning happily through every bite. The cooked spices lingered in the air and lasted for days until the tupperware containers packed with leftovers were scraped down to remnants, and we licked them clean with our fingers and tongues.

Those were the only items I could remember, that single recipe and meal he had shared with us. So it was what I texted back to Usher as a shopping list and what was now laid out in front of me on a stainless steel counter—deconstructed. The array of ingredients meant that Darius was still here and Usher intended to introduce him to the type of comfort and luxury he could expect under his care. They also meant that, like Roderick had been instructed to do for me, I was tasked with preparing meals for Darius... who, unfortunately, was about to be very disappointed with my poor interpretation of his grandmother's famous stew.

It was my fault he was here at all, and knowing what physical abuse he had already encountered at Usher's hands, I wanted to offer my best apology, even if he wouldn't know for sure it was from me.

I could open cans almost flawlessly, and as I shook the organic broth with both fists, I noticed the monitor for the first time. Whoever was typically in this kitchen had the ability to observe the various occupied rooms on a single screen mounted near the plates and bowls at eye-level. I recognized my room first, the huge empty bed and closed wardrobe. A few seconds later the screen flashed and the image was a rotating view of the purple bathtub. During my entire stay, the people in here had been able to see me in the bathroom. Fantastic.

The images continued to flip, mostly to empty and unfamiliar rooms with beds that appeared untouched. When I did finally see movement, it was Darius pacing in his quarters. Surprisingly, he didn't seem upset as much as confused while he circled around, trying to force open all the doors and windows. I knew eventually he would give up and settle in. He had endured quite a night and must have anticipated more were to come. Hopefully, the food would help.

More unoccupied rooms cycled until a single shot of a bed with a naked ass and leg hanging from the covers made me stop chopping. I knew that hairy ass; it was Roderick. His room wasn't as cute as mine but suited him. Knowing he was surrounded by his beloved floor poufs made me happy, but the slight movement of his furry round butt got me hard instantly.

I didn't often experience the urge to top. In the past, other boys had told me the size I'd been gifted from the universe was wasteful. But in that moment, as Roderick's fuzzy peach sat waiting, I couldn't stop myself from imagining coming into his room and putting my tongue between his cheeks while he slept, getting the tight space between both sides of his fullness wet with my spit so I could pull myself out and tease the head of my cock around the perimeter of his hole until it pushed inside. I would pull him, still sleepy, up with my arm around his chest to rest my body on his bare back, then plunge deep inside of him while he got firmer and let the friction of the bedsheets tease his shaft while he rocked back and forth to let me fill him completely.

Growing hard, I put the knife down. I was certain it had been the wrong one to choose because it was hurting my palm. Licking where the pain from the handle seared my etched lifeline, I allowed myself to pull the apron up enough to bring the lubrication to where my hardness was pushing through the material of the objectifying costume. The aroma of boiling starches filled the air, and my fingers were slightly orange from the grip I'd held while peeling the carrots as I wrapped my hand around my growing thickness. Everything around me was steaming hot and melding into an unintentional vegetable-based lubricant while I pulled at my cock and waited for the monitor to revolve back to Roderick's room. I needed another glimpse of his juicy ass.

When the video returned, I was so lost in my own thoughts of flipping him over on the bed to stroke his cock while I fucked him, of kissing him while our furry chests touched, that I didn't notice the sweet potatoes boiling over with foam and covering the burners. I didn't sense the sizzle or the smoke while I pumped my cock harder and harder looking at Roderick's exposed thighs in his bed. He looked as if he were waiting for me—if I could just find where his room was, I could have his tongue and cock in my mouth again.

By then I was shooting out from under the raised apron, spurts hitting the glass window of the oven I'd been preheating. Alarms were going off, and I slipped in my own cum trying to silence them. I wiped everything down with rags frantically while oil splattered and threatened my naked parts. I knew the rags would end up being stiff at some point from the combination of substances they were absorbing and, with the alarms still screeching, I waved the damp cloth at the smoke. The moisture spread in viscous strings around the kitchen from the towels, and with my bare ass and spent cock still exposed, the sirens finally died down.

Looking into the monitor, which was finally displaying Roderick's room again, I could see he was awake. The alarms and kitchen sounds I'd never heard from my room on the second floor were loud enough to wake him. He could hear them from where he stayed. I wanted to find him, to tell him that I finally knew for sure I shared the love he felt for me. But I knew with Usher's rules about us interacting it would never happen again without him supervising, that I'd never again feel Roderick's lips on mine unless I was obeying an order.

I had to least know he was safe, that he wasn't confined to his room forever or only released to be dealt constant punishment. He turned on his side, and for a second I thought I saw his cock looking half-hard, as if we'd been sharing my fantasy. Then just before the image on the monitor faded back to the montage of empty areas, he looked directly into the camera, and smiled.

CHAPTER SIX

The phone Usher had left for me was still a little confusing, but useful when real-time messages and maps came through to direct me to Darius's room and explain the passage from the library would be the quickest way from the kitchen to his room. I was still recovering from racing around the kitchen post-orgasm when he sent:

Don't cum again until I return.
Your loads belong to me.

Then immediately after:

And clean that mess.

He was definitely gone and had seen me jerkoff while I burned the bottom of every pot and pan in his kitchen, but I wondered if he had been able to zoom in close enough to see what had got me hard. It was difficult to know his intended inflection, but I let myself believe his text was almost playful. Still, I worried if he'd known the source of my motivation had been Roderick, he would have traveled immediately back to the mansion just to discipline us both.

Usher's recent map led me from the library bookcase to a room a few doors from my own room to deliver the hot food. Even if we couldn't interact, it was nice knowing Darius was close by, but I couldn't help wonder what area of the house Roderick was confined in.

Since he'd heard the alarms when I'd burned Darius's lunch, there was a chance he was adjacent to the kitchen in several directions. He could be near it on the first floor or directly above. I hadn't thought before about searching for a basement in the manor. Being below sea-level didn't typically allow for underground structures, but we were in the country now, not Beachside, so there was a chance luxury could equate to secrets lying below the ground floor, leaving me even more options of where Roderick could be hidden away.

I was still only wearing the apron, but it was dingy now with food stains and hints of rogue ejaculate. The flat strings continued slipping into my ass crack as I walked with the full tray, threatening to untie and fall off my body as I neared the door indicated by Usher's description. If I had my bearings, Darius's window probably faced a similar area of the exterior woods as mine did.

Other than the distance a destination seemed to be from the areas I was familiar with, it was difficult to know for sure where I was at any time. The winding design of the hallways in the house made it impossible to know for sure without an aerial view, but I'd observed some of the layout had a system based on the colors of the walls and the paintings decorating them.

Once I set the food down, I'd need to take a left at the sexy nautical man with his groin area covered by rolling waves as he stood in the surf, then a right at the locked door near the framed portrait of a man wearing a top hat and a light blue jockstrap with one leg up on a short stool. Unlike the first story which maintained a steady theme of dark burgundy with gold accents, the second floor was mostly deep green walls which framed the portraits and lined the path back to the open bookcase in the library.

As far as breadcrumb trails go, the paintings and statues definitely weren't difficult markers to look at or memorize for future enjoyment. Every piece of art Usher had included in the house was sensual. Even the ones where a guy was bound or gagged, sometimes with a look of fear, still presented an artistic vision which couldn't be denied.

If he'd had these works commissioned, I wondered where the artist or artists lived. Perhaps Usher was there now, in some even more glamorous part of the world, walking through galleries and playing with new boys, better boys than me, ones that didn't challenge him in his methods or beg for his touch.

His texts had been about the service he intended me to provide, yet I was thankful that he was still communicating with me. When he had left the room the evening before with his parting words, a familiar anxiety allowed me to worry I had deviated too far from his expectations. Even with Usher nowhere near the manor and constantly reassuring myself that I had graduated far enough to secure my place, I knew not to ever take my new home for granted. If I broke his rules—even the ones I didn't know—perhaps I wouldn't be thrown back to the streets, but there was a real chance something even worse could serve as my penance.

Setting the tray in front of Darius's door, I thought about Roderick again. I wondered if he'd often been the one to deliver my meals directly. Maybe he'd contemplated doing our secret knock to let me know he was here earlier than when he'd finally let it slip on the other side of the wardrobe. Like I was now, he'd probably experienced direction from Usher telling him with some ambiguity what was expected of him.

I knew I was tasked with making Darius comfortable, but Usher also indicated that I should not reveal myself and keep out of sight if the new boy did decide to wander the house or exit his confinement. So much of me wanted to see and hug my friend, hold him and tell him he was safe—at least relatively—but I also wanted to do as I was told.

Knocking with a swift knuckle, I moved quickly around a corner to assure I would not be spotted. It wasn't as easy as I had assumed it would be to avoid Darius's gaze from his open door, and I smiled thinking about Roderick hiding from me near the exterior of my own quarters. Maybe then he'd been close enough to see me pick up the food and slide the tray into my room while I looked up and down the corridor, the way Darius was doing now, searching for the source of the materialized meal.

It felt like a trick, but a fun one, as if I'd become part of the whole mischievous plan of bringing mysterious delight to a new boy. I could see Darius studying both directions of the carpeted hallway then glancing back at the setup I'd presented on the silver tray.

"What in the hell..?" he said out loud as he brought the tray through the cracked door. I had to put my hand over my mouth so he wouldn't hear me snicker at his confusion. It was honestly pretty exciting to be on this side of the illusion, to be backstage for some portion of the grand production that was Usher's custom and see how it all came together.

When his door was closed again, I retreated back to the bookcase to fix the disaster I'd left behind in the kitchen. Being so close, I was tempted to just head to my room directly and climb into a full bathtub, clean the dried cum and food residue from my body, but Usher had instructed me to clean my own mess, and contrary to my assumption when I'd first arrived, there didn't seem to be staff in the mansion—none that I had encountered at least. It seemed, in some capacity, we were the guests as well as the help.

I removed the apron and remained naked while I scrubbed the surfaces and countertops. Uncertain if Usher was still watching, I wasn't putting on a show this time as much as I was trying to keep my clothes from getting dirty. If I was now somehow in charge of meals, there was a chance I would also have to wash my own clothing. I didn't even know where the laundry room was located, but figured if I let dirty clothes pile up, I'd eventually be getting a text with a new map to machines and cleansing powders. Hopefully in all his furnishing, Usher had provided a high-class dryer. I'd come to equate having the money to automatically dry wet clothing as truly *making it*. Peak luxury was truly rapid fabric dehydration. Admittedly, imagining a clothesline in the back courtyard strung between two of the stone men was a satisfying image in its own way.

While I laughed to myself about expensive statues supporting wet multi-colored jockstraps, a phone rang. As I searched for the source of the sound, I found one hanging on the wall not far from the monitor. It wasn't fancy like the one in my room. This was more retro than antique. While I analyzed its place in the history of communication devices, a message from Usher came in:

Answer the phone.
Say nothing.

How this man got anything done while observing my every move, I couldn't understand. Using the opportunity to swivel my ass toward the camera as I got to my feet, I grabbed the phone from its holder. I put the receiver to my ear, but as requested, I didn't speak.

"Um...I'm sorry, but this food is inedible, and I'm starving up here." It was Darius on the other end, insulting my cooking. "Could I get something else, please?"

I wanted to defend myself, to tell Darius that I'd never had someone in my life teach me how to cook like he had, that I'd done everything I'd seen him do; I chopped, I boiled—I even threw things into pans with oil. But I didn't respond. By Usher's orders, I could merely listen and accommodate.

Hanging up the phone, I knew the standard response was expected to be speedy. At least it had been when I'd been the one stuck in my room being served impressive treats and having my wishes fulfilled. So far, I was not providing the same level of service.

I glanced around the room and searched through the pantry until I found an unopened bag of chips, then rummaged through the fridge. Inside was a pitcher of juice. Sampling the orange liquid with a quick gulp from the side of the pitcher's rim, I tasted mangoes picked straight from the tree somehow mixed equally with oranges.

Hoping Darius would enjoy something more familiar than my terrible attempt at stew, I poured a huge glass and threw a new tray together as quickly as possible before running it up the stone passage and in front of his door. I was still unclothed when I knocked, and this time jolted all the way back to the kitchen with my sore balls bouncing lightly against my upper thighs, hoping the flourishing orchestral music in the corridor would cover my footsteps. I'd forgotten how raw my skin was from the night before until the bruises were smacking into each other. The constant sprints up and down the incline of the dimly-lit passage between the floors were already making my tender muscles ache.

Out of breath and back in front of the monitor, I discovered dials below the boxy screen. I didn't know how I'd missed them before, but I turned and pressed them until the image froze on Darius. It would have been nice to have found them earlier in the day when I'd been jerking off to empty rooms and my imagination, but technology in any form was still a blind spot in my life.

I watched Darius drink the orange juice and eat the chips until the bag was empty, then tip it toward his mouth to consume every morsel of flavor. When he was finished, he shuffled his hands clean and piled the trash on top of the gross concoction I'd produced to put it back outside for me to retrieve. It was unclear how quickly I would need to race back up to the second floor to gather the trays, but I leaned on the counter for just a moment to collect myself. All I'd wanted after my encounter with Usher the night before was to rest. Now, I needed a bubble bath and nap more than ever. Being behind the curtain was exciting, but more than anything, it was stressful.

CHAPTER SEVEN

N early done cleaning, and with the new knowledge that the monitor in the kitchen not only cycled but could be locked onto specific views, I used the textured circle to find Roderick's quarters. The screen filled with his rainbow poufs, but his bed was empty. Turning the dial again moved the view to his bathroom. I was spent for a while after the combination of my most recent interaction with Usher and pleasuring myself while cooking, but I still hoped I would catch a glance of Roderick soaping his fur in his large walk-in shower. As I used the other dial to turn the camera's angle around both rooms, I saw he was strangely absent from the opulent setting.

The phone on the nearby wall rang again. It trilled in a high-pitched and rhythmic tone a few times before I sighed and reached out to make it cease. There had been no further messages from Usher since he had instructed me to answer the first phone call, but I assumed the orders not to speak still stood as I lifted the receiver from its holder and listened.

"Alex?" the voice asked softly on the other end. It was a smart move on his part. Darius knew I didn't love being addressed by the shortened version of my name; I had corrected him and the other boys often when we'd first become acquainted. Something about the full three syllables of a name seemed more regal than my upbringing and had always made me feel important, which was amusing in a certain way, considering Usher never used any variation of my name, shortened or otherwise. I was "boy" to him or nothing. Other than the apologetic way Roderick had whispered it to me through the wardrobe, I hadn't heard my name spoken in the house at all.

It was hard to say if Darius was trying to provoke me to answer by intentionally destroying my favorite word. If I'd been permitted to talk, I would have reassured him as well as corrected him. I didn't know if I was audibly breathing the way I'd heard someone do when I'd been the one on Darius's side of the phone, when I'd held the antique cream and gold receiver in my hand asking for bubbles. At that stage, I had yet to have my first real meeting with Usher or understand how far both his generous and sadistic nature could reach in either direction.

I successfully suppressed my first instinct to respond or to let him know I was here. Rolling the cell phone Usher had given me in my other palm, I partially expected a text to come in to tell me how I should address the current situation, but nothing arrived. More than likely, Usher knew every conversation that happened in the house, even the ones on the phones that didn't seem to have a link to the outside world. If he did know what Darius was saying, that he was asking me whether I was the one fulfilling his requests, it wasn't a priority for him to give me a course of action. So I said nothing and stood quiet, just listening.

"Alright. Cool." The phone clicked when Darius hung up. He was frustrated and reasonably so. To be surrounded by so much finery after being convinced to come here by some mysterious older man, only to sit alone and hungry in a single room, he deserved more.

I stuck the phone back on the wall, feeling terrible that he was uncomfortable in the house. Not that Usher had even asked if I could cook on my houseboy application that didn't exist, but it was still my fault the level of luxury was not up to standard. Looking up to the monitor, I turned the dial back to Darius's room just in time to see him closing his bedroom door behind him.

If Darius was under the same instructions I'd received during my first day in the house, he hadn't been explicitly told to stay in his room. When I'd been the new boy, I'd chosen to stay because my bed was soft, and I had a clean bathtub around for the first time in my life. Someone had successfully managed cooking and delivering me delicious food like clockwork, so I didn't have a reason to leave. The truth was it had taken me several days to even care about what was outside of my room because I was so comfortable. But Darius wasn't, and without orders not to do so, I assumed he could explore as he pleased.

I looked down at the cell phone: no texts, no messages. Usher had told me before he left I wasn't supposed to interact with Darius or interfere with the process, but he didn't say anything about what would happen if Darius found me. Tracing the marks still present on my skin from my punishment the evening before, I thought about the whips and paddles Usher hadn't used during our session. I wondered if they were still out and waiting for me upon his return.

Even if I had accidentally violated some rule I wasn't aware existed by using the keys I'd found outside my bedroom door and using them to discover the secret passage that led to the woods, it hadn't been intentional. Perhaps that was why he hadn't restrained me while he dealt the physical punishment. The part where he forced me to watch while he jerked Darius off hadn't been expected, but the tender marks now on my thighs, ass, and chest hadn't come as a total surprise. I'd known they were due when Usher grabbed me in the woods before I could reach Darius upon his arrival. He hadn't made it a secret—before I lost consciousness—that I would pay for my transgression: leaving my room without his direct permission.

Still, being aware the beating was due hadn't made it hurt any less, and I wasn't in a hurry to give Usher new reasons to turn my ass new painful colors. Even if I wasn't going against direct orders to allow Darius to find me, I slipped the door to the passage open and slid inside to head back to my room. It simply wasn't worth the risk.

Back in my jeans and t-shirt, I left the apron on its hook and headed back through the rocky tunnel. When I reached the second floor, I surveyed the library to ensure Darius hadn't wandered inside, then slipped the bookcase closed behind me. I wondered what he would think during his solo trek through whatever Usher had left unlocked for him in the house, if he'd be impressed by the massive collection of books and art or completely freaked out by the endless unclothed otter men in compromising situations.

Violins and the reverberations of other string instruments filled the atmosphere in the empty hallway leading to my room as I poked my head around the corner to check for Darius. I tried my best to be stealthy and tiptoe across the carpet past the jewel-tone walls. There was a chance—if he was anything like I'd been when I wandered the house—he'd already headed down the spiraling stairs to find the French doors. He would discover soon enough they were locked from both sides.

I had also thought—when I'd made the journey to tug and rattle the chains on the doors myself—they were the only entrance or exit from the house. However, as I'd been led to discover, the direct path from my bedroom's wardrobe to the exterior suggested there were other hidden ways to escape. Perhaps Usher had been upset with Roderick for bringing my attention to the truth: that if I wanted to leave, I could do so at any time.

Before I collided with Usher in the woods and found myself back in my room with no idea how I'd gotten there, I explored the passage, enjoying my time in the open air on the other side, but it had never been my intention to flee. Usher must have understood that because although the ring of keys was now missing, the lock in the wardrobe had not yet been refastened. Even so, an attempted escape in any capacity wasn't a mistake I was eager to make again. The punishment was severe, and I intended to keep the information of the secret passage to myself.

Letting the door to my room creak open slowly, I planned to pop the cork on my favorite suds and strip to nothing. I wanted to soak in warm water and my new favorite scent until the bottoms of my feet and toes wrinkled. My sore body needed to roll in the large tub and dive below the surface. In my vision of the next few hours before I'd inevitably get a text from Usher telling me to make real food for dinner, I imagined blowing air from my mouth and nose while my hair and fur flowed with the waves of the cleansing water and aromas.

Instead, as I closed the door behind me and began unzipping my jeans, I heard a voice behind me. Turning quickly with my fingers still on the fly of my pants, I saw a figure sprawled across my four-poster bed. He was on his side with his hand supporting his head. "Hey girl," Darius said with a half-smile. "This is quite a room."

CHAPTER EIGHT

"Well, I guess we're not in Beachside anymore." Darius rubbed the carved wood on one of the four posts surrounding my bed, a single finger catching in the hollow portion of a spiral and following it around the curve of the glossy dowel. I stood silent by the door, balancing the risk of punishment for making physical contact with my desperation to feel his embrace. He jumped from the bed and approached me with open arms, wide and welcoming. "Hug me, girl!"

So much of me knew I needed to pull back, that I needed to walk away or tell him to leave. Perhaps the damage hadn't yet been done, and I hadn't violated Usher's orders to avoid my friend, but I wasn't moving or speaking. Instead, when Darius was in reach, I leaped toward him, wrapping my arms around his body. I fell into his chest and let my head lean on his shoulder. My breath heaved, and within seconds, I was choking back tears. I hadn't realized how lonely I'd felt in my isolation, not until I felt the genuine warmth of Darius's body near mine.

Only a few weeks had passed since I abandoned the house we'd shared together, leaving the stained rugs and mildewed ceilings behind, but that place felt like a foggy memory now that I was among the bronze and velvet. He wouldn't understand if I had told him what I was thinking as our chests pressed together. Surrounded by golden tassels and pressed lace, textured art and smooth surfaces,

I wanted to tell him the value in the bond we'd formed during our shared struggle was a currency that couldn't be spent, but it was worth more than I'd known before.

Those weren't the words that came out of my mouth, instead, I managed a few whimpers while my body convulsed to hold in the tears. He pulled back to look at me, taking in my full frame, which must have looked disheveled after being on my hands and knees for a day and a half.

"You okay?" he asked sincerely. I nodded without hesitation and wiped any water attempting escape from my eyelids.

"You?" That was honestly the more important question. I'd had time to adjust to living here, but Darius had just arrived and barely had a moment to acclimate. He walked a few steps backward to let me view his entire ensemble.

"Bitch, I am great! Look at these boots! Look at them!" He smiled and twirled in the mid-calf charcoal shoes he'd paired with pleated pastel shorts and a button-down shirt he'd tied into a crop-top to display the hair on his stomach. "Everything is designer, honey!"

"That fur though," I said pointing at the forest he'd let flourish where he used to trim or sometimes even shave.

"Well, your girl does like to please. He asked for it." I nodded in understanding. Now we both knew who "he" was: the man who had sent the camera equipment and computer to our old home, the man who owned this house.

There were so many blanks I wanted filled in about how Darius had found himself here, but when I opened my mouth to ask, he stopped me. "Listen Judy, I didn't come here to eat barbecue chips. Where's the kitchen?"

I should have taken the opportunity then to give him directions and stayed in my room. That way, I would have had some form of defense when Usher inevitably tore into my flesh with some new collection of tails. But Darius was already passed me and in the hallway, pointing his finger back and forth in either direction with a non-verbal "which way?" If the damage had already been done, I was going to enjoy some time with my friend.

Back in the kitchen yet again, Darius rounded up what was left of the stew ingredients and posed in front of the stove. He shook his hips to a beat I couldn't hear in the classical music while he cooked and talked. "There's a closet full of underwear with a guy's first and last name on the band in my room. It's incredible."

I hadn't taken Darius through the bookcase to get to the kitchen. We went the long way to the dining room where Usher had put me and Roderick on a shared leash. Luckily, I remembered the path, and every door on the way had been unlocked. Even more fortunate was my correct assumption: beyond the long table with the red runner and through the swinging door was another entrance to the kitchen.

I wasn't trying to keep information from Darius as much as trying to save him from knowing too much. Roderick's intentions had likely been pure, but the deeper he'd brought me into things without Usher's permission, the more trouble I seemed to be in. If I exposed him to more than Usher was ready for him to see, there was a chance I wouldn't be able to accept the torment for both of us. I knew as I watched Darius sway his ass in the kitchen, my intention was to do just that whenever Usher did return.

"That's what that crisp mess was supposed to be? Stew?" Darius was filling more of the air than I was with conversation, which was strange because I had so much to tell him. I worried my social skills had suffered from being secluded, but more than anything, I focused on the phone sitting in my pocket, expecting it to vibrate with a slew of messages from Usher. So far, his power seemed unlimited. If his hairy knuckles wielding a long whip somehow found their way through the touchscreen to my body, I wouldn't have been entirely surprised.

"How?" I finally asked, still tense as I watched Darius choose a knife that was probably more correct for chopping herbs and root vegetables than the one I'd selected. He didn't stop his cooking flow as he explained that he had been worried about me after we'd made contact and I'd sent him to Roderick's empty apartment. He'd spent a good chunk of time afterward asking about the previous tenant around town and giving the only name he remembered: "Roderick."

"That guy is a bad-news-gay," Darius said as he opened the top of a sealed pot and vented some of the steam inside. He pulled at his new stubbly beard as the moisture soaked into his skin. The new hair looked good on him. As attractive as Darius had always been, the hair he'd let turn to thick fuzz on his face added more allure. Considering he'd always made it a priority to shave his balls and ass, I couldn't help but wonder if the same fur had spread to even tastier areas.

"Bad news?" I asked, trying not to stare at his thighs through the leg holes of his fitted shorts.

"Yeah, girl. I get that you two were a thing or whatever, but it's good he skipped town. No one trusts—"

"Are these the same sources who told you a millionaire lived in the country with a mansion full of hairy sex slaves?" I hadn't meant to cut him off or be defensive.

For the first time, Darius turned away from his stove to look me in the eye as he motioned to everything around us. In the huge kitchen with the industrial-grade equipment and endless supply of gourmet food, his hands showcasing like Vanna White reminded me our surroundings proved at least one thing: the urban legends were true.

Turning back to the stove, Darius laughed, "And bitch said billionaire, so that better be the truth. I must have opened that webcam every night hoping you'd show up."

"What did he tell you?"

"To stop shaving."

"I thought you liked having a smooth ass," I said, laughing.

"I said I was worried about you, bitch!" Our laughter paired with the delicious smells of glutinous rice and flavored broths. "I don't hate it. Honestly, I feel sort of sexy. I see why no one else in the house bothered trimming now."

"He likes it on you," I said before thinking. If I told Darius I'd seen him with Usher, he would know I hadn't stopped it, that I'd watched the entire scene not knowing if he was enjoying himself and had even jerked off to his submission.

Darius seemed confused as he stirred what was nearing real food, and my mouth salivated for something that didn't smell like soil and rubber. After a pause and deep inhale, he kept his gaze on the food when he spoke again. "My grandmother taught me a lot of things when I lived with her. She told me there's a reason we tell each other stories that seem like they can't possibly be true." Darius plated the rice and stew as he talked, then handed me a plate with rounded edges curved like a bowl to keep everything inside. "Legends are rooted in truth and grow fastest potted with magic."

We sat on the kitchen floor with our legs zig-zagged into each other. It felt like being at home again, almost as if this could become our new sanctuary.

"I'm just glad you're safe," Darius said, patting my leg. "That's all I wanted to know for sure."

"Now I'm worried about you. You don't know what—"

Darius stopped me from talking with a sharp look then turned his sight to the camera above us. "It's okay. I know. Eat your food."

We sat with our legs pressed into each other in comfortable quiet. I wanted to tell him that as much fun as I'd had with him already, I didn't know if it was safe for us to keep seeing each other until we were given the okay. Somehow, he seemed to understand without an explanation, and as we cleaned-up and found our way back to his room, before he closed his door, he said, "Stay out of that kitchen, girl. I'm doing the cooking from now on."

CHAPTER NINE

I'd gotten in the habit of locking my door since finding Darius on my bed. Portions of everything he cooked for himself showed up in front of my room, and for a while, I worried he would bump into Roderick and find out I hadn't been entirely truthful about him or our relationship. I was letting Darius assume a lot of things and keeping so much more from him.

A few days passed, and even though I kept the phone charged and near me at all times, I had only gotten silence from Usher. The lack of communication concerned me more than any threats could have. On several occasions, I considered sending him a text asking if I had done something wrong. I already knew the answer.

From under the covers, I could imagine I was anywhere and the house was anything, that the decadence belonged to me and didn't come with an unexpected exchange. In my fantasy world, I didn't live in fear of losing Usher's affection and forfeiting everything I'd gained. The weighted blankets and soft pillows were not constantly hanging like a pendulum above my head.

As soothing as the smoothness of the sheets were against me, I often found myself lying awake into the night until the sun threatened to rise outside my window. One night, a few hours before dawn would be taunting me, I heard a series of loud bangs below my room. Sitting up in bed, my body tensed, wondering if Usher was back in the mansion. I forced myself to curl back under the covers as the bangs grew louder. Soon they seemed to be outside my room and their source was now turning the knob to enter.

I put the blankets over my face and tried to be still. If it were Darius, hopefully he would remember our agreement and go back to his room. But within a few seconds, I had my answer. Keys jingled against the wood of the door until the lock turned and the door creaked open. My body wasn't ready for the punishment I knew I deserved. Usher had never come to my room before, which meant I had really fucked up by spending an afternoon with Darius. If his first priority upon return was to drag me from my bed either to be beaten or discharged, I must have really made a mistake.

He was breathing over me as I pretended to sleep. With my fists balled around the fabric of the blankets in an attempt to shield myself, I could feel my own shaking breath radiating in the enclosure I'd created. Looming closer, he shifted the bed as he leaned his weight into one of the four posts then knocked his knuckles against the wood. Three knocks. Two knocks. One knock.

I pulled the covers from my face and released myself from the humid sanctuary. Roderick stood, smiling in the darkness, bending his face into mine for a kiss.

"What are you doing!?" I whisper-yelled, rolling away from him as a reflex.

"It's okay," he said, reaching for me and stroking my hair. "I talked to Usher. He wants you to come with me." Roderick pulled at my hand.

If Usher was mad enough at me that he had contacted Roderick to relay messages, I wasn't sure if there was anything I could do to fix things. I had convinced myself I was the favorite, but it seemed if it had ever been true, it wasn't anymore.

"Hurry," Roderick said, already heading for my door.

"What do I need to wear?" I asked, jumping toward the wardrobe and ready to pick a specifically colored pair of backless underwear.

If Usher was asking for me, I at least wanted to be on time. Maybe that would gain me some points to weigh against my indiscretions.

"It doesn't matter," Roderick responded. The door was open and he headed into the hallway. It had been so long since I'd seen him, and yet I couldn't fight against my own instincts to let him touch me. I threw on a pair of short trunks, then jeans and a t-shirt over them. If it didn't matter what I wore, then I would probably be picking out my last outfit. I needed to leave wearing something practical on my body for the chilly winter air and long walk back to Beachside.

Through winding hallways and stairwells I hadn't seen before, I almost felt like the house had changed itself in the night. Aside from the few paths I'd gotten used to, getting turned around in the maze of large rooms and connections was easy. Like the night I'd followed Roderick to the mansion, he led the way, seeming to have the layout memorized. He reached back for my hand as we kept a steady pace through a dark series of winding steps. I tried to resist the temptation to let our fingers connect. Roderick sensed my hesitation and looked back at me. His expression was hard to make out in the dimness, but he grabbed my hand firmly and pressed his body into mine, "It's okay, really. We have permission." Roderick put his hand on the side of my face to caress it softly then turned back, pulling me along at his speedy pace to our mystery destination.

We came to a heavy door with brass accents. Everything smelled like moist pine trees with an accent of something clean but synthetic. Roderick took the keys he'd stashed in his pocket, selected a long key similar to the one which opened the passageway in the wardrobe, and used it on the heavy lock. This was nothing like the rooms I had been disciplined in before. Beyond the chunky door were shadows and ripples of light reflected on cathedral ceilings from water. Just a few feet in front of us, beyond a paved deck surrounded by lounge chairs, was a giant indoor pool bathed in moonlight.

As I stared at the full celestial body beaming through the skylight of the massive space, Roderick began taking off his clothes next to me. Without a word, he was fully naked. Standing in the cool glow, he smiled. "Happy Birthday," he said, then got a running start and let his cannonball into the pool splash water half-way to the exposed beams of the roofing.

Roderick let his soaked hair whip around his face when he resurfaced, but I stood in shock, unsure how to respond.

"Come on," Roderick said, tapping the surface of the crystal blue water. He gave me the same big smile he always did when he was trying to convince me to do something, and before I could let anxiety take hold, I left my clothes in a heap on the deck and dove in next to him.

The water was warmer than I thought it would be, not harsh like the ocean. Being in its depth didn't feel like a battle as much as a reward. I must have been smiling when I came up for air after my dive, but didn't see him right away. Then, from behind, I felt Roderick's arms curl around my chest.

"How—" I started, grabbing his hand and leaning my nakedness into his, but he stopped me from speaking. Water dripped from my eyelashes as I his fingers traveled down my stomach.

"It's a birthday gift," he said, submerging his hand below the water's surface and between my legs. "Don't ask questions. Just enjoy it."

Chapter Ten

R oderick caressed me in the friction of the water as I reached
around to feel him growing firm against my ass. His lips
found their way to my neck and offered gentle kisses while
his fingertips tugged playfully at my foreskin and pulled it back
to expose the head of my cock. The precum stuck to my skin just
slightly despite the waves we were making, and he swirled it around
my tip in a smooth motion.

I needed to face him, to feel his lips on mine again. Turning
around, we pressed our torsos firmly together. Our wet fur rubbed
in the comfortable warmth of the heated pool water between our
bodies. I leaned my face into his, letting our short beards brush as we
stood on our tip-toes, pausing at the midpoint between the shallow
and deep end. With our noses side-by-side, his breath mixed with
mine like we were sharing the air of everything we'd held inside
since we were kids.

We could finally explore what we had always wanted with each
other. Not with the lingering idea that we only stayed paired because
we didn't have a choice, not because we were trying to survive, but
because we wanted each other. Finally, we were living somewhere
not controlled by the elements. Even if the only time we'd enjoyed
each other, someone was watching and dictating our every move,
controlling us in a different way, in this moment, it was just us. Me,

Roderick, and this incredible sprawling space echoing our deep breathing into each other's mouths.

My hand found his neck, and I felt the space where the collar had been the night I'd finally been allowed to kiss him. The permission had come from Usher, but it had also come from myself. I'd given myself the power to love Roderick, and we were here now, somehow, alone like we'd been so many times before I'd left him. Our surroundings were the exact opposite of the thin tent and cement ground. Submerged in the immaculate pool, he brought his hand to the same spot of my neck, the area where the collars were absent. Maybe just for a night, we could pretend this world belonged to us. I let my lips find his, and we kissed hard until it felt like our interlocked bodies were gliding across the aquamarine surface.

Our momentum found us against the dark blue tile of the basin's frame where my back was against the pure-white grouted squares. I hadn't noticed before the typical music playing throughout the house was absent in the massive atrium. The only sounds in the indoor pool area were our moans and the smacking of skin. Occasionally a splash from one of our hands reaching quickly for the other would audibly reflect from the wooden plank walls, but otherwise, the stillness created an atmosphere that made me feel like the rest of the world no longer existed, and with my tongue on his, I didn't care if it did.

We shuffled together to a more shallow area, and when we arrived, I switched our positions so Roderick was against the wall. I flipped him so his elbows were resting on the deck, and my fingers found their way between his hairy cheeks and to his hole. I slipped the tip of my index finger in, and as his whine begged for me, I let my middle finger join it, stretching his tightness open and ready. Like I'd fantasized while I was in the kitchen days before, I wanted to top the boy whose smile alone made me hard. I'd waited long enough and needed to know what it felt like to be inside of him.

Roderick pushed against my two fingers until they were swallowed up to my knuckles, then farther as I wiggled and parted them just slightly before pulling them out and pushing them back in. His hole was close to ready, and my cock was stiffer than I could remember it being in what seemed like years.

As I moved my fingers out and prepared my cock to replace them, unexpectedly, Roderick moved forward toward the wall. He used his hands to spin around and face me, then stuck out both legs on either side of my body, extending them before wrapping them around my back to pull me into him. My hips between his thighs, he used his hands and the buoyancy of his furry body to hover at the water's surface while holding tight to the rim.

I could see his eyes now and the way his mouth was parted with his top teeth resting on his bottom lip. His ankles locked around my back, I moved my cock back to his hole and pushed past the entrance. Roderick leaned his head back and used his legs to force the entire length of me inside of him. He moaned loudly as his tightness closed around the girth, and the shadows of the room changed in time to the growing waves.

He pushed off the wall, and I used my arms to hold him in place around me while he rode the current into a bounce, up and down from my tip to base. Leaning closer to my shoulder, the splashes and sounds of ecstasy sprang back in the nearly empty room. The unoccupied lounge chairs and stacked wooden planks, the rafters above our heads holding up the huge transparent skylight letting the full moon in—all offered us their permission to bathe in the vastness and glowing light. Roderick brought his mouth to my ear and whispered, "I've wanted this for so long," and it felt like any clouds threatening to alter the moon's luminance upon us paused in awe of our passion for each other.

Something about his words made my stomach flutter like a chrysalis exploded within me. Tiny butterflies were finally given approval to live and be beautiful. I was still incredibly hard inside him, and yet my eyes winced to hold back tears. Wetness was on my cheek, and I couldn't tell for sure if it was from the pool when I whispered back, "Me too."

We held each other for a few minutes longer until a final thrust with his arms and legs still around me sent me over the edge. I moved back to the side against the dark blue tile, all shiny and glossy near Roderick's skin, as I braced myself and prepared to shoot inside of him.

Both of our breathing was heavy, and just before I expelled my load, Roderick stopped his movement. "Wait," he said and moved so I would fall out of him. My hardness hovered in the water while I waited for him to reposition. He swam gracefully away from me and soon lay on the steps of the pool, stroking himself like a god inviting me to join his religion. I paddled over quickly and for just a moment took the opportunity of his appendage being above the water's surface to take him into my mouth. Despite the chlorine, his taste was just as I remembered, and his intoxicating scent was still present.

Now covered with a sheen of spit, I moved into position to hover over him. I was turned on enough that my hole felt ready to take him, and I swallowed every inch within me. Riding him hard, I gripped the metal loop meant to be used as a guide to lead people into the shallow end of the pool. It steadied me up and down on his cock as my arm muscles contracted with the motion, and I hoped he noticed the movement under my dark hair.

As I brought my ass flush with his pelvic bone, he grabbed at my cock and stroked it in rhythm to my momentum. In his fist, it felt like I was still fucking him, like we were somehow inside each other at the same time. Magic swirled around us. It was so overwhelming I stopped riding and had to lie next to him. I felt dizzy but reached out for his hardness. He grabbed back, and we pumped at each other with our lips and tongues connected.

"Cum with me," Roderick said, quickening his pace on my shaft. I followed his rhythm and brought my mouth back to his. As we came together, our loads spilled into the water and floated there, glistening like opals in the moonlight still shining down on us. Catching my breath with the precious stones near our skin—in the perfect nine seconds of stillness achieved by a quality orgasm—I knew if I could be anywhere in the world, it would be in this moment with him next to me forever.

CHAPTER ELEVEN

Y ou didn't even realize it was your birthday, did you?"
Roderick asked, leaning back on his elbows, still balanced
against the steps of the giant pool. I hadn't seen them before,
but below us, and extending to the deeper end, the pool floor had
colored tiles creating mosaics of masculine bodies. I'd seen it done
with dolphins in ritzy hotel pools, but instead of sea creatures these
were supersized cocks and what resembled men playing leapfrog. I
acknowledged his question with a light laugh, but still in my post-
climax haze, I didn't move my focus from the newly discovered art.

He was right; I didn't exactly have a desk calendar in my
room, but since it was somewhere before the end of the year and
the branches were still bare outside of my window, I was probably
another year older. Somehow, Roderick had remembered when I
didn't. I was certain now, even if my time with him would be the
only gift I received, it had still been the perfect way to celebrate.

The moon was hanging lower in the sky, and the sun didn't seem
far behind. Soon the pool would change from a mystical lagoon to a
warm oasis away from the chilled weather outside. I looked around
at the collection of deck chairs and tables, the folded towels and
sculptures; similar stone men like the ones populating the courtyard were in here, watching over what seemed to be a deserted, yet
well-maintained, swimming area.

I wanted to know what it looked like during the day, if the sun rays penetrated the skylight and windows enough to let someone catch a tan, but I was still uncertain how much of the house I'd see again. If Usher allowed this gift of time with Roderick for my birthday, perhaps I was less in the red than I let myself imagine—unless it was a parting gift for the last time I would ever see either of them. But if I was no longer welcome in his home, Usher wouldn't care whether I fucked Roderick at all.

Even if I couldn't understand how it was possible, I hoped Roderick had somehow convinced him, and I wanted to know the magic words he'd used. I was finally beginning to recover from my sexual afterglow, but before I could ask Roderick for details, he was on his feet and heading up the steps. I watched the water drip from the fur on his ass as he walked to the deck and dried his body, paying particular attention to his now soft cock and any stray bits of cum still hanging in his hair. "We have another stop to make before morning comes," he said, unraveling a nearby towel for me to use.

Around me were the shiny buoyant pearls we'd left behind as I sat still partially-submerged in the comfortable temperature. I didn't question who would be tasked to fish them out and wasn't certain I cared; I only knew I didn't want the night to end. In that moment I understood for sure, I would follow Roderick anywhere.

It was a task to bring myself to my feet, but once I did, the towel was immediately around me, along with Roderick's arms. He ran the soft fibers down the arc of my chest and stomach, absorbing the dampness of my own fur. I wanted to dive back in the pool to skinny dip and play longer, or sprawl out on the slatted lounge chairs to see if we could fill our balls up enough to fuck again, maybe this time on a mostly flat surface.

Instead, Roderick was slipping his jeans over his still slightly moist body, and I followed. We left my new favorite location behind to wander through more twisting hallways in the unfamiliar parts of the labyrinth. With Roderick guiding me by the hand though it all and my boots hanging at my side, I let my bare feet leave moist prints along our path across the lush carpet.

A few things began to look familiar: a burgundy wall here, a carved bust of a man with a gag in his mouth that mimicked a funnel there. I'd never seen one in person before, but the way the gag's style parted his lips, I could only imagine what liquids he was prepared to receive down his throat. If I ever did get a chance to have a real conversation with Usher, there were endless amounts of important things I should to ask, but many of my thoughts lingered on the art, and more than anything, I wanted to know where the pieces came from and whether real men had posed for each of his selections.

From the hue of the walls, I assumed we were somewhere on the first floor, not far from the red room. Roderick still had his keys jingling from his hip but didn't use them right away when we stopped at a flat wall which appeared to be our destination. Centered on the satin surface was a new stone man balanced on a pedestal. At its base were words etched into the granite with letters I couldn't make out in the dimness.

We stood at the dead end for a moment before Roderick dropped my hand. It was the first time he'd released me since exiting the atrium. He reached out his finger to circle each erect nipple of the statue, then stood tall on the tips of his toes to whisper something into the shaped rock's ear. When he finished, he smirked in my direction, checking to see if I was at all amused by his demonstration. I was.

The stone man didn't change his expression, instead turning in a semi-circle on the base and retracting to one side with a mechanical sound. Behind where he had stood guard, there was a red door.

"Seriously?" I said, smiling.

"Seriously." Roderick reached for his keys and shoved a long one with chunky teeth toward the lock.

"This house is so fucking strange."

"Just wait," he said, pushing the heavy door open. On the other side was only darkness until Roderick ran his hand along the interior wall and located a switch. With a click, the area was slightly illuminated, and before me was a series of buttons, monitors, and microphones. The endless array of knobs and dials added up into a collection of boards and panels with various green, yellow, and red lights flashing out of sync with each other.

Beyond the boards, at eye-level, was a mirror. I could see Roderick and myself reflected in it, partially clothed with wet hair. But when Roderick pushed a button on the panel, a light came on beyond the mirror to reveal a large space with dark walls, metal surfaces and black blocks, big toys and whips, and a huge cross with restraints. The red room. From this spot, I could see everything that happened inside.

CHAPTER TWELVE

ight now, the room through the mirror sat empty. Standing there, I felt moved for the first time to call it a dungeon. All the elements inside formed bars and cages composed from walls of sex objects, rods, and shining chains. It hadn't been as noticeable when I was inside of it all.

Taking in the sight, I wondered how many times someone had been in the control room while I was being beaten or fucked, if they'd observed my vulnerability from the safety of this side of the mirror. The one I hadn't taken much notice of when I was sitting confused with cum dripping out of my hole, silently waiting on multiple occasions for a man who never returned.

Roderick moved from the controls toward a desk against the wall behind us. It looked out of place with the high-tech equipment around, almost ancient, and was equipped with a rolling lid that locked at the bottom. If I were one of those men, the gays who wear loafers and roll their vintage pants to their ankle to shop for high-end antiques, I probably would have appreciated its design more. For me, possessing second-hand items was more of a consequence of my tax bracket than a method of demonstrating my taste level. Knowing I could pull the same clothes and furniture from any dumpster; to me, *antique* and *vintage* just seemed to be the acceptable words assigned to owning something out of fashion for an astronomical price.

With his endless set of old and new-looking keys, Roderick bent down and took a smaller one to the bronze lock. As he lowered himself, I could see the hair between his ass peeking out from the top of his jeans when they scooted down his hips. We'd walked long enough from the pool to the new location that I was ready to go again, and the sight of the dungeon's various structures and hanging tools registered like muscle memory to a very particular muscle. I hadn't bothered trying to slide underwear onto my wetness and could feel my hardness pushing against the chill of the jean's zipper. I wanted to top Roderick again, bend him over the rolling desk, to see if his hole would open as quickly for me as it had the first time.

Walking closer, I hovered above him, hoping he would notice my firmness through the denim near his face and pull me from my pants, that he would stay on his knees near the desk to put me in his mouth for just a minute. Morning felt near, and I wanted to spend whatever time we had left with the moon close to Roderick's body. Even in this new room with my new view, all I could think about was fucking until the sun came up and making us both spend another load.

Roderick continued pressing the small key into the tight hole until something finally clicked, and he pushed up on the roll top desk. He hadn't noticed while kneeling that I was trying to make a move on him. Once he rose to his feet and the lid chugged in a rolling pattern until it stopped, he looked down at the bulge in my pants and smiled. He reached out to give my boner a playful squeeze, then immediately turned back to the open desk.

"You need to see this," Roderick said, finally looking at me. Inside the desk were papers and small boxes, books and envelopes. He bypassed touching the peak in my jeans again while he reached out for a file. "You should know," he said, putting the collection of papers in my hands. I was disappointed but tried to bring my attention to the text and ignore the way his lips glistened. It took all my focus to let my fingers trace over the dark ink instead of putting them through his hair so I could direct his mouth to the pulsing under my pants.

On the front cover, outlined in an embossed gold frame, were words I didn't understand:

Son coeur est un luth suspendu;
Sitot qu'on le touche il resonne.

They looked liked the collection of letters on the statue outside the entrance, but I couldn't tell if they were the same. When I opened to the pages, pictures were pasted inside and held down with tape on all four corners. They were pictures of young men I'd never met before surrounded by details outlining specifics about their bodies: their height, weight, current location. Each profile contained a section regarding body hair that was highlighted and circled several times over.

I looked up at Roderick, unsure what I was supposed to be seeing in the file. It didn't mean anything to me. He reached out to flip forward a few pages until a familiar face was staring back at me.

Roderick moved away when I reached his image and sat in a wheeled office chair at the controls. I could hear him spinning in circles as I continued to read the stats under his profile. If the date was correct, he had been in the house with Usher since just after the night I'd left him in the tent. It was my fault; I had driven him here to this lifestyle. Maybe Usher had selected him, but I'd put him in the position to figure out what to do without me.

"Keep going," he said, seeing that I was lingering on his paperwork. I flipped the page to see an even more recognizable face: mine. My stats and description paired with a picture of me laying on my side in white briefs in my old bed.

Surprisingly, I looked impressive on paper. My cock size—in centimeters instead of inches for some reason—stood out, and next to my name was a gold star with the inked word:

Postulant.

The next page was another face I knew, Darius, but he didn't have the same phrase or colors near his name. There were more pages after him, but I turned back to Roderick's profile first. I wasn't the only one. Next to his pictures, he had an accolade in the same position.

Novitiate.

I faced Roderick while I read the word out loud like a question. He sighed and bit his lip, then looked at the ceiling and spun a few more times in the cushioned chair behind the control board. He seemed to be contemplating if he had already gone too far, if he had let me see too much. Sensing his hesitance, it all hit me at once.

"I'm not supposed to be in here, am I?" Roderick stopped circling but didn't face me. He tapped his fingers nervously near the flashing lights and buttons with reluctance. "Tonight—all of it— did we have permission?" My voice grew louder as he looked up to stare through the clear window into the red room and all its fixtures, still avoiding my eyes.

"I spend a lot of time here, alone," he said, fingering one of the knobs to let the light in the dungeon dim and glow fluorescent over and over again.

"Did we have permission?" I needed an answer.

"You had to know," he said, shaking his head as he turned the dial all the way down and let the room beyond the transparent mirror darken. I threw the collection of papers back to the desk.

"Why?" My voice was even louder, and I felt angry tears welling up inside. Every beautiful butterfly became a knot in my stomach, knowing he had deceived me—again.

Roderick lowered his gaze once more and ran his flattened hands over all the buttons of the control board to create a quiet clicking sound. When he stopped at a small lever, he pushed it to the middle position until the room we stood in was showered with moderate white light.

The new level of brightness revealed things in the control room I hadn't been able to see before. It was bigger than I had originally thought and extended out in one direction not far from the roll top desk toward a velvet curtain. The burgundy panels were accented beneath a single spotlight and reminded me of a secret back room in a gay book shop.

Roderick nodded toward the closed curtain, rose to walk over, and parted the hanging fuzzy lips for me to enter. I couldn't see anything beyond them but needed answers, so I ducked my head through the opening and let my body follow. Behind me, Roderick closed the drapes and stood inside of them while he flipped another switch.

Tiny spotlights on the wall lit up, each illuminating a different portrait hanging in place. They were evenly spaced out and similar in artistry, but as Roderick watched me take them all in, I could see the obvious differences between them.

Some were painted and some were photographs, but none of the images were dated. In sets of two, the first portrait was always a standing man in a suit with a boy on his knees next to him like an obedient pet wearing a collar. But they weren't the fabric or neo-prene collars with fun colors. The chokers in the pictures were solid and silver with massive locks mounted like a charm holding the ring together. I couldn't read the tiny text, but each collar had engraving which seemed to match the language I'd seen on the front cover of the file and the statue which had been guarding the room.

I wanted to ask Roderick if he knew what the words meant, but the anger was still red hot inside of me. If I turned toward him now and saw his face, I wasn't certain if I would cry or lunge at him. Even as I continued to explore the portraits, I wondered if the intimacy we shared in the pool had been real at all. If it had all been part of a scheme, I didn't want to know. Not right now.

There was empty space beyond the last hanging portrait, but it was the final entry which stopped me where I stood. Younger and naked, on his knees next to a fully-clothed man, was... Usher. However, on the plaque below, the name "Usher" was not accompanying his likeness. None of the pictures mentioned the name of kneeling boys at all. In fact, like every picture before it, the title of "Usher" was always under the standing man.

I gasped at the sight and covered my mouth. Jumping back, I prepared to finally face Roderick and ask what it all meant. I had to know why he brought me here, why he had let us fuck without permission and created such an elaborate evening to lead me to this place. I needed to know what he wanted me to do now. But as I turned to him, I was directly grabbed by the neck and hair. Roderick was gone, and in his place was Usher forcing me to the ground under his strong hands.

"This was not meant for your eyes, boy." He had returned to the house. Surrounded by the museum of centuries of chosen boys, I fell on my knees to the carpet below at his mercy. My knees rubbed into the woven fibers under his force while his glare penetrated every orifice of my body. He grabbed around the roots of my hair to tighten his hold. Despite the pain, I couldn't help noticing that he looked older somehow. His facial hair looked even more grey than it had when he had first begun letting the salt portion fill around the darker spots.

As confused and terrified as I was, he looked incredibly sexy, and if he had fucked me right then and there—forced his cock into my mouth or let knees scrape and burn on the thick carpet as he moved me around his dick—I would have been grateful. But similar to the day in the woods when he found me with the shells and phone by the tree, like he seemed to be able to do any time he made a boy cum, everything went black.

CHAPTER THIRTEEN

❧

The best night I had ever had in the house had quickly become the worst night. Suns and moons rose and set while the occasional frost collected outside the single window in my room on the branches below. My room had again become a prison.

Usher must have accepted Darius as the new head chef in the house or had again tasked Roderick with the responsibility. I was receiving meals, nothing special, but food. My basic necessities, aside from attention, were being met. Unfortunately, the purple bathtub and giant bed had lost their appeal as I paced the same square footage over and over throughout the course of each day. The phone I had been gifted had gone missing from the room. Like Usher's communication with me, it too seemed to have been revoked.

Every source of pleasure felt tainted now. Even jerking off when my cock got hard thinking about fucking Roderick in the pool was overshadowed by his betrayal. Fantasizing about Usher was clouded by my own itemized lapses in judgement. Not only had I interacted with Darius; I'd cum before Usher's return. Even worse, it had been at the hand of someone he had told me specifically not to be intimate with outside of his presence. I wasn't sure how heavily seeing the control and portrait rooms would be weighed after all of that, but I knew my indiscretions had led me to a punishment worse than physical pain. Solitary confinement.

A quick knock on the door stopped me from pacing valleys into the rug. I didn't rush for my food, but when I brought the tray in and began unpacking my lunch, a folded piece of paper fell out. I doubted it was from Usher but the handwriting and message confirmed it:

Get me out of here girl.

Darius. Something had happened to him while I'd been locked away. I hadn't been able to watch out for him while trapped behind my door, and now, for whatever reason, he wanted to leave.

Along with the note was a pen which I took as an indication he expected an immediate reply. I walked toward the wardrobe and, pushing the clothes aside, surveyed the back panel. Either Usher didn't know the lock still hadn't been resealed, or he didn't care. He probably kept the passage open as a challenge to me, to see what I would endure before considering an escape back to a more simple place. As if I could retreat to a time before I knew about tea cakes, infused bath products, and strange competitions within a seemingly enchanted spooky sex house.

Grabbing the pen, I scrawled a quick message on the blank side of the note and slid it under the door. I couldn't see his hands or fingers, but the paper disappeared into the hallway as something pulled the words I'd chosen:

Be ready to leave tonight.

I wasn't certain if any of it was "designer" like Darius had commented on his own curated clothing, but I'd developed a sort of "go-bag" now with my favorite outfits and boots. After the countless times I'd let myself believe I was about to be extracted from the house, I'd packed them along with a few extra pairs of skimpy underwear. I wrapped what remained in the glass bottle of lavender bubbles safely in some slutty knee-high socks then stashed it in a section of a gym bag I'd found in the jockstrap drawer.

Waiting until the moon seemed high enough, I pushed the latch on the back panel of the wardrobe open. Surveying the state of my room one last time—the four-poster bed, throw pillows, and giant television that would never be in my budget—I closed the panel behind me.

Using my hands to guide me along the rocky surfaces and around a corner, as I'd suspected, the tunnel did connect to other areas. There was a chance every secret passage joined at some point to match the intricate maze inside the house. But tonight, I had only one destination in my mind and just hoped I was going the right direction.

My fingers answered my questions in the darkness until they found slight creases in the stone that gave way to a more wooden texture. Pressing my body against it, I listened with my ear flush to the new panel. With no voices, I whispered my call into the flatness, "Darius?"

His answer was immediate. "Omg girl, where even are you?" He had to have been listening all night, waiting for me to find him. I tried to explain where I was in the passage without speaking too loudly, but more importantly, I needed to know if there was a lock on his end.

"Well shit," he said in response to my inquiry. I was about to turn around to come up with a new plan but heard, "One sec" as his footsteps traveled away from earshot. A few minutes later, I heard light pecking against the wood before the panel opened and Darius stood framed by his expensive clothing hanging on either side. He held up a thin sounding rod with a pointed end and smiled. "Skills," he said, letting the slim rod fall to the rocky ground with a high-pitch ting.

"Skills," I agreed, feeling his arms around me in a tight but quick embrace. As much as I had learned living on my own, Darius was endlessly resourceful. His family hadn't abandoned him the way mine had, but when they were no longer around and he made his move to Beachside, he'd taught himself more than I could ever imagine learning in order to survive.

"I swiped that after that first time he used it," Darius said as I led him through the passage and back toward the area I knew would lead to the woods. "Call me vanilla. I mean, I can do some pain, but your girl needs some pleasure with her Rocky Road." I'd never seen the sounding rods among Usher's collection of toys myself and wondered if it was something specific he had chosen for Darius. "You liked him though, didn't you?"

"Roderick?" My stupid brain was letting my mouth move on its own again.

"Wow. What? No. I mean, you liked what *he* did to you?"

I wasn't sure how to answer, how to tell Darius that it wasn't the same for me with Usher as it seemed to be for the other boys. "I can only take so much bruising on this body without some dick to make it better," Darius said, lifting his shirt to reveal slash-like marks on his chest. I nodded in acknowledgement, pointing toward my own sore places.

"You don't have to tell me why," I said as we got closer to what I hoped was the end of the passage. It was more difficult to navigate without the sun providing a sliver of light to guide us.

"It's Sonny mostly," Darius said as I pushed at the wall for the hidden door. He admitted that after weeks in the house, away from home, he wasn't sure his favorite half-boy, half-house-cat, was feeding himself. Like me, he hadn't known before coming to this mansion the expectation was for him to permanently relocate.

With the stone door pushed aside, I looked out to the stillness of the woods, and I dangled my foot over the threshold to find the dirt below. Grabbing Darius's hand and helping him out of the house, I watched as he walked into the dense trunks.

I didn't follow.

"Come on, girl!" he said, walking back in my direction and holding out his hand for mine. "It's not worth it. All the pain to be stuck in a fancy room all day and just taken out to be used?"

I laughed a little and shrugged, "It's the same gig. The clothes are just fancier." Darius pulled his hand back and stood in the clearing with the hair below his crop top blowing in the breeze. Only the wind whistled through the remaining leaves in the silence between us as I brought my view to the frozen ground.

"I'm staying," he said, breaking the strange quiet to bring his foot back over the threshold.

I blocked his way inside. "I can't protect you here, and you can't protect me either." Half in and half out, he knew what I said was true. "Please go, for Sonny. For Brent and Marco even."

I must have rolled my eyes when I mentioned the bleach-blonde brothers who came to Beachside for the surfing and cock because Darius laughed. Even as roommates, they had never been my favorite people. I didn't go out of my way to talk to them much, but I understood enough to know they were probably totally lost at home without Darius.

"If they haven't burned that place down yet, it will be a surprise for all of us," Darius said, nodding. I'd never thought much about how Darius took care of not only me, but all the boys. It didn't seem to be a position he had sought but just organically accepted. Unlike me, he just couldn't see a boy struggle if he knew he could help.

"I'm sorry you ever came here and—"

Darius cut me off abruptly but was calm as he spoke. "You know I had to...but I also wanted to."

A fresh silence hung between us as we looked into each other's eyes. I shifted my focus to his lips before I spoke. "Just get home safe," I said, leaning my body closer to his and letting our mouths align.

He held me close, and we swayed together as we straddled the passage's exit. With nothing else to say, he brought his lips to mine. We'd kissed before on the night we messed around and shared little pecks since then, to say hello, to say goodbye, to say thank you...for everything. But this time, our lips lingered longer than usual, and for just a moment, our tongues sparked in a way that felt electric. It was friend-tongue for a strange experience we'd shared together, non-verbal appreciation for us both risking our lives in order to save each other.

With his taste still on me, when our lips separated, he said, "What will he do to you when he finds out?"

I didn't know the answer, but I handed him the go-bag. When he took it, I said, "Have the boys clean the tub at home. I think Sonny will fit in the boots."

Darius sighed and turned toward the dark woods. I didn't have a flashlight to give him, but I hoped the sun would be up soon enough to guide his path. "I better not find out you're still messing with that Roderick guy."

I nodded instead of taking the chance of telling him the truth about Roderick living in the house, the truth about anything. It was safer for him if he didn't know.

"I can't believe I grew a damn beard out to be here. What a waste."

"Don't shave. It looks sexy on you," I said with a wink that for some reason made my throat tighten like tears were not far behind. Luckily, Darius shook his head and disappeared into the depths of the foliage before a single warm droplet found the top of my cheek.

CHAPTER FOURTEEN

When breakfast didn't arrive the next morning, I knew it would only be a matter of time before Usher discovered Darius was missing. Whether learning that would force Usher's hand to acknowledge I was still up here, I could only hope. Even if he burst through my bedroom door and dragged me by the scruff to be tied spread eagle and feel his boot on my cock, or ripped off all my clothes and used every stinging whip on my body, or shoved the biggest plug he possessed inside my hole without a warm-up—I could deal with any level of pain if he would just feed me his attention.

By lunch, I was offered minimal sustenance, but more importantly, another note was paired with my food. It wasn't friendly like the one I'd received from Darius. If the hand-written words were any indication, not only had it been discovered that Usher's newly appointed head chef was missing from his manor, but he knew I'd been the one to help him escape. Adding that fact on top of everything I'd already done to offend the master of the castle, I knew even more severe punishment was in my immediate future.

In the swirls and dips of Usher's impressive handwriting, the note commanded:

Downstairs,
now.

No specifications were outlined as far as the proper attire. Despite winter being fully upon us, no seasonal underwear had been requested. At this point, I would have liked to have been asked to wear a festive jockstrap, something red with candy canes or tinsel-decorated pine trees, or maybe a set of reindeer horns to go with a bright green pair of tight briefs so he could order me to prance around before he turned my ass cheeks the color of poinsettias in full-bloom.

When I arrived on the first floor, the passage beyond the credenza was already open, its mysteries revealed and lighting a clinical white instead of the dim scarlet wash I'd come to associate with the scenery from my previous experiences. Not unlike the last time Usher had left me alone inside, the full-power overhead lights felt like seeing a peeled watermelon. Whole, raw, and exposed. No modesty or caution. The room at the end of the hall highlighted all the equipment and toys, along with what must have been weeks' worth of bodily fluids. My own dried cum, near the block I'd sat on to watch Usher's first encounter with Darius, chipped when I walked my bare feet across it.

The huge rectangle of the two-way mirror reflected my frame. Beside me, in the reproduced image, I noticed something new in the room. Piled together was a bucket, a mop, and a collection of cleaning supplies. While I poked at a lemon-yellow set of rubber gloves hanging over the bucket, I wondered if I would be serving Usher his custodial fantasy until I spotted an inked piece of paper. Near the unsexy hand accessories of my new janitor costume, another note simply read:

Clean up, boy.

Maybe he didn't have a fetish for sanitation, but by the time I was on my hands and knees taking a soapy sponge to the cement floors, I knew he was right about it needing to be done. The way the spots of lubricant and cum were layered upon each other on every surface made it difficult to determine what the original liquid had been. Whether each overlapping splatter was synthetic or natural bodily fluids, the space was in desperate need of purification.

Not far from the table and walls full of sex toys were special supplies for cleaning the variety of dildos and plugs. Some were so big I wondered who was actually able to fit them in their body. Holding each of them between my hands made them feel giant and bulbous. If they had been seeds, they would have grown into redwoods.

An interesting thing about gay men is the way masculinity manifests itself within us. Being the biggest and strongest isn't an instinct that disappears; it just becomes something more exciting. Instead of lifting heavy objects, we see if we can impress a sexual partner by showing them how much we can fit in our holes. Puffing out our rainbow crests and chests, taking pain for each other and calling it pleasure, we prove our manhood through servility. The practice lies on some pastel-colored Venn diagram where submission and power overlap. People who enjoy taking toys and dick want the challenge as much as the glory. It's virtually unspoken and would change everything if we ever did admit it, but truly, bottoms, regardless of gender, are the most powerful people in the world.

There were more toys mounted to the wall, silicone dicks and polyurethane tubes that looked like snakes meant to wind long and deep into a boy's ass. An industrial size bottle of lube, matching the one I'd seen in Roderick's fake apartment, sat in the corner drizzling slowly onto the same spot like a drip castle, the kind I'd made with wet sand as a kid on the beach where the moist sand would build onto the dryer portions until it became a solid tower. Searching for something among the supplies I'd been given, I didn't find anything designed to destroy a fortified castle made from artificial precum.

It took hours to glide each smooth toy through my hands and polish it until the different colored plastics and silicones were shining and returned to in their assigned spots. I wiped down each bench and restraint. Everything smelled like citrus from using the foaming dust spray to make the wood of the Saint Andrew's Cross sparkle under the bright lights. Even if I wouldn't be using the space any time soon, it was nice to have it smelling less like a neglected locker room for once. I knew the scent of man and sexual pheromones would return soon enough and hopefully I would be part of producing them again.

Other than punishing me with manual labor, Usher's reason for deciding that now was the time to clean everything was confusing, but more than anything, I was just glad to be finished. With the supplies packed away I headed toward the door. The lights turned off as I opened it. Looking back to the two-way mirror and control room, I smiled through the darkness, hoping whoever had turned the dial to zero had enjoyed watching me scrub and stroke each toy.

The various chemicals I was covered in penetrated my nose as I exited the hallway, and I didn't bother trying to close the credenza panel behind me. A breeze pushed the hair on my forehead and felt refreshing after inhaling overpowering pine and orange for what must have been several hours. It was coming from in front of me, and to my surprise, the French doors—the ones that always seemed bolted shut—were wide open. The thin white curtains were blowing in a crisp breeze from a winter temperature that always threatened to become frost, but rarely did.

Leaning against the tall doors were garden shears and tools with long wooden handles. *No.* I approached with caution and pulled at a piece of paper taped to the glass and flapping in the wind:

You're not done yet, boy.

Seeing the doors open for the first time since I'd arrived made me think about what it would be like to run through them, to leave with just what I had on my body and turn the corner through the courtyard and into the woods. I could follow the half-loop back to the end of the brick and past the gates that were rusted and welded shut, cross the train tracks and return to a still complicated and yet simplified life. But I'd proven something to myself the night before as I'd stood at the threshold kissing Darius goodbye—despite the punishment growing like a hunger within me, I craved Usher's attention for a reason. There was little he could do to drive me away. This was my home, it was my life, and I wanted to stay.

If learning how to landscape would get me any closer to atonement, I was willing to dig in the dirt for a while. Luckily, my new sexy gear included a set of gardening gloves. As cold as it was, I decided to take my chances and remove everything I was wearing. My shirt and pants were all moistened with fluids anyway. I disrobed until I was in nothing but a jockstrap and the gloves, then I slung the gardening hoe over my shoulder. If he wouldn't give me his attention, I would take it.

I'd never had the chance to admire the flowers in the light of day. Their colors were much more vibrant, and as I knelt near a nearly overgrown bed, their scent was just as impressive. I dug my fingers into the soil while I looked up at a chiseled man plotted at the center of the garden. His shadow cast over me made me feel small, and at the base, carved into the rock, was again the phrase I didn't understand:

> *Son coeur est un luth suspendu;*
> *Sitot qu'on le touche il resonne.*

It could have been the nearly frozen earth up to my elbows or exhaustion from sweeping clean an entire fall season's worth of leaves from the spiral stones leading to the house, but as I looked up to the man, soaking in his defined jaw under the caved scruff, the tight band around his waist cupping his round ass—I heard the translation clearly:

"His heart is a tightened lute;
as soon as one touches it, it echoes."

CHAPTER FIFTEEN

⌘

With the courtyard cleared and the dungeon pristine, I was still uncertain what Usher had been preparing for with the sudden sterilization of the manor. Finally submerged in my beloved tub and fighting off intrusive thoughts about further labor, I knew hours had passed since I'd eaten anything. As the evening edged to what felt like close to midnight, my stomach ached with hunger. I'd spent so much energy cleansing the spaces and could only assume the physical and mental torment would continue into the next day. I wanted to be prepared and continue serving my sentence, but it seemed dinner would not arrive on its own. Not only was I being starved of human interaction, but now even the privilege of my meals had been revoked.

My bedroom door was unlocked, which I took as an invitation to feed myself. Slipping on a pair of white briefs, I left my shoes behind knowing they really didn't go with the outfit. The stone of the passage in the shortcut between the second-floor library and kitchen was cold against my feet, but I wanted to be prepared in case I did run into Usher. More likely, he would continue to avoid me in the expansive house. But on the off-chance I did encounter him, I wanted to look sexy—not in a way that made it look like I was trying to get his attention but more so as if it had been a total accident that I happened to be wearing a similar ensemble to the one I'd had on the first time I jerked off for him when I knew he was watching.

Munching on some chips while leaning against the counter, I looked up into the camera fixed to the corner of the kitchen. The day my roommates had helped me set up all the equipment Usher had sent to our house, the computers, cameras, and various cables I didn't understand, his voice had gotten me hard even before I had seen his face. Perhaps it was knowing how much money a man had been willing to spend to buy my time, that he thought I was worth not only the effort, but that I deserved more than I had been born into. Lying there on my old sheets with my dick popping from my waistband, I'd felt like royalty.

The memory alone was making me firm below the thin white cotton, and I didn't break my stare with the lens of the mounted camera as I put my chips on the counter and let my hand drift down my torso. My hair felt soft as I brought a finger under the elastic and let it flick at the head of my cock. I could already feel the precum leaking out as I circled it around and hoped Usher was watching. He had power over me because I desired the home he'd made for me as much as I wanted his touch. But I'd forgotten my own power, that as much as I craved him, he craved me even more. I would regain not only his attention but his full affection.

A few minutes passed as I brought my other hand to my chest and pinched at my own nipples beneath the hair. They stiffened quickly, and I circled them with spit from my tongue while I teased the release of my cock through the top of the briefs. It all felt so familiar, like the day I'd first felt Usher's presence in the woods and imagined him tasting the sweat on my stomach, like the moment he commanded me to cum and the words rang through my mind until I shot on the forest floor. The memory made my balls feel full, and as I brought the elastic down below them to push my cock up higher and on display, I let myself believe it would only be a matter of minutes before Usher burst through the door to forgive me for everything I'd done. In no time, I'd be bent over the counter with his cock inside me, pumping together until we both came.

I wanted to wait to cum, to keep myself hard for as long as possible and give him time to find his way to me. But my imagination was spiraling with vivid images of Usher and our mutual need to please each other. Whether I wanted to or not, I was about to burst. Squeezing lightly at my own balls and stroking faster, I prepared to shoot, but a loud bang stopped me where I stood. Dropping my grip on my cock, the sounds of metal on metal grew louder. My arousal turned quickly to fear, but the excitement remained.

With my hardness still sticking out above my tight underwear and exposing the top of my ass, I turned around to flip the monitor on. I wanted to know the source of the noise, but as I cycled through the empty rooms, I saw nothing. As if black material had been put over every other camera, each shot was dark. Messing with the dials in an attempt to fix the lack of color, I moved something that suddenly made the sound come through speakers I hadn't realized existed below the glass screen. All this time there had been audio, it was just turned down. I wish I had known earlier, when I'd been using it as my own personal jerkoff material.

Continuing my channel surfing, I changed the buttons until the sound of the bangs were the loudest. The screens were still black, but in one corner of the loudest broadcast was a static face that seemed very familiar. He wasn't human, but I knew where to find him.

Putting my cock away, I was still pulsing with warmth but growing soft. I left the kitchen through the dining room and followed the path I'd only taken on my knees before, when Roderick and I had been attached by our collars and led by Usher. That night, I'd found myself kneeling and taking his spit inside me. Coincidentally, the same eerie tones seemed to be playing as they had that night during the ritual.

It was a guess, but I bypassed the entrance to the grand foyer where I would have run into the French doors and credenza, instead following the back end of a path that had been revealed to me only days before. There, protecting the doorway, was the stone man I'd seen on the monitor, the one Roderick had introduced me to. His eyes seemed more welcoming somehow, more familiar, as if the statue recognized me and beckoned me to enter. The translation his friend had whispered to me in the courtyard echoed in my mind, and I hovered on the tips of my toes to reach his large ear. I vocalized the words in English, hoping he would understand, and felt the hair on my face tickling my lips against the stone as I spoke.

The carved man seemed to smirk in a half-smile before moving aside and revealing the door. I didn't have a key like Roderick's, but it didn't matter because the door was open as if someone had been inside recently. Beyond it, the colored lights cascaded on the control board. Through the two-way mirror, in the red glow of the freshly cleaned dungeon, Usher stood tall in his suit. Next to him, naked and holding a silver tray from the kitchen, was Roderick.

Inching closer to the glass, I could see that although Roderick's bottom half was out and exposed, he had something metal covering his cock. The enclosure looked tight around him, like a cage looping around his balls and preventing him from getting erect. His collar was in place but in addition was a matching ball-gag buckled tightly around his cheeks and fastened in the back.

I leaned over the controls and flashing lights for a better look. In the area that had been out of my vision when I entered, closer to the floor of the dungeon, were more familiar faces, large bare feet, and furry asses framed in backless underwear. Each lined-up round backside was resting on heels, toes curled to keep each boy in position with their knees spread apart and hairy chest leaning forward.

On the tray Roderick held was a modest collection of whips. As Usher grabbed a familiar one with a single tail from the shining surface, he waved it in front of the formation. In view of their worried eyes, he paused with the whip in his hand and looked up to the two-way mirror. I didn't think he could see me, but I stood frozen anyway, as if he were a deadly predator whose vision was based solely on movement. I could hear my own shallow breathing out of time with the moans and whimpers coming from the kneeling boys as I waited for him to make his next move.

Finally, Usher smiled, ran his hand through one of the captive's long mane of hair, and winked devilishly in my direction. Returning to his kneeling line of boys, he moved his lips around to prepare a generous amount of spit. All on their knees in the scarlet hue with collars around their necks and mouths wide open below Usher were Brent, Marco, Sonny...and Darius.

The End

LEO SPARX

Saving
ALEXANDER

HOUSE OF UTTER 3

Dedication

To my readers
for being otter worldly.

CHAPTER ONE

C haos.

Chaos is what you get when seven men occupy any house, no matter the size. When they sat around the long banquet table during the day, it was easier to see the marks on arms and shoulders: the shape of the same hand, dark across nearly every shade of face. On any part without a beard or mustache or fur, there was some lasting sign of discipline.

But today the thing on everyone's mind was food. It was whatever Darius had cooked up in the kitchen that smelled so good. Usher was on a trip for the first time in weeks. With just me and the boys in the house, it was home, but in a much larger floor plan.

"If we're gonna do it, then we're gonna do it right," Darius said as the door from the kitchen swung open and settled back into place. He was wearing his apron, and not unlike the small quarters we used to call a house, everyone was as close to naked as possible.

Darius set a large dish in the center of the table where we'd all gathered at the middle seats. Taking off the apron, he settled into an empty chair and let the plushness of the seat cradle his ass.

Sonny was perched nearby, literally up on his bare feet more than sitting. With his knees bent, he hovered over the table setting identical to the one in front of each of us. He gripped an oversized fork and spoon that were definitely intended to be serving utensils. As they glimmered in the afternoon sun next to his nipple rings, I wondered what it was about gay men that made it impossible for us to sit correctly.

Neither Brent nor Marco's feet were flat on the floor either. Both of the blondes had dark roots growing from their scalp now. One draped his legs over the arm of the velvet dining room chair, and the other was on his knees. When one switched positions, the other followed. It had been like this for days. All of us sat just lazily eating and lounging in the various unlocked rooms of the house while its owner was away.

Something had changed after the boys arrived. Bedroom doors that would typically be locked were suddenly wide open. But as fun as it all felt, I knew well enough the freedom we were being allowed paired with a steep payment. Maybe not a bruise or sting, but something worse. A strange emptiness sat in my stomach, and it wasn't hunger. While the boys shoveled hot food into their mouths, the feeling loomed in the mansion like a ghost story I hadn't heard yet.

"Let's swim after lunch," Marco said, plopping something with gravy and vegetables on his plate. Darius shot me an *oops* look from across the table. I hadn't told anyone else about the pool, but apparently they all knew now.

Telling Darius the truth about Roderick being in the house hadn't been an easy conversation, but I didn't have an option after they'd seen each other. Even if their introduction had been less than informal, Darius seemed to know exactly who Roderick was while he knelt on the floor near him.

That night when Darius encountered the man he'd only heard stories about around town, I stood on the other side of the two-way glass. Looking at the collection of hairy men inside the dungeon, lights flashed on the control board and reflected in the window.

Just beyond it, I could see Roderick's cock dripping through the cage that had been put around him. The silver tray he braced on his flat hand held three whips ready for Usher to use at any time. They didn't seem heavy, but I could tell from the way Roderick's bent arm shook near the elbow that he had been suspending them for quite a duration.

He was being punished, and I should have been grateful that the blame was on him instead of me for our pool encounter. After all, he had lied to me. I'd scrubbed the house clean inside and out as penance for believing him, but this punishment was more severe. Observing his confinement, the way his cock and balls were secured behind the metal rungs of the cage, I wanted to feel vindicated.

I wanted to be angry at him.

But among the emotions I felt observing my former house-mates knelt on the cement and Roderick in agony, anger wasn't one of them. Usher had noticed me, even if I wasn't certain how he'd spotted my form through the glass. No one else had. Perhaps they were too focused on the hurt about to be inflicted upon their bodies.

With a wink in my direction, the man in the suit, the only one wearing real clothing, grabbed the smallest whip from the silver tray. Roderick's arm trembled, and he straightened his legs. Small drop-lets drizzled from him until they hit the floor.

Usher smirked and stuck a single finger through the rungs of the cage. He ran his thumb over the moisture and rubbed it along the length of the skin he could access beyond the barrier. My former partner-in-crime winced, knowing the harder he got, the more the cage would push back against him. It looked like Usher laughed, but I couldn't hear him.

I glanced at the buttons and dials on the control board. A lever with an ear symbol and ascending bars seemed a strong possibility to add audio to the movie playing out in front of me. Unsure if I should risk it, I moved the tab slowly upward, expecting to acci-dentally turn on some sort of music or completely cut the lights. An intrusive thought crossed my mind: I could ruin Usher's façade, abruptly fading his scene to black. It was almost funny, but I knew the swift punishment that would follow would not hold the same humor. Right now, for whatever reason, he was sparing me from participating in the ceremony, but he could have me on the other side of that glass whenever he wanted.

Luckily, the lever I'd chosen seemed to open a channel, and now I could hear the whimpers coming from the boys. They posed with mouths open, tongues out, the whip tapping at their inner thighs. When Usher's spit landed inside each of them, they held it there until he commanded them to swallow. I watched the bulge of his DNA travel through their throats. If it hadn't been official before, it was now.

Usher looked up toward me again and smirked. Turning away from the four vulnerable hairy men, he stood in front of Roderick and his caged cock. He set the whip he'd been using on the tray and exchanged it for one resembling a riding crop. Roderick didn't move his face, but his eyes stared down at Usher's selection. I'd forgotten how long his eyelashes were, the way they could make his eyes glitter when he experienced extreme emotion: happiness, sadness, horniness, fear.

With a few slaps on Usher's palm, the riding crop cracked, echoing through the concrete room. The boys behind him seemed to tremble, but for just a second, I thought I saw Sonny smile. I shook my head, assuming the last thing Usher would want is for a boy to be amused by his sadism.

Using his shiny shoe, Usher pushed at Roderick's bare foot just below the ankle. "Wider," he said. Roderick obeyed immediately and another drizzle found its way through the cage and to the floor below. With his thighs farther apart, Roderick's balls were exposed and available to Usher. The suited man used his grip on the riding crop to issue quick controlled movements, three taps in a row to Roderick's sensitive hanging skin.

It looked like his knees may buckle until Usher said, "You had better not drop my tray, boy." Roderick steadied himself, and a tear fell from his eye in rhythm with new droplets of precum from his cock. Behind Usher, Sonny bit his lip to stifle another smile, and

Darius moved his body close enough to jab him with his elbow. He looked at him with wide eyes as if to say *stop*.

Darius had seen more than the other three boys in this house and learned quickly the extent of Usher's playtime. I still had yet to experience the sounding rods he had told me about, but I saw them shining from a rack, fully sanitized and prepared. Since Usher had developed a fascination with inserting the long metal dowels into Darius specifically, the last thing he needed was for Sonny to invite punishment with a little giggle.

Maybe he was nervous or maybe still stoned from the outside world—I still had no idea how long they had been here before the ritual began—but whatever the reason, Sonny couldn't stop his glee about being in bondage. Usher must have heard the interaction because he spun around quickly, catching Sonny mid-smirk. The long-haired man let the expression dissolve from his face the moment the man holding the whip had his eyes on him, but the damage had already been done.

Leaving Roderick standing in place, still balancing the tray and in visible pain, Usher focused on Sonny. He walked slowly toward the line of boys and stopped at the end, letting the surfer's face fall directly in front of the closed zipper of his slacks. "Look at me, boy," Usher said and grabbed Sonny roughly by the trimmed beard on his chin.

"Are you having fun?" Usher asked when Sonny's eyes turned upward. Sonny looked at him almost fearlessly, but just next to him, Darius inhaled deeply, bracing himself for whatever was to come. Sonny didn't answer, and a strange silence hung in the air while all focus was on the interaction.

Unexpectedly, Usher began stroking Sonny's long hair and tucked a lock behind his ear. When it was in place, the suited man pulled his hand away and smiled, wide. Sonny's body relaxed. Then, more rapidly than a lightning strike, Usher cracked his open palm across Sonny's face. He grabbed a handful of his luscious locks and said, "You'll be first, boy."

CHAPTER TWO

"The word of the day is Voyeurism, boys." Usher paced between the weight bench and the suspended sling fastened to the ceiling with chains. There always seemed to be something new in the red room no matter how many times I was in it. The sling with the stain-resistant canvas hanging from eyelets by four points was the latest addition.

Usher tapped a new whip on the outside of his leg. Not far from the bench Usher had fucked me on before, Sonny was balled on the floor, still reeling from the impact on his stubbly cheek. Closer to the swaying sling, Roderick's forearm shook under the platter full of toys, and he gritted his teeth, determined to keep it level.

When Usher wrapped his hand around one of the linked metal ropes, I wondered what it would be like to be cradled then pushed and pulled by him in the hammock. He had probably only added the new apparatus to gain easier access for inserting toys into holes, but even considering the possibility of his cock sliding in and out of me using the sling's rhythm was getting me hard.

"Do you like being watched, boy?" Usher's shiny loafers clicked across the spotty cement until he reached the other side of the line where Marco sat like a statue in his collar. Not far from him, just past Marco's brother, Darius fought to stay in position, his eyes on Sonny, who was still on the floor.

"Perhaps with your twin?" Usher said, abandoning his flogging tool with a clatter to the floor to free his hands and stroke each of the brother's fuzzy chests. He pinched a nipple on each then perched himself in front of them. Lowering his body, he traced a finger down their stomachs, stopping just before the thick bands of their matching jockstraps. I couldn't help but stare at his ass in those tight linen pants as he hovered just above the ground.

Brent and Marco squealed in unison under his touch. When Usher rose to a standing position again, retrieving the whip in the process, they both flinched and drew their faces back. The synced movement seemed to please Usher—as if some balance had been restored.

He grabbed the chain connecting the four men's collars—the way Roderick and I had been connected—and followed the links until he could tug on the line leading directly to Sonny. "Up, boy," he growled, apparently done with Sonny's dramatic display of anguish from the single open-handed strike.

"Does it arouse you knowing that someone is seeing you submit to me?" Usher spoke to the room, in no particular direction, while Sonny wiggled to his feet and tossed his long hair back in place behind his shoulders. With his cat-like friend back on his knees, Darius leaned his body into Sonny's side as if to ask if he was alright or reassure him in some way. I looked at Usher, who luckily hadn't caught the tender moment with his back turned.

"Do you feel it, boys? His eyes on you now?" Usher turned toward the window, toward me. It had taken me until that moment and his eyes piercing through the mirror to realize he was talking about me in his monologue.

My breath became quick and shallow. I worried I'd opened more than a one-way channel when I'd been searching for the room's soundtrack. Maybe the entire time, he'd heard me breathing. Maybe they all knew I was watching.

"This type of voyeur gets just as much excitement out of seeing domination as they do being dominated. Possibly more." He wasn't telling the boys anything they didn't know. As professionals, we'd all been paid to have an audience before, but that wasn't the point he was making. His words weren't for the men in the room; they were for me. My cock dripped and pooled precum in the thin cotton of my white briefs while he talked.

"Someone is getting hard," he said, still focused on the two-way mirror. Reaching down to his slacks, he rubbed over his zipper. The bulge of his thickness was unmistakable, and with all the men only having a view of his back, he stroked through his dress pants. No one else could see from their position behind him when he pulled his zipper down and reached his hand into the depths. The display was for me alone.

A brief moment of pleasure overtook his face while he gazed through the window that wasn't intended to be transparent. Our eyes locked, but I still wasn't certain if I was actually visible. I was afraid to breathe, but following his hand rubbing up and down on his hardness, a trembling sigh escaped my mouth. My cock pulsed.

His expression changed abruptly, and he pulled the zipper back up in a single motion. Usher cleared his throat and turned on his heels, dropping his arms to his sides. "Take them to their rooms. We're done now." His words were directed at Roderick, who seemed both surprised and skeptical.

Nervously, he attempted to bend and set the tray on the cement, but it slipped. Solid metal and rubber-wrapped tools bounced against the indoor pavement. Roderick froze in humiliation and embarrassment with his swollen balls between his legs.

Usher closed his eyes and shook his head but didn't turn to acknowledge the crash. "Go now!" he yelled. Roderick gathered the whips and set them back on the silver platter quickly before motioning for the tied boys to stand. They followed him from the room like a strange BDSM Pride parade, and the door slid closed behind them.

When the room was clear, Usher stood in the dim light and wiped his hands clean. The gesture seemed ritualistic as I'd seen him do it before, almost as an indication of completion.

He looked up to the panel again. "Did you enjoy the show, boy?" he asked, tracing his reset hands over the whips he hadn't used. "I did have to cut it a little short."

I was uncertain whether or not he could hear me, but that wasn't the only reason I didn't respond. There was a chance, I thought, maybe, if I stayed quiet enough, I could avoid being punished for disturbing the ritual. When I was involved, it had seemed so important to him.

So much of me wanted to transport myself through the window. It had been too long since he'd touched me, and I'd been trying so hard to get his attention during my punishment. But he had an all too familiar twinkle in his eye, like a wild animal poised to tear me to shreds.

"Come inside, boy," he said and tapped on the glass like a fish tank. Even on the side of the predator, in this control room, I was still his prey. Knowing that made me so hard my cock pushed at the cotton of the white briefs. On the other side of the barrier, Usher rubbed his hand over the growing bulge under his slacks and said, "Don't keep me waiting."

CHAPTER THREE

◈

The path from the control room to the dungeon wasn't straightforward. It seemed odd to me that while they were connected by the pane of glass, they felt miles apart when I walked with my boner across the tile floor and down the hallway. When I opened the door, he was standing there, still prepared to pounce but with a strange smirk on his face.

"Down," he said, not wasting any time. Immediately, the chill of the cement was on my kneecaps. I could have opened my mouth to say sorry for accidentally disobeying him or to tell him I understood why I had been punished. I could have told him how much I'd missed him. But he was already taking out his cock for me, and all I wanted, more than telling him how I felt, was to have his dick in my mouth.

"Did you wear those for me, boy?" he asked, rubbing the warm tip of his girth against my closed lips. I couldn't remember if there had been precum when I'd had the opportunity to taste him before, but tonight he was spreading it over the soft skin on the outside of my mouth.

"I do remember them," he said, parting my lips with his fingers and pushing the taste of him to my tongue, "but it wasn't what you were wearing the first night I saw you."

With two fingers in my mouth now and thrusting them in and out, I couldn't have spoken even if I'd wanted to. He had told me before that he knew he wanted me back when he'd watched me jerk-off in the woods outside the house. But, to me, the first night we met was when I'd heard his voice on the computer. In a time that seemed centuries away now—when he was a black screen and nothing more.

That was before he'd become the object of so much of my affection, before the need to have him in my life had gotten so strong. Before I knew, to gain a place in his world, I would trade anything: my skin, my freedom, my sex.

"What was it that brought you to me?" Usher asked, lifting my chin with a light touch so he could see into my eyes. He'd moved his fingers from my mouth so I could answer. A mix of my spit and his precum stuck to his fingertips, and he rubbed them together. Even with my mouth free, I didn't have the words to answer his question.

Roderick had been the one to orchestrate everything that brought me into the mansion. He arranged the false pretense to make me think being here would be something other than it was. If there was more Usher expected me to know, I didn't.

"It was the house," Usher said, turning his gaze to the room around us. "The house gave you to me." He stroked my hair and ran his hand down the side of my face. The suited man suddenly seemed sad and turned away. Walking toward the whips that remained within reach, he took a deep breath as he prepared to speak. While I waited to see if he would return his taste to me, I stayed silent.

"It drew you here and you told it yes. You consented to everything that has been done to you. Every ounce of pain and pleasure, you told the house you wanted it when you kept coming back. Every time you spilled your load to the dirt, you told the house to take you. That you belonged to it."

Usher approached with a whip that looked more like a thin fly swatter. It had holes like a wiffle ball or cheese grater for less resistance and, I assumed, harder hits.

"I need you to say two things," Usher said, twirling the loop of the swatter around his finger in a spiral motion. "First, tell me you're sorry for letting someone else touch you. Then tell me yes. Not to the house, but to me. Tell me you want all of this. Tell me that you want me."

Inhaling deeply, I didn't feel scared of the whip when I answered without hesitation, "Yes, I only want you." At first, I wasn't sure if the single sentence gave him the satisfaction he was after. But then his eyes were back on me, and he knelt directly in front of where I remained on the concrete.

He loosened his tie and brought my hands to his shirt buttons. I quickly pulled at them until his chest was exposed and, without permission, ran my hand through his dark fur. He didn't stop me.

My fingers rolled around his nipples, and he threw his head back before bringing it in close to my cheek. Usher moaned in my ear and whispered, "That feels incredible."

When he pulled back again, his stubble rubbed on mine and his lips lingered near my mouth. I thought he was going to kiss me, but he didn't. He was still taller than I was, but our height difference seemed less important when we were kneeling together. Turning my head, I let my lips hover near his but stopped myself from moving forward. My cock pulsed again as I imagined what our tongues would taste like wrapped together.

I thought the moment was over when he stood up, but instead, he took his dick out and motioned for me to open my mouth. Wrapping his hands around my head, he guided my wet lips until he could thrust himself deep into my throat.

With him fucking my face, I kept my eyes on him but rubbed over the white underwear. His precum dripped farther into me every time my lips met his pubic bone. Usher moaned again and said, "You never fail to impress me." He must have noticed me teasing my hardness because he nodded his head. "Go ahead."

Deep-throating the length of him, I concentrated on breathing through my nose so I wouldn't have to take a break from sucking him. His approval sent colorful butterflies through every part of me, but especially my balls, which were full and throbbing in step with my cock while I pumped and rubbed the tip.

His fingers wrapped in my hair, he pulled and pushed until he twitched in the tunnel of my tight throat. He was ready to burst. When I felt his warm cum explode and slide down toward my stomach, I stroked fast enough to erupt a full load to the hard floor below.

"I want to show you something," Usher said. I watched his cock grow soft. I couldn't believe he was still in the room after using my throat. His warmth was inside me, and yet, he was here.

He grabbed my hand and pulled me gently to my feet, then led me to an area just off the side of where the mirror was set into the wall. A rack of toys I'd polished only a day before hung in front of us.

If he was ready to pick one out to put inside of me or beat me with, my body wasn't prepared. I wanted to relax and breathe an adequate amount of oxygen for a minute.

Not that I was complaining.

Usher lifted the bottom of the pegboard, letting it rest on the two holding hooks above. Underneath was a button, not unlike the one he'd showed me the first night in the house, the same night I'd learned the meaning of the word *credenza*.

When he pushed the shiny button, the wall holding the rack developed lines on either side and above. Something made a popping sound like a spring had been holding it back. "Push, boy," Usher said, motioning to the wall. When I did as I was told, the wall became a door. On the other side was a room I'd seen once before. The one with the portraits of men.

"Short cut, for next time," Usher said, pulling the door closed again like a safe. He didn't seem to like being in the portrait room longer than necessary. I had many questions about why so many beautiful pieces of art were tucked away in a room no one ever saw when so much more of the art was prominently displayed around the house. But I was concentrating on the new secret door I'd been shown and thinking how helpful it would have been to know it was there before stumbling around the house with a hard on in my underwear. More than both those thoughts, I was most aware of him turning his body away from me once the pegboard lowered again and how badly I wanted him to stay.

"Good night, Alexander," he said as he left me behind in the dark room. It was a feeling that wasn't entirely new, but alone again, this time I was smiling. He had said my name. It was the first time he'd called me anything other than "boy."

CHAPTER FOUR

❧

After that night, I floated on clouds through the mansion. Every door seemed open to me, every passage no longer felt like a mystery. When I thought about a certain type of music, without fail, it seemed to play over the speakers.

Yet, I hadn't seen anyone—the boys, Roderick, even Usher—for days. If I had, I wasn't certain what I would say to any of them. My former best friend had gotten me in the kind of trouble that led to manual labor. For that, I knew I would never forgive him, even if his punishment of chastity for our encounter was worse than anything I'd endured.

My bliss and solitude led me to wonder: had it not been for Roderick bringing me out that night and showing me the control room, would Usher have longed for me enough to end his ritual and speak my name? Something had shifted in the energy of the house since our most recent exchange. But while I shook my hips and ass through the hallways, part of me worried the other boys weren't having nearly as much fun.

No matter where I wandered in the estate, I knew better than to go looking for anyone directly. Making so much progress with Usher meant continuing to respect his rules and his process, even if I didn't understand it. Whenever we did get a chance to be intimate again, I would ask him the questions I had been too overwhelmed to ask.

At least he seemed more ready to offer me answers, and I finally felt prepared to hear them.

I thought an opportunity for a real conversation would present itself sooner rather than later until I woke up late one afternoon to a note on a tray outside my door. *How nostalgic,* I thought, as I opened the folded paper.

> *We will return shortly, boy.*
> *Make sure they behave.*

So, I was "boy" again, but I assumed that meant him using my real name was intended to be something private and shared only between us. It still felt special that way, and I was content believing it for now. But who was "*we*"?

Wherever he was going, this time, a phone hadn't been left for me. Having the device had felt like a privilege when it was awarded before, but seeing only the note gave me a sense of relief this time around. The constant messages and instruction were no longer necessary. He trusted me to take care of the house and everyone inside without monitoring and dictating my every movement.

No sooner had I set the note down when a body came flying through my door and landed on my unmade bed. "Oh girl! We have been released!" It was Darius, back in his favorite designer underwear on his thick ass. He seemed much happier than the last time we'd seen each other.

"I thought you were leaving," I said, collapsing back-first on the bed next to him.

"Girl, I was walking; I remember that much. Then I woke up back in my room."

"Yeah, that happens."

"You know, I'm not even mad about it though." Darius grabbed at one of my pillows and fluffed it. He examined the softness as if he were sizing it up against his own provided bedding, shopping. "Like,

I spend all this time trying to get money, and here's this situation where it's just being handed to me. I'm gonna say no?"

He set my pillow behind his head to give it a test drive but immediately moved it and squinted. Displeased with its comfort, he set it back against the headboard. In a quick motion, he bounced off my bed and to his feet. "Anyway, I'm back, bitch!" Darius fell forward from where he stood between my legs and piled his bare chest on top of mine.

A familiar voice yelled some mumbled surfer-lingo happily from the hallway, then the weight of another male body was on me. I could see just the glint of Sonny's eye and some of his wavy hair from the bottom of the sandwich we'd created around Darius.

Two additional voices whooped and screamed until more naked chests were on either side of me. Smothered in chest and stomach hair from all angles, the dog pile of fur cocooned me in certainty I didn't know I needed. They weren't mad. They were okay. And while I knew I wouldn't have all the answers to whatever questions they needed to ask, while we were all out and free, I wanted to make sure they had a great time.

Days later, after our huge lunch, I guided the boys through the halls with towels over our shoulders. As we walked, I couldn't pinpoint exactly why I'd felt the need to keep the pool a secret. It wasn't Darius's fault he had told the other boys about it. The location wasn't sacred just because Roderick and I had fucked there.

It had felt magical that night, and part of me wondered if seeing it in the daylight and having the brothers doing cannonballs into the pristine water would taint it. But the house wasn't mine. If this was going to be our home, then it belonged to all of us.

At least until Usher returned.

The expensive flip-flops we'd each pulled from our closets squeaked against the tile as I tried to remember the path to the indoor pool. With the other boys trailing behind, Darius walked next to me. "I'm sorry I told them, but I'm just gonna say it: If he never comes back, you'll be better off," he said.

I didn't respond while I backtracked our group down a hallway lined with statues of men in singlets, their pebbled hair tufted in marble. "I told you before he was a bad news gay."

"Hot though," Marco said, peeking his bleached tips between us before moving back to a pedestal to stroke the elbow of one of the picturesque carvings.

"Even with clothes on," Brent said, circling the chiseled nipple near his brother's exploration. "He looked cute the other morning before he left."

I seemed to miss so many things when I allowed myself to sleep in, but it didn't take too long to string the details together. That was what the note had meant by "*we.*" Usher had taken Roderick with him on his trip.

The clouds I'd been bouncing on dissolved from under me. Both men missing from the room had a unique ability to make me feel so special and then immediately blindside me with betrayal. They could do this separately just fine, but as a team, they had successfully ripped my heart into pieces. If Usher had brought Roderick instead of me, it meant he was his favorite.

Not me.

"Are we lost?" Sonny asked, leaning against a pillar. I hadn't realized we'd been walking in a circle and had stopped at a dead end.

Admittedly, I was distracted with the new information, but more so, the house seemed to have changed around me again. The path I'd remembered to relocate the atrium wasn't the same, and instead of the decorative doors leading to the pool deck, the five of us stood at a full bookcase.

Our sandals sinking into the lush carpet, I was able to manage, "Sorry guys," before plopping down with defeat in a tufted chair. Resting my elbows on the polished handles and my head in my hands, I didn't mean to pout, but soon Darius had his arm around my shoulders. He balanced his weight against the furniture and circled his fingertips across my naked back.

"Which one are you sad about?" Darius asked. I knew he was posing the question because he wanted to help, even if it sounded like a read. We hadn't discussed everything during the short moments we'd had alone in the kitchen while he cooked, but he knew enough to understand the extravagance wasn't my only reason for staying in the house.

I'd learned a lot about the feelings I was capable of having for another man since living in the mansion, not all of them sexual. But as much information as I'd taken in since the last time I'd had a sad walk on the better side of town, I still had no idea how to answer Darius's question.

The other boys kept their distance, exploring the room that was new to all of us. It seemed to be a study or den considering the number of books.

Brent pulled a thick black-spined novel from the shelf and thumbed through it. I could hear him rustling the pages and showing them to his brother and Sonny.

"Wow, who are these guys?" Marco asked in my direction, pointing at the contents. They brought the book over to show me endless sketches of men in harnesses and jockstraps, tight jeans, and knee-high socks. In thick lines, some had on leather and some latex. There were masks and hoods and gags and blindfolds. But through the hundreds of pages, they were all just as furry as the real boys standing in the room around me.

"Every book is like this," Brent said, pulling out more volumes and licking his finger to flip through them. The bookcase reminded me of the secret passage that led to the kitchen. I'd been told at the time which of the books to remove via text from Usher when I needed the information to move unseen through the mansion, but I'd never taken the time to browse through the other books. I'd assumed they were more sad literature. I was wrong.

No artist was credited to identify who had drawn the men. Nor were the provocatively posed models inside named. I did know there had been a letter on the outside of the book which opened to the kitchen passage.

"Is there a book with a P on it?" I asked Brent as he stood with a stacked armful of the pornographic encyclopedias.

He bent down and scanned through the selection then pulled one book out slowly. The large case slid with just the slightest tilt of the masked lever. Behind it was the massive atrium. The carpeted room had felt so solid and landlocked, now the expansive area in front of us made our surroundings echo.

The boys smiled and laughed, grabbing up their towels and running straight into the still pool. They dove and splashed while the tile mosaics lining the pool floor shimmered in the sun. Somehow, the water was even more beautiful than it had been under the moonlight.

CHAPTER FIVE

From my spot on the white lounge chair, I could see boys that had been whimpering with their hands behind their back no more than a few nights before—playing naked. With the sunlight illuminating each ripple in the reflective surface, the art above and below them held the luminescence in blue hues, making the water even more inviting.

Lifting a half-empty bottle of wine from the collection we'd hauled from the kitchen to my lips, I saw the nudity of an approaching man fisheye in the curve of a green glass.

"Come in!" Darius said before setting himself down on a long reclined chair next to me. I shook my head but smiled while he ran his hands through his moist hair. For a moment, I looked at his lips and thought about the night we'd said goodbye, the kiss we'd shared. I wondered if we'd ever mess around again living under this roof.

If I'd ever kiss any man at all.

Turning my eyes back to the bottle, I was basking in a buzz from room temperature red wine. It would have been nice to play with everyone, but thoughts about Usher and Roderick cycled endlessly through my brain. Being this close to a place so tied to deception only made me ask more questions.

In the pool, Sonny hoisted himself on his hands to the deck where another bottle of wine rested. His slightly muscular surfer arms flexed holding up his weight. The fur on his round ass clung with beads of pool water which, as he drank, ran down both cheeks and down his thighs. I looked at Darius, and he pursed his lips.

"Don't," I said, handing him the vessel of wine I'd been holding, hoping to sway his attention. "Whatever you're thinking, don't do it."

"Oh, is it an official rule?" Darius asked, swigging the burgundy back quickly. He wiped his mouth around the corners and smirked, knowing he wasn't asking a real question as much as commenting on the uncertainty of the entire situation. "All the men in this house and we're what, supposed to just take the pain and—"

"You didn't have to come back." I hadn't meant to cut him off. The alcohol and general anxiety made me irritable.

"I told you I woke up here after I left."

"Haven't heard you behind my wardrobe lately. You know he's gone now. You could try again." *I finally have friends here. Why am I being so bitchy?*

Darius popped his tongue. "Any chance you've got a point, girl?"

"All I'm saying is: he'll know. Whatever you do, he'll see it." With the bottle back in my hand, I sucked on the hole at the top. I let too much liquid bitterness enter my mouth before I winced and swallowed with one gulp.

He watched me drink as we sat in a moment of brief silence. Maybe Darius didn't want to spoil the afternoon, but instead of copying my tone, he shifted his tactic and smirked. "Is that why you're still wearing this bathing suit?" he asked, running his hand near my waistband.

I pushed his hand away. Defeated, he rose suddenly and stood in front of my chair. Scanning the area, he put his arms in the air. "I don't see any cameras in here."

Just behind Darius, Marco and Brent took turns sitting on each other's shoulders and walking into the deep end until the one on top was underwater. Sonny was balanced on his elbows, half in, half out of the water like a merman. He smiled when Darius turned to meet his eye.

Looking back at me, he said, "Try to have some fun while you can, girl. I know I'm gonna," then turned fully toward the water and dove in.

I followed his bubbles popping on the surface of the pool until he reached where Sonny presented himself. Darius pulled him playfully into the water, and the two naked men kissed and tussled among the waves. The brothers stopped their game when Darius set Sonny on the steps and put his head between the merman's legs to lick and suck.

Sonny moaned, and I gulped on the bottle. I wasn't certain if I was jealous or just aware that their every action would somehow be blamed on me.

Every day went like this for a week: waking up late hungover, eating something, going to the pool, getting fucked up all night, only to do it again the next day. There hadn't been a word from Usher—no notes or messages. Glass bottles lined the hallways and dishes stacked up in the kitchen. The house was a disaster.

Like everything else, I assumed we were intended to be the housekeepers, but no roles had been assigned by Usher. No instructions had been left other than for me to keep them in check, but as the days and sips blended together, I gave up reminding them to clean up after themselves. I gave into letting them believe they had found the only room in the house without surveillance. There were many things that could be called punishment in the house, but it seemed they would need to learn that on their own.

When I felt myself passing out on the lounge chair, my eyes were closing to a scene of the four men on each other's shoulders: Brent on Sonny and Darius on Marco, their dicks, balls, and wet hair all rubbing together as they laughed. Forearms slapped moist skin, chests against open palms, until one duo pulled the other down into the water, and they started over again.

Their joyous yells became white noise among the clicking bottles bobbing in the sparkling pool until I awoke to intense moaning. My eyes parted slowly, revealing motion unfolding only a few feet away. Next to me on the closest lounger was Darius, his head between Sonny's legs again.

With Sonny's fingers wrapped in Darius's hair, Sonny grabbed his head and guided his mouth back and forth on his cock. Sonny thrust his hips forward to fuck Darius's mouth and growled with pleasure. Darius pulled back from the grip only to lick the precum from his lips then dove back in to devour Sonny whole, gliding his tongue across every part of him.

Behind them, Brent and Marco sat on another fully-reclined lounge chair. Their hairy knees touched while they stroked their cocks. Below the weight of their furry asses, the stretchy plastic straps lengthened and their balls hung full near the metal piping supporting the chair. In predictable unison, the brothers spit into their hands and brought the lubricant to their shafts to pump.

Their saliva added to the sounds of wetness between the four men, and with only a single eye peeked open, the scene was making me firm under my bathing suit. I had seen this play out before. In the place we used to call home when I'd walk through the front door to a version of the same group play but make a straight line to my room in order to avoid it. It wasn't that it wasn't hot then, but when sex still felt like a chore, I had always declined any verbal, or nonverbal, invitation to join.

Maybe it was the wine, but something felt different this time as I watched Brent stand over Sonny and bend low enough to fit his cock into his mouth. Sonny enthusiastically turned his head and opened wide, ready to have his face used while Darius continued bobbing between his thighs.

The other brother stood and soon Marco was behind Darius, using the precum from his dripping foreskin to spread on Darius's ass and wiggle a finger in the opening. Marco straddled his thick legs and dripped spit to the round cheeks and hairy hole between his knees. When he slowly worked his cock inside, Darius moaned and hummed on Sonny's cock which caused a ripple of excited sounds through the connected line of men.

I wasn't sure if anyone could see, but I was rock hard. Some part of me felt stupid for never taking advantage of living with such attractive men who seemed to desire me. It had taken until now, when it was forbidden, for me to return that desire. Now, I wanted them more than ever.

I wanted to be behind Marco or hovering above Sonny, letting him lick between the two dicks while I kissed Brent and stroked the thick fur on his stomach. In my head, I imagined myself next to Darius on the chair, our bodies pressed together and making the plastic strips stretch down to the deck below under our combined weight. I could almost taste Sonny on me while I thought about what it would be like to kiss his precum from Darius's lips.

Where I still lay on the nearby lounge chair, I could see the long-haired man, flat on his back, reaching his hand between the standing man's legs. Sonny tickled at Brent's balls then sucked on his own fingers to bring the spit between Brent's ass cheeks and shove it into his hole.

As he was penetrated, Brent spotted me watching the scene unfold and smirked. He nodded and smiled, looking down to his brother on the other end of the orgy pile. I'd never fucked either of the brothers. But, admittedly, despite my generally mixed feelings about their stupidity in general life and conversation, they were both incredibly sexy.

The wine swirled in my stomach, mimicking butterflies. I felt nervous and excited—as if in this place I was seeing the men in a whole new way. Basking in the stained glass of the atrium, the stone men, the art, and blue water reflecting in all of their eyes, I wanted them all. But as I prepared to stand and join the group, in an instant, my stomach went sour. I froze where I lay, paralyzed by the vow I'd made. The promise we'd all cemented the moment we accepted Usher into our bodies. We didn't belong to ourselves anymore.

We belonged to Usher. We served the house.

Despite my better judgement and realization, my hand still found its way to my cock and I stroked, watching the men suck and fuck each other. A quick switch of positions and Darius was on his stomach with Sonny behind him, working several fingers inside the now widened hole, loosened by Marco's girthy uncut dick. The brothers hovered to the sides, pumping tip to base until Sonny moved to the side to let Brent into his place fucking Darius. Sonny was immediately on his knees and swallowing Marco to the hilt over and over again while he gripped and pulled at his own dick.

Now facing me while Brent pounded him from behind, Darius was next to spot me watching. He followed the motion of my strokes under the thin material of my bathing suit. Rubbing my precum over the more sensitive skin of my head, I was close to releasing. Everything was building and pulsing, ready to explode. The sounds echoing through the massive atrium built into a crescendo of moans; we were all ready. Darius reached his hand toward me and smiled, pulling at the waistband of the short trunks again. I didn't stop him.

With my cock exposed to the humid air from the enclosed pool and sex, my balls tightened seeing Darius's fist prepare to grip me. With only a few pumps, I knew I would shoot. But in that exact moment, as the eruption of our collective climax began, the house shook and vibrated with something sinister. My body clenched, and we all stopped.

Standing in the strange vibrating earthquake of knowing we were about to be caught, the feeling was undeniable. Usher had returned.

Chapter Six

The slamming of a single door sent a shockwave through the manor. I felt sheer panic, unsure whether to clean the mess, hide, or just stand frozen and accept the consequences.

Knowing he was back hit like a swift punch to my stomach as I looked around at the merlot and cabernet stains around the pool, the dirty underwear and towels balled up in the corners. I thought about the wet footprints we'd left through just about every accessible room over the course of a week and could already sense Usher in the grand foyer calculating our punishment for desecrating his home.

I had not made sure they boys behaved themselves. Now, they were experiencing the same fear I'd held inside of me for too long. The men scrambled to their feet and grabbed up what they could hold in their arms while wiping precum and spit from their cocks and holes.

Darius huffed, dabbing a spilled pinot noir from the porous cement. "Girl, help us!" he yelled as he continued to pat the full-sized towel frantically over the moisture.

I didn't move other than slipping my softening cock back into my shorts. Putting my arms behind my head as a pillow on the lounger, I breathed in deeply and exhaled. The damage had already been done.

We'd been entering the atrium each day through the new bookcase but directly across from it were the double set of doors Roderick had showed me. Those same doors shook and burst open, revealing Usher with two shorter figures on either side of him. One was Roderick, wearing real clothes for the first time since we'd reconnected. His outfit looked fierce, but his face was predictably judgmental above his tight sheer shirt and black pants. He folded his arms, cocked his head to the side, and smirked at me as if he knew something I didn't.

On the other side was a young man so handsome all of the boys stopped their frantic cleaning. Sonny gasped and the bundle of bottles he'd collected fell to the ground. On impact, they shattered into hundreds of emerald and crystal shards around everyone's bare feet. As they stood naked, surrounded by the broken glass, all of the boys' eyes were on Usher. No one moved. I exhaled again.

Already I could feel the familiar sting of whips and hear the silence of impending solitude. Soon enough, I'd meet the rubber gloves and be on my knees scrubbing marble statues, probably using small abrasive brushes to clean the spots behind their finely-chiseled ball sacks.

In a way, those were the options I preferred after seeing the harsh cage Roderick had been equipped with after disobeying Usher. I couldn't tell if he still had it on, but just thinking about not having access to my own cock made me squirm where I lay.

That sort restriction from even my own hand used to cross a line in my brain. But now, the way my kinks had a way of pushing the threshold of what seemed sexy further and further from what once turned me on, I knew if Usher put the chastity device on me, I would wear it. If he poked and prodded my nuts and made me wait to cum until he rewarded me with the key, I would say thank you and ask for more. As long as it pleased him.

Even from several yards away I could see, the newest boy at Usher's side had eyes that sparkled under perfectly arched eyebrows. His lashes curved in just the right way too. Framing his thick lips, he had a jawline sharper than the pieces of jagged glass protruding from the crimson puddle creeping down the pool deck in Usher's direction. It had become a red blend of alcohol and mistakes no one felt like drinking anymore.

The suited man watched the liquid drip like blood in a single running line until it stopped in front of him. As conflicted and angry as I was knowing he'd taken Roderick on his trip instead of me, I still thought Usher looked incredibly hot between the two shorter men. Rugged but shaped facial hair surrounded his lips. He bit the thickness of the bottom portion then pressed them together, surveying everything. The mess. The nakedness. The very obvious sex that had taken place.

Even if he hadn't witnessed it remotely, the scent of cum hung in the air along with smashed fermented grapes, sweat, and chlorine. A silence stretched eerily with everyone frozen in place. Our fates were sealed. We were ready for the verdict to be delivered by the master of the house, standing steady, inhaling our missteps.

Then he smiled. "Well. Did you boys have a good time?" Usher lifted his head in our direction and ran a finger across one brow.

My stomach dropped. His attempt at humor couldn't be sincere. This was worse than I'd anticipated. I wanted everyone in the room gone so I could beg him for forgiveness with his beautiful cock in my mouth. So I could feel him touch me and hold me. So we could really talk.

Above the handsome grin, his mustache curled toward his cheeks. He flashed straight white teeth. Something unsaid lingered in the space between the two groups of men. An impending battle. Whatever happened next was going to be terrible.

No one moved from their position, but the deep breaths I'd been taking had spread to the naked side of the room. The other four boys inhaled in odd synchronicity nearby while the pyramid of men in the doorway stood firm. With a quick exhale, Darius unexpectedly spoke, "I'm sorry. We—"

He was cut off immediately by Usher's booming voice bouncing from the textured walls and statuesque men filling the decorated space, "Enough. Let's not be rude to our guest, boy."

Usher motioned a graceful hand toward the new handsome young man. The one wearing tailored jeans that hugged his fit body. From the V-neck of his shirt, a tuft of thick chest hair curled its way over the fabric. Even from where I sat, his nipples were erect enough to push through the cotton.

I could tell by the way he held himself—one leg crossed over the other, the toe of his shoe resting on the ground, a hand in his pocket while the other pushed swooping hair back in place—he knew every man in that room wanted to fuck him. Even more so, this wasn't a new feeling; he radiated a breed of confidence that took years of compliments to cultivate.

By the way Usher looked at the new addition as he posed so aloofly, it seemed no man among us wanted to fuck the fresh meat more than Usher. No matter how attractive and self-assured the new boy was, I immediately wanted to hate him.

"Upstairs, all of you. We don't have the time for this." Usher pushed the sleeve of his pressed suit back and looked at his gold watch. He wasn't smiling anymore. "We're already behind schedule."

Usher looked at me where I still lay stupefied on the lounge chair. When he pursed his lips and shook his head to demonstrate his disappointment, I was glad not to have my dick out. Being naked while he clicked his tongue and wagged his finger at me could have gone in either direction.

Almost anytime his eyes were on me, I seemed to get a little hard, but disappointing him made something retreat under the safety of my shorts. Then, before turning on his heels to exit the atrium, he waited for the other boys to look away. With one side of his mouth curved up, as though he were amused, he winked.

It seemed the gesture had only been for me. If it hadn't, no one else had noticed the quick eye movement. Something had happened wherever he had been for the last week. From even the brief inter-action, I could tell he seemed excited to be home. He was happy to see us, or at the very least, me.

Whether that meant we would bypass harsh punishment for our actions, I didn't know. But what I did know was I didn't entirely rec-ognize the man who had returned. His face and body were the same, but his softened expressions and warmth felt fraudulent.

It could have been a performance intended to disarm us, or perhaps he really was actually in a good mood. Either way, the uncertainty had me on edge. Walking from the chair and leaving the desecrated indoor pool behind, the world I'd known here sus-pended above the unknown, and I found myself bracing for impact.

CHAPTER SEVEN

ow there was a hand-written note waiting on my bed
the second I opened the door, I had no idea. As far as
I knew, Usher and his jet-setting sidekicks had arrived
only moments before they'd burst into the atrium. But, like most
things in the mansion, there was often something I was missing.

Not only was there a note. With no one watching, I'd stopped
picking up after myself days ago. Yet my bed was made, my bathtub
was scrubbed, and all the clothes in my closet were clean and pressed.
So much housekeeping had been accomplished. Maybe I had been
drunk and asleep longer than I thought.

Whipping off the wet wine and precum doused trunks, I stood
nude in my newly cleaned room as I unfolded the note.

Clean yourself.
Orange jockstrap.
Dining room.

In another life before joining the house, I'd gone to a party that
handed out colored bandanas at the door. The large security guard
would size you up before entering. He'd look at your clothes and
hands; analyze your shoes and mouth. Then he'd hand you a color
from a plastic trash bag packed tight with a cascade of rainbow
polyester.

Back then, he slid something vibrant orange through his closed fist like a magician doing a party trick. The massive authority figure turned me around by the waist in a swift motion. Pulling at my ass to make space in my back-left pocket, he stuck the bandana in, letting half of it visibly dangle.

When I asked him what it meant and what others would know about me simply from the color protruding from my cut-off jeans, he said, "Anything. Anytime."

Like a queer fortune teller with runes or illustrated cards telling a customer about a prosperous future, I wanted to believe his intuition was correct.

Even though I was yet to discover new bubbles since adding them to Darius's go-bag that was most likely lost somewhere in the woods, the purple bathtub felt welcoming. I could have stayed submerged with my toes curling over the edge all night, but as the classical music shifted to something dark and moody, I knew it was calling for me to pick up the pace.

I was still aching to cum from my partial participation in the pseudo-orgy. While I dried every part of my body outside of the wardrobe, I thought about finishing myself off. In case I arrived in the dining room to the bad news that Usher knew we had all touched each other while he was away—then presented the worse news in the form of a strict enclosure around my cock locked with a single key—I wanted to get off one last time on my own terms.

As if it were a dream I had abruptly been awoken from, I imagined what would have happened had Usher not stopped us. At the thought of Darius stroking me while the other boys fucked him, sucking the brothers and Sonny, us all cumming hard together, my cock was standing firm while I dried my hair.

I reached down to stroke, but the moment I had the shaft in my fist, the music seemed louder than before. Then even louder. Then louder still. I dropped my grip. Not only because it was impossible to concentrate with blaring violin concertos and classical piano recitals in my ear, but because I knew how to take a hint. Someone didn't want me to cum, and rather than tempt fate for more punishment, I opened the drawers in the wardrobe and found the orange jockstrap.

On my way down the stairs, I didn't see the other boys come out of their rooms. The lights were dim and night had fallen outside. Under my feet, the cold tile felt familiar and reminded me of the first time I had officially met with Usher. How he had approached me from behind and grabbed me by the hair. The way he had inserted himself into me in spite of his intentions to keep a separation between us.

No matter how many boys filled the rooms now, that was still something only he and I shared. The warmth of his occasional intimacy kept me tiptoeing to my destination even though I was afraid of what I was about to encounter. Whether I ended up gagged or bruised, tied or confined, he had called me by my name before he left. Even if I was "boy" when we weren't alone, I still knew, in his eyes, I was special. That fact was all I had to hold onto when I reached the bottom step and let the flickering taper candles guide my way to the dining room.

Taking the lit path, I passed the area where Roderick and I had crawled on all fours to the red room together. Where we'd been connected by a single leash at our collars and I had felt like he was the only thing I wanted in the universe. Then, I'd needed to ease his pain. I'd needed to feel his body and lips. Usher had seemed like the enemy that night, but the only adversary I had in the manor now was Roderick.

The candles continued into the archway, but as I entered, things in the dining area looked different. The mess of used plates, forks, and silver trays had disappeared. Chairs and tables had been replaced with thick rugs and pillows.

Seeing the alterations made me realize any bit of destruction we'd left throughout the house had been remedied. Everything was spotless and pristine again. I wondered if I'd lost track of time in the bathtub, but before I could attempt to calculate how even a group of housekeepers could have gotten everything back in order during a quick wash and wardrobe change, a voice was behind me.

"Deliciously spooky," Marco said, posing near the fiery glow in a dark blue jockstrap. Next to him, his brother leaned on his shoulder in contrasting bright pink.

From the kitchen, Darius emerged with Sonny behind him. Sonny tapped at Darius's framed ass in the green backless underwear and laughed.

"You're gonna get us in more trouble," Darius said, swatting at Sonny's waist near a fluorescent yellow band. Before he could respond, a creaking sound came from the corner, and a door I'd never seen before opened into the dining room.

Coming through what looked like yet another secret passage was the new boy dressed in his own black jock. All of our eyes were on him as he slowly closed the passage. He was silent as he approached before he exhaled and swung his arms at his sides. "This place, huh?" he said with an accent I couldn't place right away.

When he reached out his hand to introduce himself to the cluster of mostly naked men, I could see his fingernails were painted to match his underwear. He had just the slightest charcoal smear under his eyes to accent smokey grey irises with flecks of turquoise.

"Julien," he said and formally shook each hand before pushing his shaggy black hair behind his ears. He was rock star hot. And as much as I wanted to dislike him because he had somehow captured Usher's attention enough to have brought him all the way from what sounded like... France? Julien was, admittedly, really easy to look at.

The other boys smirked and looked at each other. Brent and Marco were especially infatuated and probably would have been banging him from either side with their lizard brains had it not been for the next sound entering the candlelit space.

From behind them, in time with the music, Usher and Roderick appeared. It seemed everyone had arrived in pairs aside from myself and Julien. In this duo, Roderick had on a deep purple jockstrap, matching his collar, and held an oval chafing dish complete with chrome lid.

He walked in front of Usher like a horse pulling a carriage. Two metal loops hooked to Roderick's neck, and on the other end, Usher held a set of reigns in one hand. He gave the lines a quick snap with a flick of his wrist.

Roderick jerked at the motion, and halted in place in front of us. He held the large tray with his forearms stretched out, presenting it.

"Well, this seems about right doesn't it, boys?" Usher detached the strips from Roderick's collar and threw them to the side of the room beyond the pillows. "The ambiance is there, but something is missing."

Usher closed his eyes and tapped his temple as if he were recalling a memory. The music shifted from haunting piano to a single violin that ebbed and flowed with notes of longing. Usher kept his eyes closed, but smiled. "Yes, there you are."

I didn't see him reach into his pocket or anywhere else to use the remote I'd seen him use before to control the atmosphere of any room, but nothing about him and his need to be mysterious surprised me anymore. It had been timed somehow, the shift, and while I was impressed by his dedication to keep the experience interesting, so much of me wanted to live behind the curtain.

When he opened his eyes again, they seemed glossy, and he inhaled deeply, stifling some sort of emotion. The moment was fleeting as all of us stood together with our hairy asses exposed to the open air. I wanted to sit on one of the large cushions covering the floor, which I was certain Roderick appreciated. They reminded me of his tweed floor poufs and the way he tried to pass them off as actual furniture.

But before I could entertain the idea of continuing to nurse my hangover from our week-long bender, Usher was lifting the lid of the shiny dish. Roderick's arms shook under the weight, and I wondered why he was always being punished with such tedious physical training. He did seem to be developing a certain endurance. If he was in pain, it didn't show on his face.

If anything, he appeared pleased when Usher presented the contents of his offering to all of us: colorful ropes wrapped into coils. All were different: purple, pink, green, yellow, black, blue, and orange.

CHAPTER EIGHT

I t didn't make sense to me at first, but next to the wrapped cords was a single paddle, flat and wide. No one moved. Usher nodded to the vibrant colors on the tray then to our hips and between our legs. He was bringing our attention to the waistbands and pouches, the strips of elastic cupping our furry ass cheeks.

"Take your color, boys," Usher said with a sinister smile, sliding the wooden paddle from the tray before sauntering to the other side of the room. He tapped it against his palm and leaned against the wall, closing his eyes to take in the music.

The boys hovered in a semi-circle around the options. With Usher almost out of earshot, Roderick whispered through strained breath, "Hurry up." His arms trembled, and he shifted his weight back and forth on his feet.

Surprisingly, it was Sonny who made the connection first. Glancing down at his blindingly yellow underwear and matching it with the corresponding rope on the platter, he palmed the coils and strutted between the pillows like an obstacle course. We hadn't been instructed to, but after Sonny sat down on a cushion and began unraveling the rope ball, the remainder of us followed his lead.

Usher didn't speak while Roderick retired the empty tray and settled with his matching purple rope on the floor with us. He massaged his tired arms. With our lines unwrapped, Usher opened his eyes only to say to no one in particular, "Doesn't he play beautifully?"

Nervously twisting the orange rope around my fingers, I wasn't familiar with the artist of the piece flowing from the speakers in the house. But Usher was right; the music was beautiful.

For whatever was about to happen, the mood had been set, and he allowed us to bask in it for a few more minutes as the violin continued to play its ominous score. When a piece ended and drifted into a moment of silence, Usher audibly sighed and sauntered to the center of where we were perched on the grouping of pillows.

"Up," he said quickly and gestured for us to rise. When we stood, he nodded to Roderick who hastily grabbed Marco's rope from him then turned him by the shoulders. "Hands behind your back, boy," Usher said, observing Marco's apprehension at being handled so roughly by another boy.

Still, Marco obeyed Usher's order and allowed Roderick to loop the dark blue line around his wrists. He winced as Roderick tied the rope off tightly and looked at the group of us watching.

"All of you," Usher said, nodding to the lines in our hands. A collective hesitation fell across us, but it only lasted a few seconds before we fumbled around, trading the colored ties.

It felt strange trying to decide which man to present my rope to, but Julien approached me before I had the chance to choose. I still wanted to hate him. Even in that moment, I could see Usher staring at Julien's plump furry ass as he bent over to fasten my wrists. His touch was gentle. As the fur on his arms brushed against my lower back, I thought about how badly I wanted to cum.

Only Roderick was left to be secured, and Usher took the purple rope firmly in his hand before pushing his collared boy against the closest surface. Roderick's face pressed to the eggshell wall with Usher's elbow across his back to hold him in place as he was tied. The swift motion was so aggressive the rest of us jumped back. I nearly tripped on a floor pillow, and it made me wonder what I would have done if I had landed on the hardwood panels without a way to get back on my feet without humiliating myself. Perhaps that was the intention. He wanted us to be helpless.

The sudden force Usher was demonstrating extended past the interaction with Roderick. Moving from the wall, he returned to the middle of the dining area and kicked each floor cushion out of the way. "Circle up," he said with hostility in his voice. "Face the outside."

I was nervous again. His constantly shifting mood surged adrenaline through my body, tensing me in a rapid cycle. Usher breathed in deeply as if he were trying to prepare for something, then I felt it.

On my ass framed in the orange jockstrap, something thundered against my skin. It immediately burned so intensely I was certain all of the air had left my body forever.

A storm of rapid hits followed the echo of the first contact, but not on me. Usher was making his way around the circle of boys, putting paddle to bare ass over and over again. I could see from my peripheral vision that when a boy seemed to be losing his balance from the pain, he'd stand them up straight again and continue.

The music ascended with furious stings. As the anguish grew, an image came into my head of a boy playing the violin in time with our percussion. He strummed the chords out in succession, and as the track ended, my premonition blended into the agony of my reality. As my skin scorched, flames surrounded the young musician. He looked into my eyes and whispered, "Run."

I was in the room again. Candles wavered in reflections on the wet faces of every boy I could see by turning my head in either direction. Usher had gone around the circle with his paddle at least a dozen times based on the multitude of spots where my ass burned red hot.

He must have tired himself out because he stood hunched over in his suit before dropping the paddle to the polished wood floor. During his break, he walked to a small table nearby that I hadn't noticed before. From a decanter, he poured and sipped a glass of red wine.

While he caught his breath, the seven of us stayed in formation, afraid to move. I kept my legs parted in a wide stance to keep my raw cheeks from touching each other as much as possible. Either a drop of sweat or a tear rolled from my face to my chest where it settled in my fur.

Seemingly refreshed and back in the center of our circle, Usher spoke firmly, "Now the front, boys."

Hesitation no longer seemed to be an option after the pain had broken down my defenses. I spun my throbbing backside away from the man in control and offered him my cock which was still safely resting in the orange jockstrap.

With a clear view of each other and our hands still tied behind our backs, Usher traveled to every boy and wiggled the band of our underwear down to our ankles. I'd seen the cocks in that room before, aside from Julien, who hung long even when he was soft.

It wasn't long before I got to see that the young French man could grow even larger when he was hard as Usher spit in his own hand and began stroking him from base to tip. "Don't cum," Usher said to the boy, loud enough for us all to hear.

After a few minutes, Julien wiggled in place trying to escape the milking. He clenched his teeth and winced. Usher stopped. The French man's cock still stood at attention when Usher moved onto Brent. Julien sighed with relief.

Using the same tactic, the older man cycled through each boy the way he had with the paddle, but instead of inflicting pain, he was edging us over and over again.

From the second he gripped me with his lubricated fist when my turn came around, I wished I had ignored the music and jerked-off before coming down the stairs. I'd spilled my load before Usher had wanted me to in the past and suffered the consequences. I wasn't going to make the same mistake.

By his third time around the circle, I was biting my lip hard and squirming from his touch. Letting up, Usher swatted at my cock and smirked. Quiet enough so no one else could hear, he said, "Just a little longer, boy."

It was Brent who came first, his droplets landing to the floor below. Then Sonny, who didn't seem to care very much about losing whatever competition was going on as long as he could relax again soon. Darius gave in, then Marco. Sticky pearls gathered like an abstract painting in front of each boy across the dark wooden floor.

I couldn't take my eyes off of Julien's cock while Usher stroked it furiously. He ran his hand up Julien's furry abs and chest until he reached his mouth, "Spit, boy." When Julien complied, Usher brought the warm liquid down to continue pumping. The French man was close.

"Beautiful," Usher said, when Julien arched his head back and finally exploded. Even losing whatever strange game we were playing, Usher somehow still found him perfect.

With only Roderick and myself left, our keeper motioned for us to meet in the middle of the circle. He untied both our colored cords and placed our hands on each other's cocks. My wrists throbbed from being released, and my balls pulsed with a mix of pleasure and anger. We knew each other's weaknesses, and as badly as I wanted to cum, I was even more determined to beat him.

Roderick ran his finger from just above my balls and all the way to my tip while I rubbed the flatness of my palm on the underside of him, where I knew he was most sensitive. We stared into each other's eyes with something that made me want to breathe fire. It was passion mixed with betrayal, anger mixed raw sexuality. I wanted to take him down.

There was something in him that felt just as relentless. He wouldn't release my gaze. And for a moment his eyes softened, almost like an apology.

As I had my guard down to process the meaning behind his look, he stroked faster. The crowd of boys and their spent cocks watched intensely, former a tighter circle around our battle. Usher was stoic at our side like a referee, paddle in hand, prepared to step in at any time.

I tensed up but worried it was too late. I tried to think about unsexy things, but all I could see was the visible anticipation of six attractive men focused on my hard cock. I heard the paddle slapping against Usher's hand and thought about the last time I'd held him in my mouth.

At the point of no return, I came hard on Roderick's hand. He smiled before taking a few steps back and shaking my load from his fingers to the ground.

CHAPTER NINE

We'd been dismissed to our separate rooms after the new group ritual. Although I didn't understand it entirely, Usher seemed amused by the outcome. He also stood around for a few minutes once I'd came, looking at the ceiling and through the windows but not sharing with us what he was searching for. The suited man appeared nervous, bracing himself for something which never arrived.

All in all, I was happy to be alone again. Having friends around had been nice, but when a tray arrived for breakfast the next morning, I was relieved I wouldn't have to go back downstairs. I wasn't in any hurry to see Usher either while my stinging ass healed from being swatted over and over again with the paddle.

Days passed outside my small window when, one night, something called to me. A voice I'd never heard in the house before woke me from a deep sleep. It drew me down the stairs like a siren before I knew even I was walking. Now, I was standing in front of the stone figure guarding the entrance to the control room. The secret words fell from my mouth into his stone ear, and he slid to the side, granting me passage to the already unlocked room.

Curtains had been drawn from inside the dungeon to block out the two-way mirror. I pushed the button to open the mic on the other side and heard what sounded like a conversation at first. Two voices went back and forth, but they weren't discussing anything as much as trading the incoherent grunts and dirty talk people do when they're having sex. But hearing Usher's cadence and tone among the two, I knew that couldn't be what was happening in the red room.

Through the velvet drapes of the portrait room, I didn't take the time to greet the painted men before bending down to feel around for the opening to the panel Usher had revealed to me behind the pegboard holding toys only days before.

When my fingers found the crack, I pushed lightly and peeked one eye through the opening. In the new sling, Sonny was on his back, legs in the air, furry toes against the chain. Usher stood in front of him, and from where I spied, I had a full view of them both.

I watched as Usher took out his hard cock but still didn't believe what I was seeing. He tapped his hardness on the suspended boy and using his tip, rubbed the precum from Sonny's front hole all over both their dicks. The surfer moaned with pleasure of the frottage before Usher moved his moist cock head to Sonny's ass to tease the opening. Sonny stroked his dick between two fingers while the man standing above him pushed just slightly into one hole, then the other, never fully entering.

The sleepy boy with the wavy beach hair had always been a favorite of the men who came to the old house. Not in a fetishy way—Sonny was just exceptional in bed. He'd told us before that having three fuckable holes didn't automatically make him a bottom. As much as he liked to get fucked, he'd always favored being versatile. Having an option the rest of us didn't have, and making his own lube, made him unique.

Sometimes when he was stoned enough, he'd laugh and tell us, "Sorry about your luck." Then he'd throw back his luscious mane and parade his perfect ass around the boardwalk. No one needed to know what was in his pants unless they were planning to fuck him, but once most men saw him tossing his board around the waves, that's exactly what they wanted.

Usher had apparently found him just as irresistible because right in front of me, he wasn't just inserting toys or hitting flesh. Sony wasn't receiving him at the end of a paddle or riding crop. The man who said fucking wasn't the way things were done in the house, the one who chastised me for making him break his own rules, was on the cusp of penetrating Sonny's holes.

It was only teasing for a while, but when Usher finally pushed inside, they both moaned and Sonny pulled at the chain. The standing man's eyes rolled back as he thrust in and out of one hole and moved to the other, back and forth, coating his fur in slippery precum. The sling rocked back and forth, making it easier for his entire length to be swallowed by the hairy openings.

My heart sank. I closed the panel and leaned back against the wall below a hanging portrait. The men in the room, their faces illuminated by a spotlight, seemed to be mocking me. With my head between my bent knees, my face felt warm and my body went empty with embarrassment. How could I have been so stupid to think I was the only one Usher was having sex with?

Slowly, I pushed the panel again and focused my sight through the slots in the pegboard. I didn't want to force it too far this time and have one of the thin metal rods or double-ended dildos fall to the cement, giving me away. Through the dots I could see a swiss cheese version of their encounter, but the score was still clear. The moans of pleasure and rattling of chains. Slaps to Sonny's chest and the back of his thighs as Usher went feral, forcing himself deeper and deeper.

At least they weren't kissing. Not that we had either, but seeing Usher's lips touch another man may have broken me in that moment.

Still observing the scene, I watched Usher grab Sonny's cock and stroke it while they fucked. He wanted him to have a good time, to enjoy it. He jerked it hard until they came together. And in that exact moment, my stomach felt sick.

Usher was slumped over Sonny's body on the sling, and I closed the panel to return to the ball I'd been sitting in. I worried that if I kept watching, I'd see him stay. The way he finally had with me after leaving his load inside my body so many times. Sonny already had Usher's warmth, and now I worried he had his attention.

I crawled my way back through the red curtains on my hands and knees. The mic was still open in the control room, broadcasting a rhythmic panting. I couldn't tell if it was one man or two catching their breath post energetic coitus, but I didn't want to find out. With a quick flip, the sound was gone, and I sat alone in the silence.

From the roll top desk across from me, a drawer protruded from the middle section. I didn't remember it being pulled out on my way in, but I had, admittedly, been mostly asleep. When I crawled over, I saw that the folder Roderick had shown me weeks before with our names and images was inside, opened to a page with a face and set of stats I hadn't seen in there the first time.

Just below Julien's picture, not far from text detailing the location he'd been found in France, his known sexual skills, and a generally high rating of obedience was a familiar word:

Novitiate

I still wasn't sure want the seemingly ancient title meant in relation to our adorable little sex cult fraternity of furry men, but when I flipped the complied book back a page, Roderick's glossy bearded face was staring back. Under his name was the word:

Postulant

Slamming the folder back into the drawer, there were assumptions I could make. One was that among all of the boys, Roderick and Julien were at the top of the list. If I'd ventured further into the pages, I was certain I would have seen Sonny somewhere as well.

The other assumption was that the ranking Usher was keeping could change at any time, and right now, my position was slipping. If I was on it at all anymore, I was apparently not at the top of his list for favorite boys.

CHAPTER TEN

❦

I t took me until mid-afternoon, when food didn't arrive at my door, to drag my growling stomach down to the kitchen in search of sustenance. I could hear talking before I even turned the corner into the sitting room with the bookcase leading the kitchen. The chatter made me wish I was alone again, that they would all disappear, and I could return to my solitude—just so I wouldn't have to explain myself.

Julien was wedged between Brent and Marco on one of the sofas with the tufted back. It was definitely an antique and older than all of us; it would be impossible to have it cleaned.

Brent ran his finger down Julien's bare chest and down his stomach. "So France?" he asked. Julien nodded. "You must know a lot about Eiffel Towers then."

The brothers laughed at the joke Julien definitely didn't understand.

"Maybe you call it something else? Like whatever you call French fries there," Marco suggested with a tilted hand and a shrug before leaning in closer to the man in the middle.

Brent raised the volume of his voice as if that would make it easier for Julien to parse out and followed up by asking, "Since you travel a lot, maybe you're more familiar with the London Bridge?"

The French boy cleared his throat nervously, looking back and forth at the two men ready to pound him from both sides as soon as they got the word.

From the passage, the bookcase slid to the side and Darius emerged. "Maybe he calls it what the rest of us do: a spit roast. Speaking of which, looks like I'm banned from the kitchen. Someone else is cooking today."

He was talking to the group of men, the three about to gang-bang on priceless furniture and Sonny, whom I hadn't noticed when I walked in, passed out with his arm over his face on the matching loveseat.

When Darius saw me standing in the doorway, he put his hands on his hips, "Oh, she has risen."

I couldn't understand why we all had free reign of the house. After spending weeks locked away by myself before the arrival of the other boys, it didn't seem fair. Rage built inside of me, and seeing Sonny casually curled up after what I had witnessed the previous evening was making me burn even hotter.

"I don't travel," Julien said. The response seemed delayed as if he'd been searching for the correct English words. "His plane was the first."

"*His* plane?" Darius said, closing the bookcase behind him. "Didn't know we had our own airline too. Alexander found us some *money* money." He smiled at me, trying to make me smile back. I didn't.

"He found me at the house," Julien continued. There was something oddly serious in his tone, and for just a moment, the brothers pulled back. "People used to say the ruins were haunted. It was burned a long time ago."

"In France?" It wasn't my intention to speak to any of them, but I needed to verify where Usher went and what exactly drew him there. Would he really travel across the ocean just for a new plaything?

Julien nodded and wiped at the remnants of his smokey eyeliner. He picked at his chipping black nails then motioned to the house around us. "Like this one, but destroyed."

The French boy had been brought here from his home on an entirely different continent and was doing his best to communicate with us. He'd obviously been through a lot. I wondered if maybe I'd been too hard on him.

Darius walked farther into the room to perch on the arm of the loveseat where Sonny slept. He stroked Sonny's mane while he watched Brent and Marco poke at Julien again. They rubbed at his hairy thighs, and Julien squirmed in his seat.

"Stop bugging that kid," Darius said and snapped his fingers. He pointed toward either side of the couch, telling them to separate like unruly children. "He's obviously smarter than the two of you combined. Even if he wants to be the filling to the little croissanwich you're trying to make, he's not trying to break the rules."

"Oh, we've got rules now?" I smirked at Darius, who only days before was trying to jerk me off by the pool during a five-man orgy while I resisted.

How things had changed.

"It helps to know what he wants, now that he's actually told me," Marco said, bringing his large feet up to the glass coffee table and crossing his legs at the ankle. There was something about the way he used the word "me" that made my stomach feel uneasy.

"He likes to tell us separately, I guess." Brent brought his own wide soles up and set them on Julien's lap. The French boy sighed with defeat and started stroking Brent's leg lightly with his fingertips.

"Whatever. I was getting bored fucking y'all anyway," Darius said with a slight sigh. He pulled at Sonny's ear playfully, and the cat man responded by stretching wide then balling up even tighter. "Guess no one can fuck anyone in this house except for—" Darius stopped talking when he saw my face.

"At least it's good," Marco said, filling the air. Darius nodded in agreement but didn't take his eyes off me or my obviously surprised expression.

"I thought you didn't like pain," I said. There was no way I didn't sound angry. Darius probably worried I was about to lunge myself across the room and tackle his body into the books behind him.

Darius chose his words carefully before he spoke. "Not without pleasure. No."

"Not without fucking." I wasn't asking as much as clarifying that I knew what he meant. My face burned again and the silence returned. Every boy awake in the sitting room stared at me.

In slightly broken English, Julien broke the quiet hanging between us all. "Did you think you were the only one?" he asked.

"I've been trying to tell you," a voice said from the side of the conversation. Roderick leaned in the space where the bookcase normally sat. He was the human embodiment of the judgy face emoji wearing tight underwear and giving me side eye.

When I didn't respond, he looked past me. "Food is ready," he said to everyone else. The boys stood and made their way to the kitchen, glancing at me with what could have been sympathy but was probably pity. I wanted to disappear then reappear when all of them were gone. Not just from the room, but from the house.

Darius shook Sonny's shoulder. "Food," he said in an attempt to wake him. Sonny gave a thumbs-up but didn't move from his comfortable spot.

When Darius scooted by the doorway, he reached out to put his hand on my arm, but I shrugged it away. If anyone should have told me, it was him. All of them, including Darius, needed to go.

With the room mostly cleared out, I slumped to the antique couch and put my head in my hands. All the pain I'd been taking for him, the confinement, the uncertainty—it had been for nothing. I'd not only fallen out of his favor; I didn't even deserve the truth.

I sighed heavily and wondered if I should leave the house, if I should gather the things I could call mine and try to open the wardrobe to escape into the woods. Maybe Usher was over me. Perhaps if I left, he wouldn't try to stop me. Even if I did wake up in my room again, Usher needed to know I didn't want to be here anymore. Not for the fancy things. Not for Roderick. And especially, not for him.

Sonny rolled over on the couch and cracked his eyes open. He rubbed them and waited until I realized he was awake to speak. "Sorry, dude. That sucks," he said, then turned on his side and returned to sleep.

I was going to leave. That was certain. But first, I was going to make sure Usher knew why he was losing me.

CHAPTER ELEVEN

Never even once had I thought about where Usher resided within the manor—not until I'd gone back to my room and started packing my bag. I realized then that nothing in there, aside from the clothes I'd arrived in, belonged to me.

Leaving the bag I'd started behind, I put on my old jeans, T-shirt, and boots. Stuffed in the corner of the wardrobe, they were clean but not fresh. They weren't like the clothes and gear I'd gotten used to parading in around the house, but at least they were mine.

As I prepared for my exit, a voice called my name from the hallway. I didn't know which of the other boys was outside my closed door, but I had no interest in speaking to any of them.

Opening the wardrobe, I pushed on the back panel. The lock was gone. Between where I stood and the end of the passage lay only a few hundred feet of stony path, a winding tunnel back to a life before I knew what happened inside the mansion I'd be so captivated by at one time.

I understood what Julien was telling the other men about being pulled to a place. We shared the feeling he had for the house in France which mirrored this one. Though, for some reason, that one had been burned down to the foundation. Part of me wondered what had happened there, but more of me wanted to step my boot onto the first cobblestone below the wardrobe and never turn back.

From the hallway, the voice called my name again. It knocked in a familiar pattern. Three knocks, two knocks, one knock. *Seriously?*

Taking a breath, I stood huddled in the closet with my left sole hanging over my next decision. I could leave right now without telling anyone. Whatever Roderick was invoking our secret knock for, I wasn't interested in hearing.

He pounded out the secret signal again, this time with more force. I pulled my leg back into the wardrobe and dropped it to the carpet of my room. Speed walking from the open wardrobe and still angry, I was prepared to let Roderick receive the brunt of my displeasure.

"What?" I growled angrily, whipping open the bedroom door, prepared to see his stupid face. But there in the hallway, no one. I looked both ways up and down the corridor but not even a hint of a human man hung in the unexpected vacancy. He was messing with me.

I was ready to close my door and continue my exit plan with more rage, but something caught my eye. A painting. One of the portraits from the room with red velvet curtains had been moved and now hung at the end of the hallway.

Moving slowly toward it, I could see two men captured in the art. One was standing in a suit and the other, a younger man, knelt by his side with a collar around his neck. I knew the more youthful of the faces. Usher.

Closer now, I saw that something was different from when I had seen the painting before. The plaque below it included a name I hadn't observed the first time. The older man was footed by a gold plaque engraved with the name "Usher" while the naked and kneeling one, the man I'd come to know as Usher, was identified by a different name: Madden.

Just reading the name, my body stung with a tremendous sense of longing. The older keeper in the portrait had his sight on me, and no matter what direction I faced, his eyes followed.

Without changing positions, he seemed to be calling to me, begging for my help. "Find him," the man in the suit said. His words, in a French accent, echoed through me. My feet began shuffling on their own up the nearest staircase.

I climbed higher in the house than I had ever had access. Passages I hadn't known existed were open. Traveling over lush carpet and bracing myself with the polished banister, I ascended until the atmosphere around me grew dim.

Chandeliers hung unlit and covered with cobwebs when the stairs ran out, and I stood on what must have been the top floor. The music that typically played non-stop throughout the massive house was replaced with an eerie quiet. Twisted copper strings dangled from the upper part of the landing. Exposed and pointed wire protruded as if the speakers had been ripped from every wall.

A single door sat at the end of the platform. I approached it with caution. Every step I took made the floorboards creak under my boots and tug at my throat. I could hardly breathe or keep up with the rapid pace of my own pumping heartbeat.

Then, a few steps from the door, a flash of Usher fucking Sonny played in my brain. A series of the all the times Usher had lied to me or led me to think I was special paired with the punishment I'd taken for rules that never mattered, boiled back into fury. With that fire within me, I walked more quickly and used my anger to force open the entrance.

We gasped at the same time. Me and the naked man lying in a king-sized bed just below a porthole window. I'd seen the window from the exterior of the house. It was at the very top point of the mansion and could only be seen from the front. Before calling this castle home, I'd stared at the circular glass from outside the rusted gate. I'd grabbed the brown-red metal and wondered who could live inside such a room with only a single window. Now I had my answer.

Usher sat up quickly, his cock sitting on his thigh. He didn't attempt to cover it, and I tried not to stare. "It's your fault." Usher's voice trembled with something unfamiliar: vulnerability. The only time I'd heard anything like it before was the night he'd said my name, but never like this.

My boots tapped against the wood as I got closer to him, but for once, I didn't feel afraid. "My fault?"

"We weren't supposed to—" He stopped himself and analyzed me where I hovered near the bed. He looked at my jeans and boots. It seemed to click for him that they were my traveling clothes. My grand exit look. My escape the haunted mansion realness. "It will all be over soon."

"Because of me?" I asked, sensing a strange cynical coldness in my own voice. Weaponized and pointed.

Hanging over a chair, opposite to where I stood, Usher's suit seemed less menacing when it wasn't on him. It was not unlike the way his naked body in front of me made him seem more like a man than a constant threat. He was an attractive man, an incredibly sexy man with a hairy chest and an exceptional cock between his legs... that I was definitely looking at.

Perhaps it was the combination of the two which created such power, like a superhero with a cape and mask. Without the costume, he was someone else.

The naked man didn't answer my question. Instead, he rested his elbow on one bent knee and looked at the balled-up satin sheets surrounding him. How long had he been in this house?

"This happened before. When he loved us." Usher scrunched the soft fabric in his fist when he finally spoke. "I knew I was breaking the rules. This house will fall just like that one did."

I didn't understand the cryptic nonsense he was speaking, but it sounded ridiculous. Rolling my eyes, I felt angry again. "Yeah, okay." My arms crossed my chest on their own. "So that's why you fucked all the boys when you told me you couldn't? Because you fell in love with all of us?"

Usher sat exposed and silent for a moment, pushing again at the bedding. "No," he said but didn't look at me.

"No, you didn't fuck them?" It felt strange being direct with Usher, even if it was just my tone of voice. Impatience had taken hold, and I wanted answers. I needed to know how many men in the house had lied to me.

"Yes, I fucked them. All of them." Usher raised his head to meet my eyes, but hearing those words, I was already turning my body to leave.

One quick jolt down the steps and right out the back doors with the flowy white curtains, that's all it would take. I could bid my goodbyes to the stone men in the courtyard and be back over the tracks on the bad side of Beachside before nightfall. Maybe the old flop house was still unoccupied or Roderick's old fake apartment would be available to rent once I had the money. Until then, an alley would suffice. As long as I could get out of this house and away from everyone inside, I would be fine.

Usher leaned over quickly and grabbed my wrist, stopping my momentum. "But no. I didn't love them."

Hovering where I stood, his hand felt softer and moved from my wrist to my palm where he interwove his fingers with mine. "Why did you have to be so perfect?" he asked.

My eye caught his cock again, and as it rose from where it had been sitting against his leg, he pulled me closer to the bed. I landed next to his bare skin but tried not to touch him.

I was still upset, but my cock was getting firmer in my jeans just feeling him close. When he turned my face toward his and looked into my eyes, it was pushing at the zipper.

Pulling me in tighter by my shirt, he put his lips on mine and kissed me hard. Deep and passionate, our first kiss felt electric in a literal sense. The lights on the top floor sparked and flickered, but we didn't stop.

My cock throbbed as we rolled around the bed until I pinned him on his back to straddle his hips. Usher pulled me down to his lips, and when we finally went up for air again, he whispered, "Let it burn," then put his tongue back in my mouth.

Chapter Twelve

⁓⸎⸎⸎⁓

There were parts of him I never thought I would have the chance to explore. I licked his chest and sucked each erect nipple. He allowed me to taste and nibble his entire body and run my fingers through the fur that started just below his neck and ended at his hard cock. I tickled at his balls, and for the first time, he didn't hold back when he moaned in my ear.

"Alexander," he said, as if he knew the sound of my own name from his mouth would make me stiff. He was right.

My shirt off and my body positioned between his legs, that urge to top I hadn't felt since being with Roderick came over me like a wave rolling into an undertow. Sliding my jeans below my ass, the tip of me pushed at his hole, and I searched for the right words to open him enough to plunge inside. I ripped off my boots and pulled my jeans down to make sure he would get the full length of me.

"Madden," I said, stroking his thick cock and hoping for precum I could use as lubrication between us. The man below me jolted unexpectedly and tossed me from my stance. I fell back on the bed while he hoisted himself to his knees and towered over me.

"What did you say?" His voice had changed again. It was the tone I knew better than the despair and remorse he'd demonstrated when I'd entered the room. This was the man who had dragged me by the ankles and smacked my most sensitive parts for his enjoyment. My heart was pounding again as our naked flesh barely touched.

"Isn't that your name?" I could hear the trembling vibration of a question stuck in my throat, desperately trying to escape in time. The man I suddenly didn't know how to address leaned his ass on his heels. He brought his hands to his upper thighs and looked down at the sheets we'd unraveled in the tide of our passion. Now I was drowning in the choppy waves of his unpredictable nature.

Afraid to move from where I'd fallen, I watched him continue to kneel as if he were listening to something I couldn't hear. He ran his hands through his dark hair and rubbed his lips together, deep in thought.

I had never said his name to him before, even when I'd learned the title from seeing it around the house. He hadn't asked me to call him anything, only to comply with his demands as he made them. But in that moment, while I braced myself for an expected impact, my lips parted slowly. The word came out just above the volume of a whisper, "Usher?"

Watching his face change to anger, I immediately wished I hadn't spoken. Whatever I'd done to stop and upset him, I regretted it. We could have still been kissing. I could have been pressed against his chest and caressing the neat beard on his face. If I'd just stayed quiet, there was a chance I'd be deep inside of him, instead of fearing his next movement.

"There is no Usher. Not anymore," he finally said. I didn't understand, but that must have been clear by my facial expression as I still lay below him with my cock growing soft through the fly of my pants.

"There was one, a long time ago, but he's not me. He wasn't the man who brought me here either." The naked man moved suddenly, swinging his wide foot from the bed to the wooden floor in one quick swoop. I didn't mean to flinch and cover my balls, but it was a reflex.

He reached for his black dress socks, which lay on the floor in front of the chair near his shiny shoes. "You know more than I thought, but you still have no idea what you're part of, do you, boy?"

With his socks on, he went for his fitted black briefs next. They'd been folded into a tidy square that Usher unraveled to slip each leg through. While he brought them over his hairy ass and adjusted his balls inside, I was already missing his cock.

"I didn't know either when he brought me to France, but it's no excuse for your behavior." With each piece of clothing concealing his nudity, his tone grew harsher. I ached for the vulnerability he'd shown me for the limited few minutes when I'd first pushed through the door to the strange attic which seemed to be his room.

"How long have you been here?" I asked, unsure why I was speaking.

"You're asking the wrong question," Usher said tersely as he grabbed his linen dress pants from the back of the chair. When he fastened the button and pulled at the zipper, the lights flickered again. I assumed it was the strange wiring up here, but I was so nervous it felt as if the bed was shaking below me.

Usher steadied himself against the arm of the chair and shook his head. He reached for his belt and even in my confusion from the sudden movement around me, I blocked my chest and face with my arms, certain he would hit me with the long strip.

"I think we may be passed that now." He laughed and looped the belt through his pants, fastening it below his navel. "It's already begun, boy."

My eyes fixated on the hair resting between the silver buckle and his belly button until the rumble below me happened again. I gripped the sides of the bed. It wasn't just my nerves; the entire house was shaking.

"What's happening?" I yelled to the man slipping an arm through his white collared shirt. He buttoned the end around his wrist with a silver cufflink before he spoke calmly. "Ritual. Revenge. Retribution. I knew the moment I saw you this is how it would end."

As he followed with the other sleeve and brought the fabric to his chest to button together, the floor shook. The walls vibrated.

I jumped to my feet and glanced around for my clothes. Before I could ask if he thought it was safe to be in the old house with it moving around us, Usher was suddenly near me. Alarmingly close to my face, he brought his hand to the stubble on my cheek and stroked it lightly.

I leaned into his open palm seeking comfort and asked, "Should we leave?"

A cruel laughter erupted from the man, and without withdrawing his hand, he said, "Sure. Go ahead. Go. That was your plan, wasn't it?" He patted the side of my face, patronizing me.

Despite his sudden return to coldness, I wanted the man I'd met in this room to return. I turned my head slightly to let my lips touch his hand and kissed his fingers. My hand rose to join his and bring his hand closer to my mouth. As the house trembled and the lights flashed, I whispered quietly, "Come with me."

His hand pulled away immediately and with force, smacked against the spot on my cheek where it had been resting. The floor beneath me felt like it was about to crumble while Usher screamed loudly enough for his voice to echo across the walls, "Go now!"

CHAPTER THIRTEEN

I left my clothes and Usher in the attic. My balls slapped my thighs as I ran down the shaking stairs, pushing the cobwebs from my face. When I reached my room, I hoped to grab shorts and continue my pace straight out the back door. As I gripped the doorknob, a series of screams came from a few doors down.

The house continued to vibrate while my detour toward the sounds of terror brought me to the sitting room. There I saw three faces I recognized: Brent, Marco, and Julien. The brothers were naked and frozen in a high-five. One was in Julien's mouth and the other was behind him.

All balanced on the antique couch, the young Frenchman was on all-fours between the twins. His cock hung long and hard, but it wasn't swinging with the momentum of being fucked from both sides.

Each man in the threesome was so hard, in fact, they were stone. Statues with expressions of pleasure plastered to their scruffy faces. A trio of men fused together forever in a top-tier sexual position, turned to priceless art.

I ran. I aborted my mission to cover my naked body and sprinted from the sitting room to the staircase. At the bottom beyond the grand foyer, the double doors were open. Their white drapes were gently sucked into a light breeze framing my path to freedom. All I had to do was walk through.

I hesitated. No matter how we'd left things, I knew I needed to find the other boys and take them with me. There were so many questions, even more since my latest conversation with Usher. Among them was how I would find my friends in a crumbling house of endless mystery rooms and secret doors. In the midst of my uncertainty, something around the corner called to me and soon my feet moved again on their own.

Now the back doors were completely out of view, and I found myself in front of the control room with the stone man I'd whispered to so many times. He was looking down on me. Unlike the times he'd granted me access before, in this moment, his eyes seemed to look passed me. When I turned to see what he was focused on, a door I'd never noticed before across the hall was bathed in a strange light.

The statue shook. His muscular body quaked with the house until I reached my closed fist toward the door. Then he stopped, almost as if to tell me I was finally on the right track. I had planned to knock, but as I got closer, the room opened on its own, revealing a real man in the flesh sitting by himself.

"There you are," Roderick said, barely looking up. He seemed unaffected by the now constant jittering of the entire manor.

I hadn't realized I was close to tears before I started yelling my questions at him.

"What happened to them?"

"It was probably the twins, right? They never had a chance," he said calmly, shaking his head.

Brent and Marco weren't actually twins, but it seemed like a less than an important detail to tell Roderick as the tweed poufs in his room wavered back and forth with the rolling of the house.

The man on the floor flipped through paperwork and rummaged in binders. On his lap was the folder from the control room, the one he had shown me with our pictures and descriptions. He opened it to cross reference something from another book.

"Julien too? Huh." He shrugged and with a red marker drew two crossed lines over Julien's face on the page. From where I stood dick-out and almost crying in his doorway, I couldn't see if Roderick was smiling.

"Unexpected," he continued and tapped the marker at the section of file with Julien's perfect ass captured on film and fastened with a paperclip above his stats. "The only candidate from the other house already taken down." Roderick turned the page.

"We need to find Darius and Sonny and get out of here!" I yelled as a piece of Roderick's ceiling fell to the floor next to him, leaving plaster dust on his hairy leg. He brushed it off and continued rifling through the papers and pictures.

"It's all right here," Roderick said, poking his marker at a page with both of our photos on it. "Everything is happening the way it was supposed to happen."

"You sound just like him. Have either of you heard of a self-fulfilling prophecy?" If the house hadn't been falling down around us, I would have crossed my arms.

Roderick smirked. "You always were the smart one, weren't you?" He was finally looking at my face, but then his eyes were on my cock. If he hadn't realized I was naked before, he knew now. "Come over here."

Terror was doing something strange to my body. In Roderick's room, the one I'd searched for only weeks before, I wasn't that far from the back door. I could just start running again. There was a chance the other boys had already found their way out. But for some reason, I was getting incredibly hard, and being anxious only made me thicker.

When I moved from the doorframe and through the maze of cushions toward him, it wasn't because I felt any safer. The house continued to shake and bits of dust sprinkled from above.

Roderick got to his feet, leaving the paperwork and books scattered around us. He pulled his shirt over his head and let his shorts fall to his ankles. Just as turned on as I was, he pressed his chest into mine and let our hard cocks push against each other.

"It was always going to be us. We were always the golds." His words made me think about the first day we met. When we sat on a picnic table at the beach painting shells in bright colors. The ones that had to be the best to receive a shimmering coat.

"This may be our last chance," he whispered. Through Roderick's lashes, his eyes sparkled with something I'd so often mistaken for sincerity. All the information on the ground, the way he always seemed to know what was coming next—even before I'd arrived, he'd been calculating.

Even knowing that, when he ran his hand over the curve of my ass and said, "I tried my best to keep you safe." I chose to believe he meant it.

A firm grip around my cock and stroking, I reached toward him and mirrored his motion. His lips on mine still tasted like the ocean, the one I never thought I would miss when I left it behind.

Both of our precum tasted just as salty as that beach when I reached up to my mouth for spit to slide between us. With our cocks stacked on top of each other, we jerked them together and thrust into our closed palms. Our parts frotted and writhed while we kissed each other's necks and chests.

"Forgive me," Roderick said in my ear. It wasn't a question. A chunk of a nearby pillar launched against the wall closest to our heads. I gasped and tried to pull away, but he yanked back with force on my cock, determined to take me over the edge as the house fell down around us.

"It was all for you." The boy I'd called my best friend, then my lover, then my enemy tugged at my foreskin. He wiggled his finger inside and circled my wet tip. I threw my head back and moaned, not strong enough to fight the pleasure.

"I need you to say you forgive me. Say that you understand why this all had to happen." His demands made me want to escape his grip, but I was close and couldn't stop fucking his hand. Roderick's breath quickened; he was about to shoot too.

"Say it," he said loudly, moisture rolling down his cheek.

"No." As the word came out, I burst between our hands. At the same time, his load shot on his furry stomach.

Directly after we came, Roderick pushed me back with a flat hand on my chest and pointed his finger at my face. "You had a choice to come here. Even when we were kids, you never did know how to turn down a dollar."

Catching my breath, I looked down at the carpet below blanketed with scribbled nonsense and pictures of bearded men. On one sheet was what seemed to be a drawing of the house and grounds. I bent down, grabbing it to rub Roderick's load from my stomach and pubic hair.

While I held it, Roderick scooped the warmth I'd left on him from his abdomen and brought it to his tongue. Swallowing, he seemed angry when he said, "If only one of us makes it out of here, do you think it's going to be you?"

I didn't have a chance to respond before something gave way in the ceiling of Roderick's room and a giant piece of the house fell between the two of us. My first instinct was to make sure he was okay under the piled rubble, but from outside the room a voice yelled, "Alexander, where are you? Hurry!"

Chapter Fourteen

❦

When I reached the grand foyer again, Darius and Sonny were digging at large chunks of rock pillar that had piled up in front of the French doors.

"It's too high now. You couldn't have gotten here like thirty seconds ago, girl? What were you doing?" Darius said the moment he spotted me. He looked at the cum starting to dry tacky in my fur and my soft cock still flopping in the breeze. "Never mind."

"This is my first earthquake!" Sonny yelled over the constant rumble with some odd excitement in his voice. I didn't have the heart to explain the details I knew, not that I even entirely grasped how or why everything was falling apart around us.

Darius rolled his eyes and grabbed Sonny by the hand. "The wardrobes," he said and led the way up the stairs. Following him, I scraped Roderick's cum from me as quickly as I could and dropped the paper I'd been carrying to the cracking tile.

Shielding our eyes with bent arms above our heads, I didn't know that climbing higher in a crumbling structure was the smartest idea, but we didn't have another choice. The only entrance or exit on the ground floor had always been the back door.

My room was the closest to the stairs, but we had to pass by the sitting room to get there. As Darius pulled Sonny and I followed closely behind, he paused our journey abruptly when the antique couch came into view. Inside, the three men turned to one solid structure still sat paralyzed in shades of off-white and grey.

It was a struggle to find the words, but Sonny summed it up perfectly when he gazed upon the statues formed from men he'd been messing around with only days before: "What the fuck?"

Darius picked up the pace immediately, throwing open the door to my room and heading straight to the open closet. While the boys pulled at designer jeans and threw boots across the carpet, I looked to the bathroom, at the purple bathtub now full of wooden planks and cracked building materials. All this luxury was about to be swallowed up by a force I still didn't understand.

A collection of rainbow jockstraps landed on the bed followed by matching tube socks and neoprene harnesses in different configurations. I scooped up one of the only undergarments with a full back and stuffed a leg through a hole, but as Darius and Sonny cleared the panel and started to push toward the cave, it wouldn't budge.

"Help us!" Darius yelled. I let the underwear fall back to the ground. Putting all my weight against the door with the other two men, it didn't move. Behind it, falling rocks against the stone floor echoed. They seemed to be piled up against the access point and filling in the tunnel. This was no longer an exit.

In desperation, Darius grabbed Sonny's hand again and screamed over the constant bangs and thumps, "Let's try mine." From what I knew of the house and its winding passages, Darius's wardrobe was set farther back from the opening to the woods than mine. When I'd brought him through it, we'd passed my wardrobe to get there, but we were out of options.

They moved quickly to the hallway, and I scrambled to keep up, grabbing the underwear I'd been trying to slip into from the carpet on the way. Approaching the door frame after the duo, I ran directly into an unexpected wall. My face smashed against black fabric and more specifically, a breast pocket.

I pulled back to see Usher standing in my way. He walked into the bedroom, pushing me into the caving space and closed the door behind him. "It would end here. In this room," he said and folded his hands in front of him. "This one used to be mine. A long time ago."

"Why are you doing this?" I yelled, tripping backward onto the bed.

Usher laughed and pulled at the hair on his chin. "I wasn't given a rule book, Alexander. I've only done as the house commands. Just like you." His eyes moved to something behind me, and he smiled, only slightly. "Just as I thought," he said.

I turned my head to see the portrait that had spoken to me from the end of the hallway now hanging behind us on an empty wall. Usher continued to speak, and I flipped back to give him my attention.

"I almost asked you to run away with me once. To leave this place and start over, but the house refused to let me go." He put his hands in the pockets of his dress pants and rocked on the heels of his fancy shoes. A piece of plaster from the panel behind him crumbled to dust.

"It only calls to the men who need it most. Like me, you belong here." Usher pointed behind me, and I turned my head again to gaze upon the painting. My facial features were forming on the kneeling man, next to Usher in his suit.

"I'm going to tell you more than I ever knew. For the mansions, the planes, the clothes, wine, everything that comes with this title: You must feed the magic that lives here. You must power the house, or it will turn on you."

Usher walked to a small painting of a man basking nude in ocean waves that had always hung above my nightstand. He traced the face of the older man as if he'd once known him well.

"There's no saying how many men line the grounds of this house and will forever. Sometimes it will feel like you find a new one every day, and some of them, you'll always remember. But you can never feel guilty for being chosen, even if it never stops hurting."

"I don't want any of it anymore. You shouldn't have chosen me." I sat up on the bed. Usher moved in front of me from where he had been gazing at the picture above the nightstand. "We don't have much time now." He shook his head and bit his lip. "There's only one thing I want before the end. I want to finish what we started." The man who had tied me to the house pulled at his tie to loosen the knot and unbuttoned his shirt. With his hairy chest exposed, he leaned in close to where I sat on the bed.

Among the cascade of gear pulled from the wardrobe, I thought about the days and nights I'd longed to dress myself up for him. I remembered all the times I waited for his approval and the craving I developed for his cock and cum inside of me.

"Make it rough," I said, the four-poster bed shaking under me.

Usher smiled before grabbing me by the hair. He tugged hard while I unfastened his belt and released him from his pants. Plaster dust fell on top of us, coating both our hair as our lips made contact. Pushed to my back, I brought my legs above me to offer Usher my hole. I'd cum only moments before and wasn't certain I could again just yet, but I needed to feel him.

With no hesitation, his tip was at the entrance, and I swallowed him inside. His hands around my neck and holding down my hands, I knew I was smiling. We kissed while he stroked me, and when he arched back, something large fell from above us. The portrait jumped from the wall and hit with a crash as Usher shot his load. Soon the house would be rubble.

He withdrew and immediately stripped the rest of his clothes off. Handing over the bundle of his suit, he yelled over the vibration, "There's only one way to stop this now."

I held tight to the clothing as he kissed me one more time. "I did love you, Alexander. Obey the house. The boys will never belong to you. Tighten your heart and—"

The face that had never failed to make me hard and my stomach flutter froze mid-sentence before me. His mustache and beard, the piercing eyes, the fur on his chest. Even his cock, still half-hard from fucking me, was now a provocative nude statue standing in my destroyed quarters.

Posed with one hand on his chest and the other reaching out for me was a man who had never been permitted to truly love another man. I was led to believe he'd possessed everything I could ever want, but it had never been true. According to the House of Otter, this was the kind of man I was destined to become.

CHAPTER FIFTEEN

I hadn't noticed the music was still playing until I was gazing upon Usher's powerless form. He'd told us he'd heard the music before, and now I could feel the boys trapped inside the speakers. The violist, the piano player, the dark electronic synth enthusiast—all their talent had been woven into the ambience of the house. This was the choice: be the new leader and give the manor what it wanted or be absorbed. Eaten. Consumed. It seemed we had all been accepted into the structure's lore and would stay part of it one way or another, forever.

Throwing the wrinkled layers of Usher's suit to the carpet, I curved around his stone figure to force open the bedroom door. I looked back only briefly to gaze at the man who had been the source of so much passion and confusion. The only warmth left of him in this world dripped from between my cheeks as I walked away.

In the corridor, everything had been demolished. Sticks of polished furniture splintered with brass tacks and shreds of high thread count fabric lined every inch of the path to Darius's room from mine. I held tight to the walls as they continued to collapse, worried any second the once sturdy floor would give out below me.

When I reached his quarters, I'd hoped to be greeted by nothing at all. I wanted to believe there was a chance Sonny and Darius had found a route through the closet and into the woods. Even if they'd had to leave me behind, I just wanted them to be safe.

But inside, a book lay on the bed, open to drawings of out-stretched arms and interlocked hands connecting two men. On one side was Darius in a chef's hat, looking over his shoulder with the bow of an apron resting just above his full ass. On the other page, Sonny was next to a surfboard upright with the ocean behind him, running a hand through his long wavy hair.

Upon seeing the thick black lines, the soundtrack to the mansion's destruction picked up tempo. A beam came loose from above and landed on the bed, splitting the king-sized mattress in two pieces. The thick section of wood was on fire and quickly ignited the canopy and drapes.

I wanted to grab the book, as if I could still save the boys by tucking the collected sketches under my arm. But the blaze spread fast to the pages pinned under the plank. The corners lit and curled until they were dark ash. Their images were gone.

Retreating from the growing inferno, I tried to take the stairs, but the path was blocked by stacked cases full of books, rapidly turning to burning embers. Switching directions, I ran through the sitting room, passed the cemented threesome. It was starting to chip and crack under the weight of the destruction. The looks of pleasure on their faces had turned to fear, as had the men hanging in paintings, pictures, and portraits on the surrounding walls. They were all watching, all begging me to change their fate.

With the bookcase missing, seemingly part of the barricade on the stairs, I was able to access the passage to the kitchen directly. As the house smoldered, the stone below my feet was surprisingly cool. For a moment, in the dark cave, it felt like nothing had changed. Aside from the smell of smoke seeping into my nostrils, I could have been preparing to make a meal and run it up to one of Usher's boys. I could have been sneaking through the passage in cute underwear to entice Usher to put his cock in me. It was then I realized that my former keeper was right: all of this really had been my fault.

Silver trays were spilled everywhere across the tile in the kitchen. Red, white, and rose wine had shattered, leaving puddles of glistening pink between shards of shattered green and transparent glass. I tiptoed carefully but quickly through the mess until I fell through the swinging door to the dining room.

The large table and collection of chairs were back in place, but bits of dried cum from the competitive circle jerk still speckled the shiny hardwood. Candles like the ones from my first dinner with Usher, the one directly before he'd officially made me part of the house, flickered inside the room. It was as if the house had its own strange sense of humor and poetic vengeance. If all the candles throughout the structure had been lit the same way, that explained the fire.

A sudden memory of Roderick and me being pulled by our collars made my knees ache just picturing it. I thought about the way he ignored me until we'd been given permission to touch. He'd followed every rule and had still been punished over and over again by Usher. The only time he'd broken the vows he'd taken was when it involved me. But despite anything he'd said before his load landed on my abdomen, I still wasn't certain if his rule-breaking had all been elaborate sabotage or a way to save me from a worse fate.

Roderick may have never had Usher's love like I did. Even if they'd fucked. Maybe I was trying to convince myself the only reason Usher had slept with the other boys was because he knew he had already broken his vow to the house. That there was no going back so he may as well have some fun. When I emerged in the grand foyer again, something told me I was exactly right. The man I called Usher—but wished I had met as Madden—was still with me. His voice in my head said, "Watch out, boy."

From the side, the Saint Andrew's Cross from the red room barreled in my direction at full force. I dove out of the way, letting my naked body collapse to the punishing tile. The wooden X kept moving until it slammed into the collection of broken house pieces blocking the back entrance to the courtyard. Fire dripped from the impact and what I could still see of the white drapes ignited.

"The pool is caved in. Everything is gone! Where's the suit?" Roderick yelled, pulling the cross-on-wheels back to its starting position. He pushed it again, launching it at the rocks. Even after making contact a second time, nothing moved.

Next to me on the floor, the paper I'd used as a cum rag sat in a scrunchy ball. A word I hadn't noticed before stuck out to me on the drawing of the house: "Front Door."

I pulled at the wad and below something moist and mostly white, but slightly transparent, were the words:

Seal the doors.
They will never hurt us where we live again.
I promise.

I could see him: Madden. A young man who was brought from this house to France. Someone who had grown up in Beachside, just like me. Shoeless feet and worn trunks, he hadn't always been rich like I'd imagined. But, even then, he was incredibly sexy.

The young furry man had gone through everything in almost the same way. Every ritual. But the keeper he'd known as Usher maintained a sweetness about him.

I envisioned a moment in the long history of a manor larger than this one near water people called a sea. In my mind, I saw burning trees and townspeople with lit torches afraid of men who loved other men.

In a ceremony like the one in the dining room, Madden had worn the orange jockstrap and won, but his glory was short lived as his Usher and all the boys inside burned with the house. Their art was transported here, along with a scared young man. Alone and unaware of the rules, he'd created his own and swore he would never let devastation come to the place which had saved his life.

Uncertain if the old one could be rebuilt, Madden's first order as the new Usher had been clear to him the moment he put on his new suit. He had to hide the front door from view and hope no one discriminating in this town would ever discover what went on inside the House of Otter.

CHAPTER SIXTEEN

"There's another door!" I yelled to Roderick as he pushed the large wooden cross into the blockage a third time. It hit with a thunderous crash but still, nothing moved. My lungs hurt from inhaling the smoke, and it was getting hard to see.

Roderick ran and grabbed the structure we'd both been restrained to on different occasions. He pulled it back by the riveted straps and yelled, out of breath, "What?"

There wasn't time to explain. I got to my feet and ran to the credenza. Lucky for me, the passage was already open from Roderick retrieving the giant X and wheeling it through. I didn't have to locate the silver button to access the hallway. Even now, it seemed to stretch as long as it always had and glow with the same vibrant red. But this time, it was hot and the illumination came from the roaring blaze.

In the heart of the red room, I gathered everything I could carry, and with armfuls of dildos and butt plugs, whips and sounding rods, I made my way to the spot marked on the forgotten plans. Dropping the collection of toys in a heap in front of the space I called for Roderick, who was still smashing the cross into the rubble.

"Help me!" I yelled and started the excavation by digging a pointed sounding rod across the flat wall opposite the courtyard. In search of a crack in the wallpaper covering it, I knew I'd never seen any indication of a front entrance from the exterior. There was no porch nor steps, no knobs or handles. From the road outside the gate, the architecture had shown nothing but a dark brick wall.

I could see it in my head again, a memory I couldn't be certain the house, or Usher, wanted me to know. Two men close to kissing while a young driver waited for them in the gravel. In a time before I'd come to this place, there had absolutely been a door.

Roderick approached the moment the rod fell into a tight slit. He gasped with amazement and wedged his fingers into the narrow space. I grabbed a whip from the floor, and using the thin but sturdy handle, pried at the opening. When we used our strength together, the plaster began peeling away.

We clawed and smacked the crumbling wall with metal collars and firm double-ended dildos until finally it appeared: a door. The fire had reached the base of the staircase and was edging close to my naked flesh as we cleared the debris and turned the brass knob.

But on the other side, it was as I feared—a brick wall. The flames licked at us, and the beams in the thick pillars continued to collapse. It was over. There was no way out of the house.

Then it appeared, on our island of tile surrounded by a sea of fire: the suit. Usher's suit. Clean, pressed, and hanging next to the gaping hole we'd made in the wall.

"Grab it!" Roderick screamed with desperation. "It's the only way to stop it!" He knew enough for me to believe it was the truth. But I didn't move.

As I hesitated, Roderick said, "Fuck it" and leapt from our oasis into the flames. He grabbed the Saint Andrew's Cross and yelled "Move!" before ramming into the brick wall. The blocks cascaded to the outside and landed on cement with a series of bangs. Roderick's stupid idea had made a space just big enough for a person to crawl through.

"Go!" he screamed, running toward me. I climbed through the space but was stuck until Roderick pushed me through with both hands on my bare ass. Landing on the pavement in a naked heap in front of the house, the first thing I noticed was the sun. I never would have guessed from inside the dark house that outside it was vibrant and beautiful.

The orb shone bright through the trees, highlighting the jagged window we'd dug with hands and sex gear. Peeking through the hole, I reached inside for Roderick but didn't see him. All I saw was fire and melted butt plugs turned to dripping magma.

I yelled for him by name. I yelled that I was sorry. He was gone.

Smoke and flames kissed the blue sky for half my walk back to Beachside. By the time I crossed the tracks, I couldn't even see the ash raining down. It was gathered in my hair though and marked on my body. Even if I could wash it off, I knew then it would always be part of me.

The tourists seemed concerned when I dragged myself straight to the ocean through the hot sand. I'm certain they watched as the dirty naked man with charcoal-coated body hair waded in deep enough to float.

There in the ocean, I couldn't hear Usher anymore. I couldn't hear any of them. With my head empty for a moment, I thought about Roderick and how he had sacrificed himself to save me. I'd misjudged him—again. He'd been telling the truth. Everything he'd done really was to help me. To offer me a better life. Roderick offered me the knowledge about the more sinister side of the house as he learned it. He had always wanted me to know.

My cock was hard for some reason. Adrenaline, maybe, I thought. Floating on my back far enough out that I was no longer visible from the sand and with no one nearby, I began to stroke lightly. Figuring if there was anything that could make someone feel alive after nearly meeting their demise, it was a small taste of the little death. The hair of the dog in the form of an orgasm.

Gripping my balls and pinching at my nipple, I thought about the boys first, the friends I was sorry I had ever led, even unintentionally, to the house. I thought about the fun we'd had together the day at the pool, the orgy we'd never completed. My ass puckered thinking about the four men taking turns with each other in the mansion and in our more humble home.

Now I was seeing Usher, but I couldn't make out his face. It was as blurred and fragmented as it had been before we'd met, like the day I'd leaned against the tree and shot my load to the forest floor, imagining him tasting me. I knew there had been more. That at one point, I longed for intimacy with him. He'd been inside of me, kissed me, held me close, but I couldn't remember. My memory of the house seemed to be disappearing as I edged closer to orgasm. All I could see clearly now ... was Roderick.

With my cock dripping precum into the salty waves, my fantasy was vivid with the first time we'd ever touched. I could feel the satisfaction of finally swallowing his tongue and cock. In my mind, we pumped at each other in his room, surrounded by files and French language textbooks, and then, I came.

My load shot like I hadn't cum in a thousand years, and that was how long I lay there on the surface of the water once I had. In that state of relaxation, decades could have passed. Days, night, weeks, years with my ears under the small waves, rocking my furry otter body to sleep.

When I finally did open my eyes and swim to shore, it was close to sunset. Oranges, pinks, and yellows lined the horizon I'd never really taken the time to appreciate. This place, this small beach town, really was incredible.

As dusk approached, I spotted two men, probably only a year or so younger than I was, standing together and talking near a bench.

My nudity didn't seem to phase them beyond a quick stare and smirk as they passed a business card between them.

"This side says, 'Do you want to make some money?'" One of the young men said, reading the card aloud. He flipped the card over and handed it to the other young man who laughed when he tried to sound out the words then said, "What is this? French? I don't speak French."

The other boy pointed to something on the small paper, "It's in English underneath."

On his second attempt, the boy read it clearly, "His heart is a tightened lute. When one touches it, it echoes."

And I knew then the only man in that house who could have ever lived up to its motto was on his way to France, ready to train his own boys, in his new fancy suit.

The End

LEO SPARX

Leo Sparx is a digital artist who is bringing his fascination with the history of queer sex to the literary erotica world. Inspiration for his work is often found during virtual orgies, trips to offbeat museums, or classic—occasionally spooky—literature. His unique blend of steamy sensations and dark passion takes the reader on a kinky exploration and allows them to experience encounters in unexpected locations.

www.leosparx.com

instagram.com/authorleosparx

twitter.com/authorleosparx

authorleosparx@gmail.com

**Discover more at
4HorsemenPublications.com**

10% off using HORSEMEN10